A Splash of Burgundy

Color by Numbers

Book Two

Danielle Thompson

A Splash of Burgundy

To request permissions, contact author.danielle.thompson@gmail.com

www.writerdaniellethompson.com

Paperback ISBN: 979-8-9896983-8-7

Ebook ISBN: ISBN: 979-8-9896983-3-2

Cover designed by MiblArt

For the optimists, and those who believe that everything will be alright in the end.

They're right; it just takes a little while.

ONE

Jaden was dressed impeccably, pressed blue pants and a white Oxford button down, looking for all the world like a graduate student fresh from campus. He sat coolly relaxed, one leg bent, one stretched out before him, his unblinking gaze fixed on Kuro.

A pleasant smile graced his lips, almost boyish in its easy charm, but Kuro knew the shape of that particular mask: his stare – the intensity of it, the slightest furrowing of his brow – told him that beneath the surface of his congeniality lay a serpent that could strike at any moment. He raised a teacup to his lips and sipped it placidly, and Kuro watched his eyes narrow over the rim of the cup, an unspoken warning to him not to react.

Caroline's delighted voice cut through his horror.

"*Kuro!* Come on!"

He tried to regulate his breathing, but his heart was pounding in his chest. He took one wooden step forward, then another.

Jaden set the teacup down, nodding. He leaned back on one hand; the palm was casually splayed open on the ground, the edge of his fingertips almost touching Caroline. It was a deliberate, slow placement; he need only move in one practiced, swift motion, and Caroline would be at his mercy.

Kuro had no idea what the demon was doing there, how he had found her, or why they were in the garden together.

A worse fear twisted in his gut: he had no idea what Jaden had told her.

Jaden gestured to the edge of the blanket. "Sit down, Kuro." Kuro could hear the iron in that tone, the command layered just under the pleasantry.

He did as he was told, slowly, his limbs stiff. From the corner of his eye, he saw the subtle shift in Caroline's expression; she sensed something was wrong, and her gaze moved back and forth between them, her smile faltering.

Jaden picked up the cup again and had another sip, draining it. He looked down at the empty porcelain in mild disapproval. "You never told Caroline about me, Kuro." He cast an apologetic look at Caroline; the hand that was much, much too close to her now lifted and passed over his heart, as though the thought hurt him, and a dramatic, playful sigh escaped him. "I'm wounded."

Caroline's mood lifted again, reassembling itself; she laughed, but she glanced again at Kuro, puzzled by his reaction. His fists were clenched against his legs, the knuckles white, fingers trembling. He became aware that a muscle in his face was twitching.

"...So you've met." He was unable to hide the tremor in his voice. He cleared his throat, wrestling with himself to regain his composure; he didn't want to frighten Caroline or provoke Jaden into any violent impulse. "How long have you been here?"

"A few hours, actually." Jaden's bland smile tugged into a smirk. "You know, when I showed up...she thought I was *you*."

Kuro winced. The demon had annunciated each word with a

pointed accusation that only he could hear, intimations of consequences yet to come; with Caroline looking at Kuro now, she couldn't see the way Jaden's eyes had gone cold with consternation.

"Feral went wild," she said. "I thought you came back, so I went outside...and your friend was here. He asked if I had seen anyone who looked like you. I said no, but he said he was sure you told him to meet him here."

"Which you did," Jaden said. His hand returned to the blanket, once more much too casually near to Caroline's thigh; he relaxed his weight against it and lifted his index finger, tapping it slowly. *Meaningfully.* "Remember?"

Kuro nodded, sick.

"And Feral wouldn't calm down...I haven't seen him like that since the night I met you, and I thought..." Caroline played with the end of her braid and shrugged. "I thought, well, this might be a little bold, but since you'd never mentioned having any *human* friends...I asked him if he was a *kitsune*, too."

All at once, it felt like his heart forgot how to beat. The color drained from him, his breath catching in his throat. Jaden's smile stretched into a grin.

"Imagine my surprise," he said, his voice untroubled, cool in his detachment. "Naturally, I told her 'no.'" His words were measured, perfectly amicable, but Kuro licked his lips, fighting against panic. "But then she told me, if I *was*...what was it you said? Ah, that's right. She told me I didn't need to be afraid, because she already *knew all about us.*" He propped his elbow on his knee, resting his cheek against his fist as if he was recounting an extraordinarily boring story. "And then I was just too curious, because your scent was just about everywhere, and here was this young woman who knew about *kitsune*, and I thought...well, *this* is certainly interesting."

He didn't sound interested in the least.

"Kuro, you didn't tell me there was another one of your kind here." Kuro turned to look at her; it took a force of will to drag his eyes away from Jaden. He could feel the hurt hidden under her excitement, and at the edges of her soul, someone else...someone creeping, *touching*. He whipped his gaze around and glared at Jaden, but the demon only shrugged.

"I only just came down from the mountains a few days ago," Jaden lied smoothly. "You mustn't blame him. He's thoughtless sometimes, but he would *never* deceive someone – especially not a friend." The words were a fast dagger thrown straight to Kuro's heart. He swallowed. "Like I was telling you earlier, I've known Kuro for a long, *long* time."

Caroline set a cup in front of him. For the first time, Kuro noticed that there was a teapot on the blanket and a small tray of cookies, lemon wedges, and sugar cubes. His mind began to pick up on other details: if Jaden intended to threaten Caroline, he had yet to do it, nor did she anticipate it. This was no hostage situation.

Inexplicably, this was afternoon tea.

He looked up to find Jaden's stare on him once more. "Have a drink, Kuro," he suggested in that low voice of his that expected obedience. "You look like you need one."

She poured him a cup, and a light curl of steam rose from it. He didn't touch it; he couldn't risk taking his eyes off Jaden again. It felt like someone else spoke when he heard himself ask, "What have you been talking about?"

Jaden held out his cup with polite expectation; Caroline refilled it. They looked almost like lovers in the easy way they lounged, the way she poured him tea. "Well, I told her how I ran into you a few days ago, and you told me I could find you here... but, we've mostly been discussing books."

Kuro fought the urge to lunge at him. The *holy dark* was

surging inside of him, and with an effort, he did his best to suppress the tide, a metallic taste in his mouth. "Books?"

"Jaden's a great reader," Caroline said. She sounded impressed. "You seem so different from each other."

Jaden let out a short bark of laughter. "And to think, we've grown up with each other, but yes...we're very different, in some ways. In others...not so much. I'd like to think we've rubbed off on one another; we've been together practically since birth."

Caroline drew back in surprise. "I didn't know that. Kuro hasn't told me much about his life in the mountains."

"Well, I'm sure you'll have plenty of time to talk." Jaden reached forward and plucked a slice of lemon from a tray, setting it down in the tea. "As for me, I have to admit, this is all so very...*new*, this talking to a human...but not *as* a human. Not quite." He took a long sip, a playful grin sneaking across his features. His eyes sparkled with a light that Kuro decidedly did not like. "I've been enjoying it *thoroughly*."

He would, Kuro thought; undoubtedly he was loving the attention of this wholly novel experience, if Jaden was indeed capable of enjoying anything.

A stiff silence suddenly invaded the space; Caroline looked from one to the other, trying to understand the growing tension that she could no longer deny. Her soul had that rattling quality to it that it got just before she began to talk too much from nerves... and Jaden was staring at her, smirking, enjoying her growing anxiety.

"Jaden won't show me what he really looks like," Caroline blurted suddenly.

Kuro's blood was boiling; he wanted to punch that look of smug satisfaction right off of Jaden's face. "Did you ask him to?"

"I did." Caroline's tone was apologetic. "I just...I was so excited. I had to ask."

"I'm not holding your curiosity against you," Jaden said. He finished his drink again and set it down. "You'll just have to excuse me; I'm shyer than Kuro...but I think, as we get to know each other more – and we will," he added, shooting Kuro a look, "I may warm up to the idea."

Kuro stood at once, knocking his teacup over.

Jaden looked at the spill, frowning. "That was rude, Kuro."

"We actually have to be going." He reached down and yanked Jaden to his feet, his hand closing around his forearm with a vice-like grip.

Caroline stood, confused. "But you just got here."

"I'll be back."

"It was nice meeting you...Caroline," Jaden said, and he dipped his head in a deferential goodbye. Behind them, Caroline watched them go, and Kuro could feel the sudden wave of uncertainty and suspicion in her soul.

Kuro didn't let go of him until he was certain he had dragged Jaden at least half a mile into the woods. Only then did he release him, furious and hissing.

"What do you think you're doing!?"

Jaden straightened his sleeve. "Kuro." He tugged at the other one, satisfied that they were even, and when he spoke, his voice was icy. "I'm going to give you one warning to change your tone with me. Do you understand?"

Kuro did and didn't care. He sprung forward, grabbed Jaden by the collar of his shirt, and slammed him against the base of a pine tree. Jaden reached up, glaring, and grabbed him by both hands. For one painful moment, his fingers were replaced by claws, and they pierced the flesh in his arms. Kuro let go and stepped back just before he could draw blood, and Jaden was fully human again, pushing his hair out of his face, glaring at him. There was an emotion very near to hatred in his eyes.

"You *lied* to me, Kuro." The air crackled with the sound of a tail snapping behind him, and Jaden stepped forward, fists clenched. "That girl has a *dog*. You were attacked by a *dog*."

Kuro slowed his breathing, navigating his thoughts. "Yes. Her dog attacked me. You're right. I lied."

Jaden opened and closed his hands slowly, flexing. "And the hunting accident. Is that true? Or was *she* the one who shot you?"

Kuro stared him down, finding the will to lie again. He knew Jaden would not be very kind to the person who shot him; sheer necessity gave his words a bold truthfulness that his previous lies had lacked. "It was a hunting accident, just like I told you. I had to hide – I crawled into her barn, and her dog found and attacked me."

"And you didn't give yourself those sutures. I let that lie go – oh, don't look so surprised Kuro, you're as transparent as glass. The moment you suggested you did a *multi-step process* requiring *patience* and *research*, I knew you were lying. I assume she did those?"

It would be easier to tell the truth rather than keep track of more lies. Kuro shook his head, inwardly seething. "No. She called a friend over, and he helped me." He took a moment to focus his thoughts in an effort to get a handle on the situation. "Jaden, I'm sorry – I didn't mean to lie to you, it's just..."

"What?" Jaden sneered at him. "She's pretty, Kuro – in a country kind of way. You think I wouldn't understand?"

No, he thought. He didn't think he'd understand *at all.*

"You were hurt; she helped you, and you wanted to keep her all to yourself. That's *fine,* Kuro. I don't care. You've always been more sentimental than I am. I think you're an absolute, goddamn *fool* for telling her you're a *kitsune,* for *showing* her what you look like..." He took a deep breath. "I can't believe you would do that. And she seems to have accepted it *remarkably* well... Does she know you're the one in the paper?"

He nodded. Jaden snorted. "And does she think you're the one who did the killings?"

"...No."

Jaden considered this for a moment. "...That's why you didn't tell her about me. You didn't want her to know about your involvement."

I wasn't involved! He wanted to rage, but he clamped down on the thought, swallowing it. He was *complicit,* he knew. That was bad enough. "What did you tell her, Jaden?" His voice was shaking again. "What did you talk about before I got there? Don't lie to me."

"*Books.*" Jaden turned on him in a rage. "We talked about you for the first thirty minutes, but despite what you might think, you're not that interesting." He stalked away in a fury then came back, shoving him. "You showed her what you *look like,* you *idiot!* What's your plan when for you're done and you're ready to move on?"

Kuro stumbled backward, gathering himself. "When I'm done...?"

Jaden gestured inarticulately, rolling his eyes. "What's your goal here, Kuro? You've never shown interest in humans before. What do you *want* from her? A warm bed, a hot meal, a quick fuck?"

Kuro's fists bunched to strike, but he restrained himself with every ounce of his will. He could have throttled him for that last comment, but Jaden stood before him now looking genuinely interested and mildly perplexed.

His mind wheeled, searching for an answer, but he didn't know. There had to be something he could say, something to convince Jaden to lose interest in her and leave her alone. *And what if he doesn't?* What if he kept coming back, what if he threatened her...? He thought of that girl in the car, saw the blood again, and shuddered.

He couldn't let him do that to Caroline.

He looked up to see Jaden frozen, staring at him in wide-eyed outrage.

"Right now..." Jaden's voice shook with barely suppressed anger. "You're looking at me like you're ready to attack *me*. You think I would *hurt* her? You think you need to *protect* her from me? Don't deny it – I can see your thoughts written on your face. I understand you better than you understand yourself, Kuro." The tone of his voice shifted; the rage diminished to hurt. "I always have."

Kuro stood up straighter. He had never seen Jaden so angry... and had never been so convinced that Jaden was so wrong. No, Jaden didn't understand him.

He didn't understand him *at all*, because he had never cared for someone, had never known the need to protect someone other than himself.

Do you really believe that? His life was filled with years' worth of examples that could have testified to the contrary...but no, he thought, shoving the doubt away, replacing it with the memory of his recent manipulations; it would only cloud his judgement. Jaden only cared about *himself*.

No matter what he had promised in the past.

He took a deep breath and shook his head. He stepped forward with what he hoped was calm confidence, already sickened by the words he was about to say. "It's not that," he said. He was surprised by the rational tone he had managed to adopt, so much like Jaden's own. "It's what you were telling me earlier. About consuming a soul, and time. And – and teeth." He watched as Jaden quirked an eyebrow, curious. "I thought about what you said, and it sounded like a good theory to me. I figured if you were going to try to consume a soul...I might as well, too. So yes, Jaden – I don't want you to touch her. I don't want you to feed off of her, either. It's not that I think you'd hurt her, it's just that...she's *mine.*"

Kuro could not have explained why, but something about the words had felt *wrong,* beyond just the abhorrent lie; they echoed in the distant caverns of his heart, swallowed by the *holy dark,* consumed by some eternal silence inside him.

Jaden said nothing, studying him. Kuro felt the air shift between them; the *holy dark* was settling, and they stared at one another in silence for what seemed like a long time until Jaden finally nodded.

"I wish you success."

Kuro exhaled. Jaden glanced back the way they had come, toward the farm. Kuro followed his gaze warily, but he could tell Jaden was thinking of other things now. Exhaustion hit him hard; he allowed himself to relax just a fraction.

"I don't know how long we'll be here..." Jaden said at length. "The girl I want...I'm working around the edges. I press against her windows in the night. I spot her at a distance; I follow her. I can see the toll it's taking on her...but I can't get close yet. And she's so...*defiant.*" He bit down on the word, his teeth flashing; there were equal parts frustration and pride in his voice.

He tried to steer Jaden's thoughts away from Caroline, back toward his obsession. "What do you mean?"

"Kuro...she dances." He said it simply, but he spoke the words like a man reciting a death sentence, his voice breaking. He clutched at his face, his eyes hidden. "There's a thin pane of glass that runs along the side of her front door. I watch her through it. I keep seeing her in my mind, dancing....She knows I'm out there, she knows *it's only a matter of time,* and each day, her fears grow a little more intolerable...and each night, she dances in defiance." He swallowed. "I wish I could break her hold on me; I don't understand it...I don't understand why I can't *master* it. The angel will give me clarity, right before I kill it and consume her soul."

Kuro had no reply to that; he merely waited until Jaden came back to himself and pointed toward Caroline's barn in the distance. "I assume if I need to find you, you'll be there."

He nodded.

"Don't be surprised if I stop by every so often. I like a cup of tea as much as the next person, and I found her quite... pleasant. Although, that dog..."

"She likes her dog," he said, too quickly. Jaden glanced at him, amused. Kuro shrugged. "I don't go near it."

"No...I wouldn't, if I were you."

He shifted his weight, eager to part. "Good luck with...with Jacqueline."

Jaden laughed as he walked away, waving. "Should we make it a contest? See who can eat a whole soul first?" He didn't wait for an answer, and the words hung in the air like a poison long after he was gone.

By the time Kuro made it back to the farm, Caroline had carried the picnic blanket inside. He could hear Feral snarling from within the barn.

His knuckles rapped on the front door screen, and she called for him to come inside. She sat at the kitchen table, a fresh cup of tea steaming between her hands.

He sank wearily into the chair opposite her and felt a wave of guilt wash over him, like a child caught staying up late.

She broke the silence first. "You didn't tell me about him."

"Well...now you know."

"I don't blame you."

He winced. There was pain in her words. He felt like they were gearing up for an argument. Her soul told him that it had spent the last thirty minutes while he was gone in quiet reflection, and within the silence had grown unhealthy thoughts rooted in shame, questioning her worthiness of his confidence. "Were you afraid that you couldn't trust me? Or that I'd hurt him?"

There was no hiding his surprise, but he managed to swallow the bitter laughter that rose up in his throat.

"*You* hurt *him*?"

A half-smile tugged at the corner of her lips. "Well, I did shoot *you*."

"No...that's not why I didn't tell you."

"Kuro." She set the cup down and fixed him with an expectant stare. "Did he kill those people?"

He looked up, stunned; she was waiting, open and guileless, fully expecting the truth. What would she do if he told her? She would take action against him, surely...and as repulsed as Kuro was by Jaden's violence, he didn't want that. He couldn't betray his only friend.

His thoughts flashed by in the span of one second, and in the next he answered readily, "No."

He surprised himself by how sure the lie sounded. The stiffness in Caroline's shoulders released; she let out a breath. "Can I trust him?"

He wanted to tell her *no*, to never go near him, never let him into her house, never speak to him again...but if he said anything, she'd grow worried, frightened. *Suspicious.* If he told her *no*, would she suspect that Kuro was lying about him being a murderer?

And then, what would she think about *him* if she knew that he was *protecting* a murderer? That he was *friends* with one?

It was an impossible knot to untie...and Jaden had told him he wouldn't hurt her.

No, he didn't say that all, his mind reminded him, but Kuro had already opened his mouth and, in the face of all his fears, answered, "Yes."

Caroline sighed. "That's good to hear. You know...he made me realize how little I know about you." She looked down into her teacup, studying the golden liquid. "I started asking him questions, but then – and I don't know how it happened – I realized he was asking *me* all about *you*. Maybe he was gauging how much I really knew...and I realized, all of a sudden, how little that really was. How many *kitsune* are out there? And how did you two meet?"

He didn't know what to say – it was too much to collect and put into words.

She filled the silence with her own thoughts. "But meeting him...I also realized something else." A bloom of simple relief flowered in her soul. "I was glad to know that there had been someone with you, that you weren't just alone out there. I don't know why, but the thought made me so sad, to think of you, out in the wilderness, alone...but it turns out, you had him."

Kuro's throat tightened. He was nearly choking on his own guilt, and the quiet hurt in her soul hadn't completely gone away; it lay there at the bottom, a raw, painful edge to it that he drew back from, even as the *holy dark* starved within him, dragging him toward misery and weakness. He reached across the table and touched the edges of her fingertips where they had curled around the cup.

"I'll tell you about me," he said, quickly. She looked up into his eyes, surprised. "And... I'll tell you about him, too. But that means, I've got to tell you about...something else. And I don't want to." He could feel himself growing nervous, his palms clammy.

Her hand moved, her fingers slipping between his. "Why not?"

Kuro squeezed his eyes shut. He had shown her moving shadows, blue fox fire; he had even revealed to her his true form. But to tell her this...? He had to; he owed her some measure of truth after all the lies. He wanted to give her something real, something to assuage his guilt. "I'm afraid you'll fear me."

"Don't be afraid. I promise...I won't."

He nodded, fighting the familiar urge to bolt. She squeezed his hand, and this time, he couldn't meet her eyes as she asked, "Kuro...what is it? You can tell me. *Please* tell me."

He drew back, took a deep breath, and with the feeling of peeling back the layers of his flesh and letting her see all the inner, hidden workings of his self, he said, "We call it the *holy dark*."

Two

When Kuro was born, roughly the size of a full-grown rabbit, he looked up at his mother through squinted eyes that could barely see and made a pathetic, mewling sound that came out like a squeak. He could not make out what color she was; his eyes were nearly glued together, swollen.

His mother licked his fur repeatedly until he was clean, then turned and padded away into the forest, leaving the helpless newborn blinking by the side of a stream in the mountains, alone. Hungry and frightened, he watched her leave, her long tail swinging from side to side as she disappeared, a blur in a world too bright to comprehend.

He was desperately hungry and thirsty, but no mother's milk awaited him. Only the sound of the river called to him.

Kuro, who was hungry, cold, and thirsty, curled into a tight ball, and fell asleep.

In the first month that Kuro survived by the river, he doubled in size until he looked like a normal fox, without the change in colors along his body. He was entirely black, from the top of his ears to the tip of his tail, and he somehow seemed to be aware that this was true of all *kitsune:* each was a single, solid, unique color. The first time he saw a fox, he marveled that so much variation was possible: the browns, the oranges, and especially the creamy white along its breast.

In contrast, he was a shadow.

He gobbled down the fat bodies of frogs, the long, crooked legs kicking as he chewed. Tiny mice crept down to the water at night, and fat, pregnant hares needed to drink, as well. A steady diet allowed him to grow, and soon he could dip a paw into the river and fling a small fish onto the bank.

Kuro had been chewing on a fish, his claws finally long and sharp enough to rend whole flakes of meat from its back, when a scent came to him on a breeze, followed by a faint, approaching noise.

His nose sniffed the air as he looked around and saw where the sound was coming from. He realized quite suddenly that it had grown unusually quiet: all of the bird song, save one plaintive, desperate chirping, had stopped.

He followed that sound into the bushes, listening. Through the undergrowth, he saw its source: a fledgling sparrow had fallen out of its nest, its long, sinewy neck stretching upwards as its beak gaped, hungry. Its eyes bulged, and its body, covered in stiff, painful-looking feathers that had begun to poke through, quaked with its pitiful cries. It was weeks away from being able to fly; there would be no returning to its nest.

Kuro sat and watched it for some time, his tail moving back and forth as he thought about what to do. He had no way of knowing that other animals did not formulate plans and choose consciously to ignore instinct. He could not know that he was developing an intellect, however limited it was.

Another creature suddenly darted forward, snapped the bird up into its jaws, and glared at Kuro with bold, maroon eyes, as if Kuro wasn't hidden at all.

It was another *kitsune,* Kuro somehow *knew.* The other *kitsune* sat back on his own haunches, mimicking Kuro as he crunched on the bird and watched Kuro curiously to see what he would do. The maroon *kitsune's* tail was stiff and his eyes wild, ready for a confrontation.

But Kuro felt only joy at finding another creature like himself. The silence of other animals trailed in his wake, and he could never find another scent like his own. He felt as if he was the only one of his kind, and might have continued to think that for years to come if not for this good fortune; the world, he would later learn, was not, in fact, infested with demons. Perhaps they were all hidden away somewhere, behind a door in the world, and here there was only the hardship of solitary survival.

But not anymore.

The maroon *kitsune* watched him, quirked his head to the left, and challenged Kuro to fight him by baring his tiny, silver fangs, bloodied by the bird.

He hesitated, his black tail twitching, then crept slowly forward, pushing out from the foliage. Three more timid steps brought him to the maroon *kitsune,* and with his tail between his legs, Kuro leaned forward and licked the other demon's nose, submissive to his will.

The tension broke. Within minutes they were tussling about in the forest, rolling and barking, nipping at one another in the joy of companionship, loneliness banished from the world as the two *kitsune* leapt over one another, buoyed by their joy.

Their intellect progressed rapidly; their animal bodies aged quickly, as did their minds. They were exhilarated, but frightened and confused; other animals, it seemed, could not speak the way they did, and the creeping terror of not understanding one's own self had begun to grow. There was a constant feeling of something shifting inside them, twisting their senses away from the natural world to some inner, dark place.

Something was within him, Kuro knew; he had no name for it yet – it had not *moved* – but there was something *there,* just under his thoughts.

And it was waiting.

As time passed, they learned language from the campers in the woods, listening to the sounds and discovering its rhythm and structure.

And then one day the maroon *kitsune* formulated a word and expressed it without barking, without even opening his mouth.

Name? It asked.

Kuro was shocked. His tail thrashed in agitation. Just as instinct had made him aware of his own name, he somehow also knew not to share it. He did not know how he knew this, like so many other things, but he *did...*and it came from that place inside him, where the dark thing was waiting in stillness. The feeling was powerful and demanding, and it told him that to give up his name was to give someone else power over him. His name felt like a secret buried within the very core of his soul, if demons had a soul; everything in him strained against the giving of it, the relinquishing of this precious thing, the *only* thing, that he possessed.

And yet, the maroon *kitsune* stared at him, waiting.

Kuro found that he could speak, too. He whispered his true name, shivering.

The maroon *kitsune* barked in delight. Kuro wasn't entirely sure why his stomach felt sick, or why his tail had curled up suspiciously at the end. He wished he had made up a name, or given only half his name – maybe something like 'Kuro,' he thought. That would work, in the future. He imitated the word the other *kitsune* had used, and spoke again.

Name? He asked.

The maroon *kitsune* stopped and blinked at him, his head tilted in thought. Its tail twitched to the right, and then to the left, slowly and with caution.

After a few moments of silence, it answered.

Jaden, he said.

Much later, Kuro would realize that this was the first time Jaden ever lied to him.

Caroline's tea had gone cold. She listened thoughtfully as Kuro told his story in stumbling, broken sentences, trying – and failing – to capture the feeling, to help her see the forest, to feel its deep shadows in the summer and its chill, cutting dampness in the fall. He had grown sidetracked telling her about the river where he was born and had spent nearly five minutes in an effort to articulate the exact scent of the soft moss along the rocks, the way it smelled musty and yet so *clean,* and how it felt more plush than even the velvet of a buck's antlers. She had smiled, entranced, but he could see that his world was too distant for her to fully grasp, himself inadequate to the task of bringing it to life before her, and he had moved on, glazing over other details.

He waited for her to microwave the tea back to a high temperature, and when she returned, he started again, focusing. It was harder to tell the next part...

Harder, but necessary.

When winter came, neither of the *kitsune* were prepared for the freezing temperatures or the ice; a vicious cold snap held the mountain range in a frigid choke hold, and a storm system moving through had coated the world in six inches of snow.

Kuro, in a state of shock, slid his way across the top of the icy river they frequented. Jaden had become dominant in their relationship, and he barked at Kuro to come back to the snowbank. This Kuro tried to do, but not before crashing snout-first onto the ice. The distorted image of a fish swimming beneath the surface caused him to fly into a fury, futilely scratching at the top of the ice as he barked in consternation. He could *see* the water flowing beneath the frosty glaze, and the inaccessibility of it drove him to frustration.

He was sent flying as Jaden crashed into him, the two of them sliding down the riverbank out of control and barking with laughter. With their fur matted with slivers of ice, the two of them clumsily climbed up onto the riverbank over a pile of slippery rocks.

For that one moment, winter had felt magical, but their mood soured fast. The reality of cold and hunger set in with the coming of night. Curling up together in the dark was no longer enough; temperatures stayed low and froze the snow that would have otherwise melted, sinking deep into their bones with an ache that left them shivering and miserable. Days turned to weeks, and still the winter clung with an icy, unprecedented grip. Hungry and thinned, the *kitsune,* now almost fully-grown, climbed high into the mountains until they discovered a small opening to a shallow cave, hidden by an overhang of rock. Jaden pressed himself in first and barked menacingly; surprisingly, nothing replied. It was there in the darkness that the two of them made their first winter home, with a bed of dried twigs they pulled from the snow and what rare leafy foliage they could find.

It was there that the *holy dark* first moved in them, awakening.

Somehow, they knew they had been waiting for this moment. Jaden had some idea that the *holy dark* was what enabled them to speak, and Kuro could often feel something that allowed him to sense when Jaden was nearby, feeling just for his *presence* alone. The nameless thing within them felt like standing in a shallow current of black water that tugged at one's legs, always pulling him toward some dark destination...it was coiling, tensing, *growing*.

And at last, it woke.

It moved in Jaden first.

"What happened?" Caroline whispered, her eyes childlike in their hugeness.

Kuro paused, unsure of how to go on. There would have to be lies from this point, much fiction woven into the facts, not to mention outright omissions...he looked down at the floor, seeking help among the blandness of the kitchen tiles. Necessity had never mothered invention in him; his imagination remained empty, unmoved, and no lie would come to him.

"It just – happened," he fumbled, and moved on.

Jaden had stopped speaking to him after the *holy dark* moved within him. It was as if they couldn't understand each other anymore – they were operating on two separate levels of consciousness, like a pet and its master. Kuro would press against him, whimpering; his friend remained by his side, but when he would turn to look at him, his eyes gleamed with an intelligence that frightened him.

As the weeks went by, the silence only stretched onward. They hunted together, kept warm together, but the companionship was gone. Something had changed about Jaden, and that something stood between them like an unbreachable wall, separating them from the kinship they had shared. Another month of winter dragged on, with temperatures dropping even lower. They had to break through icicles one evening just to get back into their cave for warmth. Food had become nonexistent; Kuro was gaunt and lonely...and giving up.

And then *holy dark* moved in him at last, awakening him to hunger and pain and *need*.

He had been trying to sleep, curled into a tight ball, his snout pressed against his chest, his nose tucked under his tail. Sleep wouldn't come; he listened to the quiet sound of Jaden breathing beside him; outside, the hushed *whump* of a lump of snow sliding from a branch was the only noise that broke through the curtain of night.

And then, all at once, everything changed.

When it happened, it felt like a single, powerful heartbeat in a world of complete stillness. His pupils contracted to pinpricks, plunging him into darkness as a rush of sensation overcame him. A wave of panic crashed into him, dragging him down like a rip current into a churning sea. The river of energy he had been standing in all this time was no river: it was the ocean itself, and it was angry now, rising up in terrible waves to pummel and drown him.

Had he been human, he would have screamed until his throat bled.

Kuro didn't make a sound.

Instead, he scrambled to his feet, rearing up. He slammed his head against the cave wall, bashing his skull repeatedly against the stone with the desperation of an animal eager to kill itself rather than face slaughter. He struggled to tear himself out of his own flesh, his black fur damp with blood as he threw himself desperately against the rock while Jaden, awake and aware of what was happening, tried to snap at his heels to stop him.

All he could think of was getting *it* out of him: it was growing inside of him, and everywhere it grew, it *consumed:* he was hungry, *unbearably* hungry and *empty*, and this *thing* was demanding to eat, demanding to fill the emptiness or else drag him to some dark place he could not understand, only sense. *That* was where the current was pulling him down to die, that horrible, empty space in his heart that was growing now with a vicious rapidity that left him half crazed and fully aware of *everything* in a way that he had never known before.

Kuro spun and snarled at Jaden, the blood already freezing into red ice on his whiskers. Jaden pressed back for only a moment, but it was enough.

He whirled around and dashed away, his heart clenching and crying out within him.

A blanket of pain enveloped him as he ran – the cold was unbearable, but worse, the *knowledge* that the cold was somehow intolerable, that he suddenly wanted to be warm and soothed and held, made it worse. His mind had sharpened, expanded. Consciousness – true consciousness – had descended upon him with an existential horror that robbed him of any chance at returning to his life before this night.

His body felt weightless; his black eyes were glinting in the dark, the snow driving against them as he ran along a river too deep to freeze over; instead, small patches of ice clumped together, rushing away, then disappearing over a sudden, sheer darkness.

There had been a roaring in his ears – maybe it was Jaden, crying out to him to stop, the first words in weeks, or more likely it was the rushing cascade of the waterfall's edge. Either way, as Kuro found himself running faster along the icy bank, his paws skidding on the slick stones, a hopelessness crushed down upon him, sharpened by his new, awake mind.

He realized that he was condemned to live and struggle in the world.

He realized he was irrevocably different from all the other animals in the forest, more different than he had ever truly realized, and that he would live and die a life devoid of meaning while his brain was forced to stare on in horror, aware now of its own senseless existence.

And far, far worse: he realized that he would have to fill this *other* hunger inside of him, that it would never truly leave him, never be satisfied.

He had never known good and evil before, and now he saw that evil lived and moved in *him*, demanded from *him*, that he would be a slave to it all his life... and then, at last, it would ultimately consume him.

All of this flashed through his thoughts in the blink of a moment with the expansion of his conscious mind, and in the wake of that moment, he realized that he wanted to die.

His back legs tensed as he sprang over the edge, his form graceful as he fell softly down through the empty space of the night, down into the roaring waters below.

In a strange, soft way, it was like a reversal of birth.

As Kuro sank into the river, the thunder of the water crashing onto the rocks slowly faded until it was only a gentle thrumming. He never even felt the impact of his body against the freezing waters as he sank, his fur gently floating around him, swaying in the current. The cold had shocked his body into an involuntary gasp, and water had rushed into his jaws, filling his lungs. It would be a swift, numbing, merciful death.

His body felt light, and yet his chest was strangely heavy. The world had grown very dark and quiet; it was impossible to know if his eyes were open or closed, if he were awake or unconscious.

For the first time, a dream passed before his eyes, a succession of images and sounds.

-A girl with a radiant smile and hair that fell in thick, silver tresses-
-blue eyes surrounded by white light-
-never-ending warmth-
-a young boy brandishing a stick-
-a little girl, laughing, applauding-
-the colors of springtime: green, pink, gold-
-the same blue eyes: wide, pleading, desperate-
-and sobbing, screaming-

The water had ceased to feel like water; the world grew steadily blacker as he drifted down into the depths, and nothing was cold anymore. Everything felt *warm*, and the warmth wrapped itself around him and held him in that one, perfect moment, promising oblivion and release.

A soft eternity came and went.

A sudden pain brought him back to reality. Suddenly, his lungs were burning – it felt as if they were trying to tear themselves from his chest. He gagged again, struggling and fighting against whatever it was that had bit into his flank and was pulling him up, back up to the surface...

His head burst into the open air, gasping, and the world exploded into sound. Someone was swimming furiously, dragging his body up onto the rocks. He rolled over and began to violently cough up water, his body trembling from the cold. It felt like knives had been shoved into his ribs; his limbs gave out beneath him, and his head ached with a pain that was all-encompassing, pressing behind his eyeballs.

Kuro! Jaden cried, his body soaked. Already the water was freezing into a crust on his fur. *Kuro, breathe! Speak to me!*

He collapsed fully on the rocks, heaving. His lungs ached horribly; a hideous pain was beginning to spread across his lower body where Jaden's jaws had clamped into him.

But there was something else, too. When Kuro closed his eyes, he could still feel Jaden there and hear his friend's frantic panting, but beyond those senses, there was something *new*.

He could sense Jaden's *presence*. Before, it had been a whisper; now, it was a shout. He could feel the power in his friend, the same *thing* that had driven him into the water, to death, coiled up in the belly of the demon beside him, waiting to be summoned. They could sense that same power in one another now.

Kuro struggled to his feet and shook the water from his fur, pausing; he looked up into the winter sky. The black outline of the new moon was visible, silent and empty.

Are you alive? Jaden asked.

He thought that was a ridiculous thing to ask; wasn't he standing, breathing? Hadn't Jaden just saved his life?

But he was looking at him with new meaning. Kuro was coated in blood and ice; he was still coughing up water, his legs trembled with the effort just to stand, and every part of him was in aching pain...

And yet.

I've never felt so alive before, he whispered. He could remember everything from a few moments ago with a clarity he had never before possessed; he could relive the crushing weight of the water over and over again with a self-awareness that made him shudder, but memories of before – of yesterday, and the day before that – were fuzzy, mostly colors and scents. It was all gone from him, fading; he had crossed a bridge, and the bridge had fallen away.

There was no undoing this, no going back.

He wasn't just alive; he was awake.

And he was *hungry*.

Jaden grinned at him, a startling image through his fangs. Suddenly, all of the loneliness and abandonment that Kuro had felt in the past month had washed away; their bond rushed in on him again, comforting and renewed. He understood now that

Jaden had become what he was supposed to be, and Kuro, until the *holy dark* had moved in him, had been nothing more than an animal at his side.

Are you sure? Jaden asked. Their eyes met and exchanged a look that expressed all that needed to be said between them.

When they returned to their cave, they shook the ice from their pelts and gave a great yawn before curling up together, their snouts resting on each other's backs as they slept in patient slumber, waiting for the rest of their lives.

Caroline had nothing to say.

That's a first, he thought with some measure of satisfaction, but his thoughts came too soon – her mouth moved to open, then shut again as she shook her head slowly in amazed wonder.

"So when it moved in you...you had a dream?" It was her best attempt at speech.

Kuro puzzled for a moment, caught off guard. He had expected questions, but not about that. "Did I say I had a dream?" He shook his head. "No, demons don't dream."

"You don't, or you can't?"

"We don't because we can't."

"But you said you had a dream," she insisted. "You said when you started to lose consciousness, you dreamt."

He had mentioned the dream, but not told her the details.

"It was a hallucination, then," he amended. He felt uneasy; he didn't want to discuss the dream, or the fact that he had continued to have it over and over again, multiple times a week, every time he slept. It never went away, those images...those sounds. He didn't know what it meant; he *knew* that demons didn't dream, that Jaden also didn't believe him about it...and he wished he had never mentioned that part of his past at all. He didn't want to think about it.

"I see," she said, but he could hear her doubt. "So the two of you have been together all this time. And the *holy dark*...is inside of you? Why do you call it that?"

"...I don't know," he admitted. "We just knew...that's what it was called. When it awoke in me, I knew its name."

"And it's why you need to feed on souls, it's how you can move shadows and change...?"

He felt disgusted with himself. "It *is* me. At least, a part of me. It's the part that hungers."

"It's killing you. It's why you're starving to death."

He attempted a smile, but it was crooked. "Not yet," he said.

"Eventually." She rose. He watched as she moved as if in a daze, her thoughts muddled – he could feel her soul moving throughout her tranquilly as it thought and pondered over something. Her hands gathered up her garden tools from the kitchen counter without much interest, her eyes staring beyond the edge of the woods outside the window.

"I'm going to do some gardening," she said, but her voice was lost in her own thoughts. "I'd like some time to think for a while... about all this. By myself," she added.

She turned around, her eyes fluttering up to his for one second before falling away. "Thank you for sharing your past with me, Kuro," she said, just before walking out of the door.

He wondered what she thought and felt about his story, but her soul was oddly still. There was so much more to tell, so much more he realized he wanted to share with her, but the edges of her soul pushed him away and told him that she wanted to be alone, and so he sat, thinking.

He had promised to tell her about himself, and by doing so, tell her about Jaden, but that...that he could not do. And now Jaden knew about her... and he didn't know how much he could truly trust him. A memory – a memory he had kept from Caroline – clawed at him now, and he took an uneasy breath, unable to shove it from his thoughts.

It had been much different for Jaden when the *holy dark* stirred inside of him.

It was one of a handful of memories from before the *holy dark* moved in him that he could recall with perfect clarity.

Kuro had been sleeping on the cavern's floor when Jaden suddenly rose and raced out into the night – no bashing his skull against the stone to stop the pulsing temple beneath it, just a sudden flight into a world bright with a full moon. Without the added heat from Jaden's warmth, the *kitsune* stirred and woke sleepily after about an hour, shivering. Kuro rose, stretched, and froze; the familiar scent of blood was in the air, and Jaden was gone.

Kuro ran to find him. His paws crunched through a thin layer of snow as he searched, following his nose.

Jaden's footsteps had already disappeared, the tracks erased by the fresh snowfall that had begun, but Kuro managed to follow them as he ran in between the barren pines, stopping only when he spotted a sudden splash of burgundy under the moonlight.

There, not twenty feet in front of him, Jaden stood with his tail raised high, his eyes flashing with malevolent revulsion at everything around him. The red irises looked darker, like old, rich wine filled with bile and hatred.

Jaden's snout was covered in blood.

Beneath him, a doe lay dead, its tongue lolling from its mouth, its eyes rolled back. The once graceful neck had been ripped open, the exposed strands of muscle pulled apart and shredded as Jaden sated himself on the animal. The steam from its innards rose around him in a thick mist, the brown hide gleaming as the snow melted from the heat of its blood.

Jaden stepped forward over the body, his eyes wild. He didn't appear to recognize Kuro, and he snarled a threat to stay away as his tail slashed the air behind him.

Kuro watched as the demon shoved his snout into the deer, grabbing the organ sacks in his jaws, and shook them viciously, shredding them. He was not interested in eating, only in the total mutilation and destruction of the creature beneath him. He ripped at the animal until its flesh dangled like ribbon, and still his body shook with fury in its effort to pulverize bone. Kuro's slender legs took a step back, his tail curling between them, and he turned and retreated toward the cavern, shaken and confused.

When Jaden returned the next morning, he slumped heavily onto the ground at Kuro's side and fell promptly asleep without saying a word. His whole body was soaked in a crust of thick, dried blood; it had turned his fur a muddy brown.

When he first glanced at him, it seemed for a moment that the maroon *kitsune* was gone, temporarily replaced instead by some brown, common animal who now slept an uncomplicated slumber: a wolf, perhaps. The real him was hidden under this new layer of death, buried beneath the viscera of another being's life.

Only now, as Kuro sat in Caroline's kitchen, did he realize that that had been exactly what Jaden had always wanted.

THREE

All his life, Kenneth had felt pathetic.

He hadn't faced any particularly difficult challenges, and the knowledge that he had lived a fairly easy life, nearly idyllic by most people's standards, and that he *still* could not be happy only made him feel that much worse. It was like he had been born with a blight rooted inside his soul, something sad and misshapen, and it had poisoned his ability to enjoy life and robbed him of everything he should have been.

When he thought about the two people who attacked him, the hardest part was picturing that other version of himself. That version was bold, powerful...that version looked perfect. That version was everything he could never be.

It hurt to think about him.

Jacqueline still refused to engage with him beyond the perfunctory greeting and goodbye in class. The silence between them was agonizing. He had tried calling her repeatedly, determined to be a better version of himself, and was met with only the beep of a voicemail.

Kenneth took a long, steadying breath, imagined he was someone other than who he was, and locked up his house.

It was close to eleven in the evening when he knocked on Jacqueline's door.

There was a long answer of nothing, and then he knocked again, waiting. "It's me," he managed to croak.

Finally a face peeked out through the glass pane along the side of the entrance, and then the door flew open and Jacqueline stood fuming at him. She hadn't yet gotten into her pajamas, and she wore a long skirt that trailed at her ankles, but her midriff and arms were bare.

"Kenneth, what the hell do you think you're doing here?"

"Can we please talk?"

Her reply was an angry scoff, but she stepped aside, letting him in. He went into the living room and sat down, waiting for her to join him. When she did, she crossed her arms over her chest, glaring. She looked tired, he noticed. Almost sick.

There appeared to be a pile of tortoise shells on the living room table, long strips of leather dangling from them. He stared at them, uncomprehending.

"What is it you want to say? If you're here to try and convince me of what Eric said –"

"I'm not. Please...just listen. I talked to Eric; I have something important to tell you."

But with her waiting, he suddenly didn't know how to begin. It was hard to apologize, harder still to meet her gaze. He stumbled through the latest developments of his life: the police search, the conversation with Eric...and all the while, he grew increasingly ashamed. He had banged on her door in the middle of the night, and here he was, once again just talking about himself. Eric had said that Jacqueline cared for him; that seemed impossible. How could anyone care about someone so self-centered? He hadn't asked how she was doing, why she looked so exhausted. He hadn't even said hello.

He hadn't told her about the uncomfortable, terrifying weight of the gun he now carried in his pocket.

Jacqueline listened, her expression carefully blank. "You think Eric's friend is hiding one of the killers?"

"I don't know. He never mentioned her name. He doesn't want to get her involved."

"It's probably his ex," she mused. "I know he dated someone down at the station, but it was short-lived..."

"He's also worried he'll go to jail for stealing medical supplies and treating someone illegally."

"And you're worried that if he reports what he saw, it could put things in motion. Bad things."

"Right." That's what Eric had warned him, anyways, and the more he thought about it, the more he feared it made sense to proceed with caution.

"If you're asking me for advice...then I don't know what you should do. If you report it, you could endanger Eric and his friend. On the other hand, if you don't, and that guy is the one who attacked you, you could be putting more people's lives at risk, including your own. It's like that old ethical dilemma...you can protect one person you know, or a whole city of people you don't."

He cringed. "When you put it that way, I know I should tell Eric to go to the police, but...I don't know."

"I'm sorry." She sighed and pulled her hair over her shoulder, rubbing her neck. "I didn't mean to make it sound like it was an obvious choice. It isn't – it never is. I don't know what you should do."

Her movements were fatigued. There had always been a kinetic, almost quicksilver sureness in her actions, but she moved now as though weighted down by some heavy burden. "Are you...okay?"

"I'm fine," she answered automatically. It was a bald-faced lie.

"You're not. You look like a wreck."

She frowned. "You don't look so great either, you know."

"Jacqueline, I don't want to fight with you. I'm...sorry."

Her eyes were flinty. "Sorry for what, exactly?"

He took a deep, steadying breath. "I'm sorry I don't believe in the same things you do. I wish I did, because then you wouldn't hate me right now, but I don't. I never have. And I respect you too much to show up here and lie to you, or tell you that I've changed my mind. I haven't. I still think Eric is right. But I want you to know...that even though we think differently about this...I'm still here for you, if you'll let me be. I'm sorry for being offensive, earlier; I was being insensitive. I want you to believe whatever you want, and I want you to know I'm okay with that. I mean – you don't need my permission to believe whatever you want," he clarified, feeling as though he were pinwheeling, falling headfirst into rambling incoherence, "It's just, I...I miss you." *I don't deserve to miss you,* he would have admitted in a heartbeat, *but I do.*

Her gaze softened. She stood and moved closer to him, the cushion barely sinking with the weight of her. She studied his face for a long time and then asked, "Do you really mean that?"

"...I do."

Neither spoke until she reached over and placed her hand on his.

"You didn't tell me how Albert died," she said.

"Oh." The change in topic caught him unawares. He cleared his throat and told her about how his liver had failed, how a transplant wasn't an option, and how one night he had told a neighbor he hadn't felt well and left a party early to go lie down. Albert had never once, in his entire life, left a party early. He had died that night in his sleep.

"I'm sorry to hear that," she said. "I liked Albert. He was always smiling."

He nodded, deeply uncomfortable that she had brought his death up. Kenneth thought of him all the time; he still hadn't brought himself to box up any of Albert's belongings. It was a bit like living in a grave and feeling like an intruder, but every time he picked something up, no matter how innocuous, Kenneth slowly put it back where it belonged, feeling grief rake its claws across his heart. "Eric mentioned your dad..."

"Cancer." The word hung with a ringing finality, as if there was nothing more to be said about it. She pulled her hand away. "He didn't want to get treatment at first. He wanted to just let it takes it course and pass on. In the end, my mom convinced him to do it, if not for her...than for me. He suffered more from the treatment than the cancer itself. She hasn't forgiven herself; that's why she moved away. She couldn't stay here...she saw him everywhere. Not literally," she added, shooting him a pointed glance, "Just... the memories. She's in Savannah, now. I think after I finish up here I'll head down there to be with her. She'd like that, I think. She'll sell this house and have some money to eventually retire on."

Kenneth turned to her. A new strain had entered her voice. "What is it?"

"What's what?"

"Jacqueline." He forced himself to be like that other, perfect version of himself who haunted his nightmares now, to do what he thought was impossible, to reach up and push her hair back, take her hand, and turn her to look at him. "What's wrong?"

For a moment, he thought she was going to crumple, to cry. Her mouth twisted, her eyes shut, and she drew a deep, shuddering breath...but no. Her spine was steel, and what he mistook for tears was merely a trick of the light. She sat up straighter, and when she looked at him, her eyes were mourning, but dry.

"I keep dreaming about him. Everything was so terrible...the months that led up to it. Hospice. And I wasn't there, at the very end. He kept calling for me. I could hear him from the other room. But you don't know what cancer does to a person. You don't know what he looked like. He died humiliated, broken, *destroyed*. I couldn't bring myself to go in there, Kenneth. I couldn't look at him like that. And then my mom came in, to tell me he had passed...and now I see him, in my dreams. And I know I can never make that right. I betrayed him. And I've never felt the same since...it's like my soul is cold, now. Like there's wind, rushing in through a door..."

He reached forward and pulled her close. She pressed her head against the folds of his jacket and sighed a long, shattering exhale, and he rested his chin on top of her head, tucking her in toward him. They held each other in a warm embrace, the minutes slipping away without comment.

At last, she pulled back and stared into his eyes, searching for something.

"Kenneth..." He could feel his heart clenching, his pulse racing. "Why did you never call me? Or write? Or...anything?"

He looked back, helpless.

"Because I love you."

She stared at him. Kenneth shut his mouth slowly and felt the energy drain out of him. The words had escaped in a choked, frightened whisper. He slumped backward onto the couch, his head in his hands.

"Because I love you," he said again, barely audible now. "Because I'm selfish and self-centered and I'm not good enough for you. I should have called you, or texted. Anything. I should have done *anything*. But I was afraid that...that you didn't care about me. As long as I didn't pick up the phone, I wouldn't have to confirm it. I'd never have to hear you tell me the truth...that I don't deserve you. Even though I read your texts, got your voice-mails...it was like there was this thing inside me, telling me it was all a lie, that you were just being polite, or nice...that I was an inconvenience. Every time I tried to text you back, I'd just stare at the screen, then delete it. I'm not worth your time, Jacqueline."

He hadn't heard her rise. He heard the sound of dishes moving in the kitchen, but he didn't look up. He kept his palms pressed firmly into his eyes.

He heard the whirr of a lighter and glanced up at last.

On the table in the living room, she had placed a small abalone shell. It was suspended between three sticks that formed a base, and in the shell, she placed a small plank of wood. The fire moved and caught it, and soon a sweet, woody smell began to fill the room as the gray smoke rose in curling tendrils; she motioned to the smoke with her hands, beckoning it to rise.

He opened his mouth to ask a question, but she held a hand up to her lips, silencing him.

"My mother is Cherokee," she said, and then she paused, as though startled by what she had said. "*I'm* Cherokee. But my mom...she wasn't very connected to her tribe. *Our* tribe. She always regretted that. Her heritage was passed down through her father's side, and disease cut away her grandparents before she knew them, so she never really came to know her culture – not the way she wanted to, she told me. And then there was my dad – he was part Chinook, did you know? This was a long, long time ago, before his side of the family moved across the country. I asked them once what percentage I was from each of their tribes and they laughed at me. Dad said I had more Creole than Chinook from him. Mom said her great-grand parents were full Cherokee, but that it didn't matter for her tribe, because we traced back to the Dawes Rolls.

I had no idea what that even meant, and I wanted to learn more.

I'd like to tell you that I went on some great spiritual journey, discovered my ancestors, but I didn't. I read a few books, went to a few gatherings. I think Mom was looking forward to rediscovering her heritage with me, together...but then Dad got sick. There was no time for anything anymore besides appointments and treatments, and long stretches of quiet so he could rest. But for a moment, it was nice to see my people. *My* people," she repeated, and she laughed. "If I can call them that. I feel like a fraud when I say it, like I don't measure up, because what do I know? When I looked at them, I thought I was looking back at living history...And I told my dad that, back before things got too bad, and he told me no, I had it all wrong. History unfolds in every minute, he said. They weren't just preserving traditions or putting on shows: they were *alive*. Our culture was changing, growing. I had it all backwards; they weren't living fossils. They were living *people*. And he said...I could still be a part of it. I would always belong to my people.

And I saw them dance.

I thought I might do that someday, too. I had this vision of my future, of what I could do and who I could be...and then none of it came to pass. It turns out my future wasn't a girl who danced with others in a circle, stomping. It was a girl who pulled a blanket over her head, pretending to be asleep, pretending not to hear her father calling for her hours before he died. That was who I became."

She stood; Kenneth didn't know what to say and was relieved to see that she expected no reply. Instead, she ignored him entirely, crossing to the other side of the table. She reached toward one of the piles of tortoise shells; to his surprise, they all lifted at once with a loud rattle; there were approximately a dozen box turtle shells all connected to what he now saw was a curved leather sheath, the cord strung through thick eyelets on each side. Each shell had a few holes drilled into them. Jacqueline bent one leg to the table and placed it along the length of her calf, just below the knee, and began lacing the straps. When she finished, she repeated the process with the other, testing them with a small hop; they remained firmly on her legs.

She stomped suddenly, loud, and the sound startled him. She took two small steps in quick, successive rhythm, her arms firmly straight at her sides...but then her lips quirked, and her hands stretched out and up; the wrists snapped, her palms moving upward in a flowing gesture like the smoke now hanging in the air, and he watched as she stomped again, harder, repeating the steps. A rhythm began to form, and her hands moved through the smoke, dipping; she paused, picking something up from underneath the table, and tossed it to him.

He caught it, surprised. It was a tortoise shell on a stick. She laughed at his puzzled expression.

"That's a tortoise shell rattle. My mother said it belonged to her grandfather; these are my grandmother's shackles. The men use that. I want you to keep a beat for me."

"...Me?" He wanted to protest; he had no rhythm, and he felt that whatever this was, whatever she was doing, he was not invited to participate in it.

But Jacqueline's eyes narrowed with insistence; she would not be denied. "Try – you can do it, Kenneth."

She began to dance again, moving rhythmically around the table, the smoke swirling around her hips, trailing in her hair. Kenneth beat the shell awkwardly at first, but he watched her feet and discovered her rhythm. She moved beautifully, powerfully, and her tiny frame pounded the ground with authority. In the smoke she writhed, and for a moment, she seemed inhuman, a soul lost in time, her arms high above her head, her skirt flowing at her feet. In the stomping and the smoke, he forgot his embarrassment, forgot that this was her way of not addressing what he had said, and he let it absorb him and pull him into a hazy place where time hung suspended, forgotten.

She had been dancing for nearly an hour when she at last stopped. Her forehead shown with sweat. The cedar plank had crumbled into ash, and the last embers were shuddering with the remains of life. She knelt and breathed upon them, and they flared in answer. He watched as she reached below the table again and brought a bit of braided grass up, setting it delicately in the flame. The embers flickered at it hungrily, and with renewed strength, burst back into life, gobbling up the sweetgrass.

She settled back on the floor. Her anger and ferocity from earlier was gone, and she smiled with a calm, peaceful expression. He understood that she had not danced for his benefit; she had been giving a gift to herself, and he had merely been here and allowed to witness it. Her eyes met his, shining; she didn't look so tired anymore.

"Why did you do that?"

"Why'd I dance? I've been keeping it up for hours, every night." She stretched her legs out, the silence slinking between them. She had grown thoughtful; Kenneth could tell she was wrestling with an internal struggle, deciding whether or not to share something with him. She had shared *this,* this beautiful moment of pure rhythm and sound...but now, she was holding something back, studying him, deciding how much she could trust him. How much faith she could truly put in him.

For a moment, she chewed her bottom lip, worrying at it...but silence won. She shook her head, sighing, and pointed out at the sliver of night beside her front door. "Call it my way of raising the battle flag, of saying *I'm here. I'm not afraid. I'm as powerful as you are.* I can dance in the face of darkness. I can defeat it."

But there was a creeping uncertainty in her words, the shadow of a doubt that kept them from being a boast. Fear had not yet been conquered.

Once again, she had rendered him speechless; he had no idea how to respond to that. He knew there was something she wasn't telling him, and all he could feel was a sinking shame at the truth that he wasn't worthy of her full confidence. He swallowed and had the decency to accept the judgement she passed upon him, and did not press the issue. Instead, he asked, "Where did you learn how to dance?"

"I didn't, not really – I'm not doing it right. My arms always want to do their own thing. I only saw the women do it once, at a festival. An old man got up there and sang for a while, and then some women danced in the middle of a dirt ring. I don't know why they were doing it, or what they were celebrating. Actually, he sounded sort of sad – maybe it wasn't a celebration. I wish I knew," she said, and he could hear the wistfulness in her voice. "So I'm just doing my best, doing what feels right. I burned the cedar to cleanse us, and the sweetgrass to bless us...so we can start over. Do you think it worked?"

He glanced away, uncomfortable. She laughed at him again and drew her legs up, stretching her arms.

"I know, I know – you don't have to believe. *I* believe it." But her smile had fallen away.

I believe in you, he wanted to say, and that was enough, but instead Kenneth took a deep breath and stared up at the ceiling, and his words came out in a breathless whisper. "I'm scared, Jacqueline."

"Yea," she whispered. "Me too."

For a weighted moment, he thought the silence would defeat them, but Jacqueline fought it, and won.

She undid each shackle and then stood, pulling the tortoise rattle from his lap and placed it on the couch, then moved to the stereo on top of the fireplace mantle. He watched as she put a disc in, then adjusted the dials. "This is more my dad's style," she said. "I think you'll like it."

A gentle, pulsing beat began, backed by the shivering of violins and the steady melody of trumpets hovering in the background. A marimba mimicked the melody as a snare joined in, shaping the beat. She turned to him then, and Jacqueline took his hands in hers and pulled him up, lifting one arm above her head as his other sank to her waist. "Do you know what I do when I'm scared?"

Kenneth could only manage a weak shake of his head; his arms trembled.

She smiled. "I dance."

She moved him, turning him around, guiding him in a gentle circle. He fumbled clumsily at first, trying to find the rhythm, and as he grew worse, her eyes lit up with merriment until she was throwing her head back and laughing. The sound lifted him up. He closed his hands over her fingers and tried to twirl her, and to his surprise, she spun and came back into his arms.

He forgot to judge himself and decide if he deserved this type of happiness. He forgot how to hate himself. He chose to ignore the fact that she hadn't answered him back when he said he loved her. He accepted that he had failed her in so many ways, that he was unworthy of this girl who granted him a forgiveness he didn't deserve. He forgot about murder and shadows that moved in the dark; he let go of guilt and shame. He clung to her arms and her smile, and for a moment, the sunken thing inside him seemed to disappear, and Kenneth laughed with uncomplicated joy. He knew the song would end, that this moment would end, and reality would crash back upon him, and he made the hard and conscious decision to ignore those facts for just the next two minutes.

For two minutes, he promised himself he would be happy.

The brass shifted, gaining momentum, and they jumped to the changed, energized beat. Engelbert's voice soared with the orchestra as they danced, laughing and spinning, faster and more frantic, swaying as only two clumsy, hopelessly happy people could do.

And in the night, watching through the windows, a demon disappeared, slipping away into the dark just as it had done many, many nights before.

Autumn arrived with a clinging dampness that melted into a persistent, gray drizzle. The tree bark deepened into black against the rain, throwing the colors of the remaining leaves into sharp relief. In the pale light of an autumn sun, nothing could glisten the way it would by December; instead, the world outside of Jacqueline's window looked almost slimy.

Jacqueline scanned the woods.

She knew he was out there, watching her...and there was the horrible, terrible truth that *he wanted her to know.*

For weeks now she'd had the uncomfortable sense of being followed, *spied* upon. There were times when she'd be walking down the sidewalk and feel as though an ice cube had melted on the top of her neck, cold water prickling down her spine...and she'd spin around to see nothing, just a few puzzled stares. Sometimes the strange warmth chased it away...but just as often, it didn't. The feeling followed her and kept her up at night. She knew it was him; at times, she wanted to scream. At first, she had even draped an extra bedsheet over the glass window that ran along the side of the front door. It took just two days until the duct tape began to sag from the weight of the sheets.

Maybe he expected her to wall up in her home, cowering in the closet. Maybe he expected her to flee. Perhaps he thought she would doubt her sanity, check herself into some hospital somewhere.

He had underestimated her.

"*Fuck you,*" she had muttered when she dragged the storage box out from under her mother's bed. The top of the cardboard was thick with dust; she ignored it entirely when she lifted out the tortoise shell shackles. "*Fuck you,*" she cursed when she pulled the bedsheets down from the front window. She wasn't a fool; she was terrified, but she didn't have to let him know that. *I'm going to show you who I really am,* she had thought in a brazen fury.

But the weeks went on, and she didn't see the man (*the demon*), 'Jake,' again in person, and after letting Kenneth into her home, she allowed him back into her daily life. There had been no new murders, either...but also no new leads. One of the photo-journalists over at the *Times* had taken Kenneth under his wing, and from him, Kenneth had learned and passed on a few more bits of information that the press knew, but had not printed.

'Trophies' had been taken from the two crime scenes, spurring investigators to look back at the Brittany Alice murder more closely. Her body had been cremated, but Kenneth told her, "Matthew said that when the investigators followed up with the family about her remaining effects, the family confirmed that something *was* missing from the crime scene." Naturally, the police hadn't disclosed what was missing. It was the sort of key evidence that, if found, could close the case on a suspect...because animals didn't take trophies.

It had been enough for the Buncombe County Police Department to swallow their pride; a triple homicide across county lines with the telltale signs of a serial killer was enough for them to kick the case over to the FBI. The headlines had picked back up for a moment, and with nothing new, the story had died a few weeks ago.

Kenneth figured it was the last bit of info he'd learn for a while; after speaking with the police himself, he had been told he could no longer submit any content related to the developing story, should he produce any, and that he would no longer be included in any further developments. It would harm the paper's objectivity, he was told, but Matthew offered to grab a beer with him and fill him in, off the record, if anything else popped up.

"I think the killers have moved on," Kenneth told her mid-October, overcome with relief.

But Jacqueline, who felt eyes lingering on her wherever she went, didn't think so.

No, she thought, shivering; *they're just distracted.*

She couldn't bring herself to tell Kenneth about the encounter with the demon in the library. There were so many moments where she thought she might, but then she would look harder at him and find herself reminded of his fragility. There were things he simply could not accept; that the world could have spirits, shapeshifters, *demons* even...that was something she believed.

It wasn't important to her if *he* believed in them or not; she felt no need to convince him, though she worried about his safety with almost obsessive dread. He'd revealed to her that Eric had given him a gun, and for half a moment she had the distinct desire to go straight to Eric's house and punch him right in his smug, empty face. Kenneth didn't know how to use a gun, and when she asked if he was practicing with it, he had said no; he hadn't shot it, not even once.

She had breathed a sigh of relief. He was more likely to hurt himself.

And that thought had stayed with her, burdensome. *He was more likely to hurt himself.* Maybe she wasn't the only one who'd been hurt by his absence, his silence. Maybe some small, mean streak in Eric had justified giving the gun to Kenneth by pointing out the truth (Kenneth needed to protect himself) and intentionally ignoring the obvious: Kenneth should not have a gun.

Eric, she thought, clenching her jaw with frustration; Eric had told Kenneth he provided medical aid to someone who looked just like Kenneth.

Someone who'd been wounded in his leg.

Eric had convinced Kenneth that life was full of coincidences while simultaneously handing him a weapon.

Coward, she had thought. No, more than a coward...was he capable of being so cruel? Had that same mean streak, some secret ache of anger, spurred him to look at Kenneth, to give him a loaded gun, and to think *he's more likely to hurt himself.*

Because Kenneth had his own demon to grapple with, and it wasn't hiding in Asheville.

It was inside him.

She wished it was otherwise, desperately. She didn't want to think Eric was capable of that kind of insidious intention; he was their friend. There were so many things she wished: she wanted to confide in Kenneth, to have him beside her as an ally in her struggle against the demon who was stalking her, but she saw him now with a level of objectivity that she had never before possessed. He didn't have the strength to face this, she thought; it didn't matter that he had seen the evidence of the supernatural with his very own eyes. He had the kind of mind that told itself that what it had witnessed was wrong, that he was merely confused; he would protect himself from a truth that could crush him.

Eric was different: Eric simply *refused* to face the truth. Anything that didn't fit neatly into his worldview simply *could not be.* He had seen a man who looked *just like Kenneth,* wounded right leg and all, and had said *coincidence.*

It was *unfathomable* to her that neither of them was willing to take action. She couldn't conceive of it. Someone had to do *something.*

And so in the evenings, she danced, defiant.

But during the day, she began to plan.

It had begun with her aborted research. Jacqueline had thought back to that beast in the forest many, many times, panning her memories for new details as she searched online for answers, clues as to what she was up against, or why one of them was stalking her: long legs, slightly lupine body...and it could turn into a person.

There was the *lougarou,* a type of werewolf, but no – it *wasn't* a wolf, she was *certain* of that. It was too lean to be a *crocotta,* the legs too long and feline. She'd been hopeful when she discovered something called a 'Ringdocus,' but no: that was much too like a dog.

Its snout had been angular, pointed. Its tail was the length of its body, beautiful in its own way: long and flowing, belling out at the end –

Like a fox. Not as bushy as an actual fox, no: it was sleek.

She knew she was right the moment the insight hit her, and the Internet returned with page and pages of answers: *kumiho, huli jing...*

Kitsune.

They weren't all the same; the Korean *kumiho,* the Chinese *juli jing,* and the Japanese *kitsune* were all foxes that could turn into humans, but they all had distinctive traits and stories specific to their respective cultures. She tumbled down into this new world of myth she'd never heard of, finally finding the discipline to sit still long enough to learn something useful. There were famous *kitsune* whose names were etched in legend; there were categories, stories, warnings and songs. Nearly all of the tales were about *female kitsune;* they could work special tricks, a type of individualized magic. They could produce something called 'fox fire.' They were not demons in the Western sense of the word: these were *yokai,* creatures of spirit and mist, and while 'demon' was a muddled Anglican translation of the concept, she grasped at once that they weren't inherently evil; some were even good, eager to serve and help humans.

And some *were not.*

Some were vicious, malevolent, and cruel. Some were devoted to destruction.

At first there had been too much to take in, too much to learn all at once, but Jacqueline sat for hours, her eyes poring over the information, and finally she was able to condense all she learned into one simple fact:

Her life was in danger, and it would be up to her to do something about it.

Her trust in herself was absolute.

And she had no intention of waiting around to be a victim.

———

She'd been reading in the evenings about *kitsune,* and every new link brought her to a new story, another old woodblock pressing, a deeper myth. It felt like stepping up to a garden wall and peering down over the edge onto the other side, where fantasy and madness crawled. Every so often she would pause and ask herself if she was losing her grip on reality; was this how it began for people who fell down the long tunnel of conspiracy theories? Did they think themselves fully sane and rational, even in the grip of their mental illness? Was that her, even now?

No, she thought, and grimaced; those people probably said the same thing to themselves with equal certainty. *No. I'm not wrong.*

In her mind, Jacqueline pulled herself on top of that wall, preparing herself for the leap down into this new world where spirits prowled.

It was her only choice, she thought. She was convinced the killers had not left Asheville, and she believed that she was the next victim. The sensible thing was to go to the police, but what would she tell them – that she suspected the murderers were shapeshifting fox spirits, and that because she felt a horrible, crawling sensation whenever she left her house, that she knew she was being stalked?

Kenneth continued to come over in the evenings; they often worked next to each other on their classwork in comfortable silence. During the stretching quiet, there had been so many times when she'd nearly opened her mouth to tell him of the plan she was forming...but no. She was worried he'd tell Eric.

She decided to skip class on Tuesday to put her plan into motion; she feared the demon stalking her knew her routine, but doing something unexpected might give her just enough time to get to where she needed to go without being followed, and there were long stretches of time when she knew he wasn't around at all.

She was heading to the police department after all, but not to speak with a detective.

There was a secretary she wanted to meet.

A feeling like a soft blanket of warmth came over her suddenly just as she grabbed her purse, flowing down her arms and wrapping around her heart.

She slipped her keys into her pocket. Her hand was on the front doorknob of her home when a voice spoke in her head.

Don't do what you're thinking, Jacqueline.

She whirled around at once, her voice hitching. "*Show yourself!*" She screamed.

Nothing appeared, but the safe, warm feeling, the same she had felt in the library, came over her again more strongly, sinking deep into her bones.

"What's happening?" She whispered. She pressed her back against the front door. "What's going on? What *are* you?" *It's not my voice,* she thought, panicked; it hadn't been her voice she'd heard in the forest, or in the library – this was something else, different from the demon, and it was with her now, *in her home.*

Jacqueline tried to swallow her fear, but she trembled nevertheless.

I'm trying to protect you.

"What are you!?"

Its answer was immediate and sobering. *I am the creature standing between you and death.*

"Why?" Her heart raced as adrenaline surged. *It's talking to me. I'm talking to...it.* "Why are you protecting *me*? Why not those other people? Why do *I* matter?"

It didn't answer.

She swallowed; her mouth had gone all cottony, and though her legs shook, she stood up straighter, willing herself to remain calm. *Keep it talking – don't let it go away!* "Are they real? The... the *kitsune*? Is that what they are?"

Yes. It floated to her as a whisper, far away now, but Jacqueline had the sense that it was somehow holding on. Doubt tried to sneak in and tell herself that she was having a psychotic break with reality, but she stamped it out: she was scared, but *sane*, and that certainty helped her to find her voice again.

"Are they responsible for the murders?"

No, they are not.

Its voice was strained, almost as though it were struggling to speak.

Just one of them.

Her head snapped up.

"Which one?"

Nothing.

"The maroon one? Or the one who looks like Kenneth?" And when the silence resumed, "*Tell me!*"

It didn't answer. She clenched her fists in frustration.

"*Why* is it after *me*?" She felt furious at the way her voice pitched; she would need to be stronger than that if she were to face down a pair of demons. "If you want to protect me, why won't you tell me?"

The voice returned, strained, as though it were caught in a terrible struggle. *Because I'm afraid of what you will do. I cannot do much to help you, Jacqueline. I can't always be there to protect you. I'm trying – I am failing. Don't do what you are thinking of doing.*

"What are you? Are you....are you an angel?"

She wasn't sure why she had asked that; it could be anything, after all, and yet...there was a promise in that warmth around her heart, a promise somehow of goodness and courage and light.

I am.

"Why are you protecting me?"

I am protecting you because I do not want you to be killed by the kitsune.

"Why?"

In answer, a light began to glow.

She watched, astonished, as a small light grew in the room, flickering, like a single, burning flame, suspended a few feet in front of her. She could have held it in her palm, but her arms were frozen to her sides now, her voice a shaking whisper. "Are you my guardian angel?" She'd never believed in such a thing before, but now...?

No. Such a thing does not exist.

"Then why are you protecting me?"

The flame flickered, but did not answer.

"...What about Kenneth? Can you protect him? They attacked him, too."

It was the one thing that had held her back for weeks now. She had figured out where to find the demons based on what Eric had told Kenneth. His 'friend' was his ex-girlfriend, and all Jacqueline needed to do was go down to the police station and ask for the names of the secretaries, pop them into an online property search, and see who owned a farm. She would know where the demons were hiding, and even if it meant risking her life, she'd confront them. She had formulated a plan, and she felt certain she could get Eric's gun from Kenneth without his noticing...

But she didn't know what would happen to Kenneth. They'd attacked him once already, sparing his life...

What would they do to him if she failed?

And could she do it: could she really look into the eyes of a living creature, squeeze a trigger, and end its life?

Especially one who looked just like Kenneth?

She'd have to...because if she didn't, she would have to resign herself to waiting for the day when they showed up to kill her, and that she wouldn't do. And if she failed, she feared Kenneth would find the courage to go after them, which would surely be his death sentence.

She had never answered him back when he said, "I love you." She knew what was in her heart, and the thought of anything happening to him, anything threatening *him* had kept her a prisoner of indecision for almost a month now.

But if this thing – this *angel* – would protect him...

"Will you make sure nothing happens to him?"

...*I'm sorry, Jacqueline,* it whispered; it sounded like its heart was breaking. *That I will not do.*

Will not – not *can* not. Jacqueline swallowed, angry. "But you'll protect *me*?"

I will try...but it is very difficult for me. I am not truly here right now.

She didn't need an explanation; she just wanted to convince it to help Kenneth. "I don't need you," she tried to tell it, pleading with this light in her home, speaking to nothing. "*He* might. I can take care of myself. Please, can't you –"

No.

"*Why?!*"

It didn't answer.

Jacqueline stared into the heart of that pulsing heat, into the golden, flickering center. It was possible that she was hallucinating, that she was encompassed now in a great cloud of unknowing and was walking through the miasma of her delusion toward some martyr's end or else institutionalized care. It wasn't just possible; it was *probable*. That's what Eric would say if he were here right now.

She discovered how preferable that would be to the truth: that there were things – giant, unknowable things – and mysteries that lived with her side-by-side that she could never understand. There were beings that could change their shape, 'angels' or voices or whatever this creature was, living by rules she could not begin to comprehend, playing a game toward a goal they would not share, for reasons they would not divulge, occupying spaces beyond either 'life' or 'death.' The comforting dichotomy of a world where things began and ended had been discarded for an entirely new reality where nothing was known any more. Nothing could be the same for her, to have heard this voice speak, confirming the existence of demons, to have seen this flame hovering before her eyes.

In her heart, she took the final leap over the wall, and came down firmly on the other side.

There was no turning back now. Her voice was a command.

"You have to protect him. Not just me."

The angel said nothing. The flame flickered.

"I love him," she tried; oh, her traitorous heart...she did. She always had. It was good and painful and necessary to hear it out loud. The light dimmed. "*You have to protect him!*"

Don't follow this path, Jacqueline. Leave them alone.

"Even if I do...he won't leave me alone, will he? ...The maroon one." She felt certain it was him who had killed those people, but that didn't make the black one any less dangerous: at the very least, he was an accomplice.

No. He will never stop wanting you.

She tried to fight off the wave of despair that came with those words. "Why?"

Jacqueline thought the silence would stretch forever, that the angel would not speak, but at last, in a voice that sounded as though it were in pain, it answered her.

There are those who we belong to, it said.

She didn't understand what this had to do with the demon, though, or why it had become obsessed with her. There was something more to be said, some further step from this toward the answer she sought as to why the demon would never stop following her, *wanting* her. She waited for it to continue, but the silence only grew. At last, she tried a different route. "And you... do you belong to me?"

No. The flame quavered for a moment, heavy with sadness. *I am not yours.*

And then, like a light bulb flailing and extinguishing, it was gone. The room was dimmer by a fraction; for a moment the warmth remained on her skin like the last touch of a summer's sunset.

Then it lifted, and the chill crept in.

For a long beat of quiet, Jacqueline considered the different possible futures beyond this single second: in one, she put her purse down on the counter. She returned to her bedroom. She waited.

In the other, she turned the handle of her front door, and took the first offensive step against her enemy.

Jacqueline paused long enough to square her shoulders for one indulgent second more, and then she stepped outside, into the rain.

Four

September fell into the jewel-toned world of October with the steady drumming of the autumn rain.

Kuro was used to being in-tune with the seasons, but more and more of himself seemed to be slipping away. A year ago, he could close his eyes and sense sunrise, or press his ears to the ground and hear twilight approaching in the calls of the bullfrogs. He felt seasons turn in his bones, his coat growing thicker in winter, a compulsion to eat roaring in him through the fall.

Those instincts grew quiet with the rise of the harvest moon. Before he had even noticed that time had stolen away, the bark in the trees that lined the edge of Caroline's farm had grown dark. The maple trunks had turned almost black even as the aspen trunks hardened into the white of bones, their leaves a burning liquid gold, and the wind turned crisp and pleasant.

When Caroline let him, he slept in her living room, his feet stretched to the very end of her couch. At some point, he had stopped sleeping as a *kitsune,* and the floor was no longer comfortable. Every other night, he slunk out into the barn, trading places with the dog. It made him feel humiliated and frustrated to be put out like that, but he said nothing; she loved the animal, and even if it barked at him to the point of a frothed muzzle, he didn't express his distaste.

She could see it in the way he scowled at it, though.

The hay was scratchy and uncomfortable in the morning; even if he bedded down as a *kitsune,* his tail wrapping over his nose, he always awoke as a human now. It had surprised him, the first time; now, it annoyed him.

Caroline had offered to let him sleep in her brother Christopher's old room rather than the couch. He had tried it once and left for two reasons. The first was that she thought she could shut him in the room and keep Feral in the house. Neither Kuro nor Feral were pleased by the arrangement, and the dog gouged deep grooves in the wood of the door in his effort to break through and maul him until Caroline managed to drag him out to the barn.

The second reason he had more trouble in explaining to Caroline, opting instead to lie and say the room smelled too much like the dog. It wasn't that at all; rather, it *felt* too much like Christopher. His imprint, the ghostly *something* that humans left behind, was on everything, and all around him it left a feeling of unease, as though everything was slightly off tilt.

Something had happened in this room; it had left a heavy dread behind, a weight that made it hard for him to breathe. He wanted to ask about her brother but restrained himself; she would share in her own time...but he couldn't stay here, not with this *feeling* all around him.

He missed having Jaden close by for the warmth as the nights grew cooler; he *hated* sleeping alone. The two of them had always pressed themselves together in whatever hollow they could find in the wilderness, warm against the wind.

Kuro had no doubt that Jaden was somewhere in the city these days, enjoying the comfort of a soft bed in a warm hotel room. The demon had a way of making money materialize with little effort and less time; a smile at a girl, an unsettling feeling to distract a man – he could pickpocket with ease, although the act disgusted him. He felt it beneath him to be a common thief, but he also thought it beneath him to sleep in leaves.

Kuro had never minded sleeping in leaves until he began to wake up to bugs crawling over his human skin. *That* he did not enjoy.

It was the second week of October now, and Kuro was helping Caroline in her garden. Every day he braced himself for the feeling of the *holy dark* to stir, to alert him to Jaden's presence at the gate...but his friend kept away, granting him a space that Kuro was at once grateful for and simultaneously anxiety-ridden about. He felt as though he were waiting for something to happen, that this quiet, suspended life of small moments couldn't last...but the newspapers remained empty, and Caroline never mentioned any further murders in the city. All was quiet, and the quiet unnerved him. He was relieved when Caroline asked him for help in her garden, anxious to turn his mind toward something other than his own worries.

He was astonished by the amount of work it took daily, and she took full advantage of having him at hand for labor. He was becoming quite the gardener.

"I've – absolutely – *had it* – with these – *tomatoes!*" She cried. She was ripping up the soggy stalks and vines. The base of a few of them were nearly as thick as her arms. He crouched next to her, trying not to gag at the pungent scent. Even a gentle touch of their stalks or leaves was enough to set the sharp smell into the air, and it rubbed off in green patches along their arms. It had been unseasonably warm long into September, and Caroline had hoped to do one final harvest and call it quits for the fall, but the plants had been too healthy: they continued to grow, the tomatoes all ripening unevenly at their own pace. The newest batch were all cat-faced due to the late pollination in the odd weather. She ripped a misshapen tomato off a vine and hurled it down into the compost pile.

"I could almost wish for blight," she said. She reached down and yanked up another plant. "I'm sick of these things. I've been harvesting them all summer – *hundreds* and *hundreds* of them. I've made salsa, marinara, I've given them away by the dozens – I can't keep up anymore. I should have planted pumpkins." Another tug, another wave of nauseating, acrid odor. "If I had planted pumpkins, I could have been watching them right now, thinking, 'What will I carve this year?' Even squash. I should have planted squash. Zucchini."

Kuro hauled out a plant, ripping up the roots as far as he could.

She stood up and wiped away the sweat from her brow. "Next year," she vowed. "Next year, I'm planting pumpkins. Maybe even corn."

They resumed digging in silence. Kuro grew thoughtful as he sunk a shovel into the ground, searching for the end of the roots. *Next year?* Where would he be next year? With a start, he realized he had never thought that far ahead...it had never mattered. Where would he be? With Jaden. But now...

There was Caroline.

Furtively, he stole a glance at her. Her arms were completely streaked with the tomato skin, and her gloves had turned entirely green. She was on her knees, digging with her hands at the roots, and her eyes were narrowed in concentration. She had tied her hair back in a loose ponytail, and it trailed all the way in the dirt, the curls limp with her efforts. It was Saturday and she hadn't had to go into work in the morning, so they had been digging in the garden for a few hours now, helping it transition into the autumn, and she was dirty and in a bad temper.

And she was beautiful. Every muscle in her body strained as

she pulled at the plants, and even the glimpse of the sweat on her arms, the way it made her skin glow, made his heart lurch.

He looked away, concentrating on the shovel, but his breath came a little faster now. She'd taught him how to use one last week and praised him for his ability to make short work of manual labor. Would he be here next year when the future pumpkins needed picking? And what if she did plant corn – would he be here to help harvest? Would he keep moving from the barn to the living room couch, over and over, slinking off to the edge of the woods when the dog needed to go outside for a run? He didn't need to think that far ahead – even just a month or two in the future was unimaginable. After all, what would he do in the winter, when the world grew too cold for him to be in that barn, alone, and his heart ached for the feeling of a body close beside him?

"Maybe not corn." She threw the last of the tomatoes onto the pile. Some under-ripened fruit in various stages of deformation sagged, wasted energy on a dead vine. "It takes a lot out of the soil, but you know what really makes me unsure?"

He shook his head.

"Mice." She stood up and stripped the gloves off, tossing them on top of the discarded vines. "You plant corn, you get mice. Those garter snakes are big enough as it is. I saw one the other day that was *fat*. And besides the mice, if it rains, the stink…the mud is gross. Your boots will get sucked completely in. No, not corn. Pumpkins. I'm going to plant pumpkins."

He liked to listen to her talk. He nodded again in assenting silence and waited as she cocked her head to the side, studying the cleared section. She sucked in her bottom lip and squinted her eyes, imagining the possibilities.

"…Then again, maybe corn."

He laughed.

Her face lit up. "You laughed at me."

He stopped, his gaze darting down sheepishly at the plants. "Sorry."

"No, I think it's great!" Her voice grew kind and soft. "You rarely laugh."

When he didn't respond, she motioned back to the house.

"Come on, Kuro – let's eat dinner. We'll burn this pile later."

After they ate, he found himself on the threshold of the front door again, hesitating. She stared at him from the kitchen table, abashed.

"Kuro...you don't have to go to the barn. Christopher's room –"

"Is awful," he said, cutting her off. He felt a feeling stir inside of his chest, a frustration all at once tight and hurt and upset. He couldn't explain it or understand it, but it was getting harder to walk out of this door and into loneliness.

Caroline's shoulders slumped. "But I've vacuumed and sprayed, the sheets are clean, and I never let Feral in there."

"It's not the dog," he snapped, then stopped himself at once; her soul had pulled back, hurt by his tone. His voice softened. "It's...*him*." He hadn't attempted to articulate this yet, but her soul was aching; it was time to try, or else she would keep attempting to fix the unfixable. "People sometimes leave feelings behind, pieces of themselves. Have you ever been to a place and felt that, that sense that something was...left behind? That something still clings there? I can't explain it. People do that with things, places; they leave imprints on them. Strong imprints last a very long time...some never go away. There's something *heavy* about that room. I can't breathe in there; it crowds me."

He watched as the expression on her face changed. Her eyes dulled, and she closed her mouth, sucking in a tight breath. Her soul gave a violent shudder, and a sorrow so acute it was nearly lacerating burned bright in its center.

Kuro had to grit his teeth against the force of it, pulling

himself as far away from it as he could. "Caroline...what is it? What is this..." *feeling,* he might have said, but he shook his head, his vision almost clouded by it. "What is this pain?"

Her gaze fell to the floor. "I should tell you," she whispered. "About him...me. Us. My life. I told you I would...but I wasn't ready to talk about it, before."

"Caroline..." He felt the overwhelming need to suddenly cross the kitchen and take her into her his arms, to press her face against his chest and breathe in the scent of her hair. Sadness was still welling like a rising tide; it was sweet and tempting, but Kuro refused it, turning inwardly away from it now. He wanted to find the source and pull the plug on it, let it all drain out of her...but such a thing wasn't possible, he knew. His arms twitched at his side; he held them back. "You don't have to share anything with me, if it hurts."

"I want to," she said. "You told me about your life with Jaden. Please...I've never told anyone..." She looked up at him with such sudden, sincere hope that Kuro had to catch his breath again. "Can I tell you about Christopher?"

He heard the pain in her voice; it was laced through her soul like a fine web. Kuro nodded and returned to her, sitting down. Before he could stop himself, he reached forward and took her hands, holding them.

She stared down at their joined hands, saying nothing, but she didn't pull away. Kuro felt her soul stir inside of her as he squeezed her palms, and then she began to speak.

Christopher had always been 'different' as a child, she said. At first, their parents had thought that he had a learning disability, or was perhaps autistic – he didn't form the same type of relationships with other people, not the way the other kids did. He was sullen and shy, nervous and angry. He would lash out if he felt threatened. They were twins, and her earliest memory was of him leaning around a doorway to stare at her, as if she was some sort of threat, and the physical wall between them could keep him safe.

Eventually, he grew to love her; they played well together, and the psychologists looked at their relationship and saw that he was functioning within the typical range for his age group. He was just 'difficult,' their parents concluded.

He wet the bed often as a toddler. He was terrified of things in the night that only he could see. The two of them shared a room, their bunk beds stacked against the wall. She could remember many nights that her father dragged him out of the bottom bunk and, his belt clutched in his hand, beat him for wetting the bed, for waking them all with his night terrors. Their father's solution to most problems was a belt, and most of his problems were Christopher.

Caroline learned from an early age not to intervene, to stand back and say nothing, no matter how awful Christopher screamed.

She had become very good at moving ever so slowly, not even stirring her sheets, in order to pull her pillow over her ears, crushing away the sound. It was the only way to muffle his sobs so that she could sleep.

When they started first grade, the teasing began. Christopher was placed into a different classroom than her, and her classmates passed on stories that her brother was crazy, mean, dirty, and children were cruel: she was guilty by association. Once a boy had thrown gum at the back of her head because "she was gross, just like her brother," and her mother had given her a dreadful bob to try and mitigate the damage.

It was the first time she began to resent her brother and the hardships he brought.

And money became tight. Something had happened at school

– an incident, Caroline said, but wouldn't elaborate – and her father had beaten her brother within an inch of his life, like nothing he'd ever done before. Caroline had been terrified. Her brother even had to go to the hospital, and her mother had finally put a stop to the violence after the looming threat of CPS intervention. They began to explore new options.

They were seven, maybe eight years old, she said. It was hard to remember the exact date.

Her parents had tried different psychologists and therapists, but sessions were expensive, only partially covered by insurance, and ineffectual. He always came home and whispered to her at night about the things he saw, the things he heard. She knew he was frightened for her and wanted to warn her of the things he feared in the woods, the things he thought he saw on the edges of doorways.

She was nine the first time she heard the word 'schizophrenia.' Her parents were yelling about it in the living room because the psychiatrist they had sent him to refused to diagnose schizo-phrenia in children, and they had argued with him that a diagnosis would help alleviate the ballooning medical costs for his treatment. Her mother was screaming, and when she screamed, her voice was shrill. Her father roared in response, and somewhere in the house, Christopher cowered, and Caroline stayed out of the way.

She was ten when she learned where the peroxide was under the bathroom sink. She needed it almost every day after school because she was constantly fighting the other kids in knock-down, drag-out brawls in dirt roads and gravel paths, and often, the kids were older than her. On the bus, the students were merciless to Christopher. Whatever private resentment Caroline felt, it was nothing to her love: he was abused enough at home, where she was helpless to do anything.

She wouldn't let it happen to him elsewhere.

Caroline had stormed up to the worst offender and bashed the boy's face in, chipping his front tooth and breaking his nose. In return, he had kicked her so hard in the shin that she thought the bone was fractured. She wore pants in 80-degree heat so that her mother didn't see the way her leg was swollen with the bruise. Christopher was emboldened by his twin's refusal to stand down; he began to fight back with his own fists, and only after a particularly nasty fight that left both their knuckles split did the bullying finally stop. He didn't make any friends, but he didn't have to cower from anyone anymore, either.

She was twelve when Christopher took up woodcarving. The hobby calmed him, absorbed his attention, and for a while, he seemed almost healthy. The bullying abated entirely by middle school; redistricting had mercifully moved away the worst offenders who had tormented his early childhood, but their parents' faces had grown thin with stress: Caroline was approaching puberty, and she heard them say it was 'indecent' for them to share a room anymore, but the house only had the two rooms.

Christopher didn't think it was indecent at all; privately, Caroline agreed, even if it was difficult to sleep sometimes because of Christopher's nightmares: puberty had increased his inner torments, though he had gotten better at trying to hide them... when he could. Their father continued to mutter about late-night wakings and a boy sharing a room with his sister at this age, and after years of being tormented by their parents, her brother's fears had hardened into defiance. He spoke up and told their father it was fine for them to share a bedroom – what, did he think he wanted to abuse his sister or something?, and Caroline watched from the doorway as her father formed a fist, pulled back a corded arm, and almost broke Christopher's jaw.

She'd heard the things her father went on to scream at him because she had run outside and sat just under the open bedroom window, too afraid to help, too terrified to completely leave him to their father's mercy.

They would need to move, but there was no money for a down payment on a new home, no savings even for a first month of rent and a security deposit for a new place. Their parents made them swear up and down not to tell *anyone* that they shared a room, because God only knew what people would say at the church, and they obeyed; although her father had never hit *her*, he was fast to fly at her brother now, after years of restraining himself; Christopher's adolescence had spurred him to new violence.

They slept in bunkbeds until they were sixteen. Sometimes, he'd whisper his secrets to her – his hopes, his fears, the things he was ashamed of, the secrets he asked her to keep; sometimes, she would vent to him about her tests, her schoolwork. Other times, she'd climb down the ladder and hold his hand, squeezing it so hard that the knuckles turned white, to try and keep him from screaming, because voices were talking to him, he said. He still saw things, heard things, he told her; they frightened him. He knew they weren't real, but it was getting hard to *believe* they weren't real.

She began to think that the schizophrenia diagnosis might have been the one thing her mother was right about, but her parents never did take him back for treatment now that he was older. They needed to save all their money toward a down payment on a new home.

One morning, Caroline had walked into their room. The bunk beds had been replaced a few months back with two twin beds on opposite walls, and the result was a crammed, narrow space that was uncomfortable for them both.

Christopher was on his bed, thin and reedy: he'd been having trouble eating for about two months, and his eyes were always darting, fidgety. He was perpetually nervous these days, his movements driven by anxiety...but when he was woodworking, she could squint her eyes and see the person he *could* be: he could fill out just fine if he could keep his meals down. He could be tall and strong, and though he was shy, she could see he could be handsome. He'd look just like the other boys at school; he'd fit in. Maybe he could even smile. Unlike her curls, he had inherited their father's wavy hair, and he tossed his head down as he worked, sweat beading on his forehead, carving a napkin holder shaped like a mallard duck. He'd been working on it for nearly a month now and was almost finished.

He was bringing the blade over the wingtips, shaving off the curves of the feathers as one of the final touches before pausing to examine it, satisfied. He asked what she thought, and she smiled, impressed.

"You think they'll like it?"

"I think so," she said. "I could paint it, if you want."

He returned her smile, and her heart was bright. He handed it to her and swept up the wood shavings, placing them in the trash, and for a moment, everything was perfectly normal, and just like that, he turned to her and gripped her shoulders, telling her that she needed to be careful at night, that she needed to keep her eyes open, to not go near the woods –

She wrenched away from him, and for the first time, all her anger came welling up in one giant, furious wave. She remembered beginning with *why can't you be normal!?* and then hurling at him how he had ruined everything in her life – she had no friends, they had no money, everything was *wrong, he* was wrong. He was a liar, he only wanted attention. He made up things and kept her up at night with his ravings. He had ruined their lives. He couldn't even let her be happy for one, single moment.

She meant all of it; she meant none of it. She was sixteen and had grown up watching him being beaten. She loved him and hated him in equal parts, and her heart was breaking with the pain of it all.

He had looked at her then with pure, untempered pain. She backed away from that look, walking backwards towards the door, still clutching his carving. His hands remained frozen, outstretched from where they had rested on her shoulders, and she realized that she had smashed something inside of him, that even though he had stopped talking to his parents about his hallucinations, he hadn't stopped telling her...because he loved her. He *trusted* her to believe him. He wanted her to be safe.

He wanted someone to help him.

She turned and fled from the room, crying. She set the napkin holder down in the kitchen, her shoulders shaking, and turned back, forcing herself to return to him, to tell him she was sorry. Less than a minute passed before she walked back down the hall, the apology clogging her throat, her face streaked with tears.

When she opened the door, there was blood all over the floor and the comforter.

Christopher was on his knees, and his small case of wood-working tools was next to him. He had slashed each wrist vertically, wrist to elbow, and was already sinking down, and there was so much blood –

The details grew hazy in her memory from that point onward. Everything in her life was divided into the clarity of before and after that moment, as though Christopher had drawn the line not down his flesh, but through her very life.

Someone started screaming. She remembered being covered in his blood because she tried to hold his wrists and apply pressure, to force it back inside, but then she realized she had to get help. She remembered how the telephone had fallen out of her hand because the plastic slipped from the blood that slicked her palms. She remembered the scent of fresh air; their parents were outside, and she must have run out of the house to get them, but all she could remember was the scent of dust on a cool breeze. There were flashing lights at some point, red and blue in the driveway, and then time seemed to leap all at once, rushing her forward, to the moment where she became aware, later, that the paramedics had saved his life.

She was later told that her brother was getting help somewhere, in-patient treatment. She was told she wouldn't see him for a little bit.

They took his bed away. The room became her room. There was no longer any need to move, not that they could have afforded it now, anyways.

And they did not talk about him, ever.

She saw him intermittently over the next couple of years, an unpredictable amount of time passing in between each new visit. She wanted to scream at her parents at dinner, demand to know where her brother, *her twin*, was.

She sat in silence, too afraid to ask.

Her parents were tight-lipped; even when she finally worked up the courage to ask for an address to write to him, they refused. When he came home to visit, sometimes for days, sometimes for weeks, never longer than that, he only told her that he was getting help...but he didn't seem well, and the phrase felt rehearsed, practiced under the looming threat of punishment. Their parents had forbidden him to say more, and a new, cagey bitterness had left him reticent and mistrustful; whatever medication they were forcing him to take had rendered him muddled and incoherent. He slept on the couch, and their father had him up with the dawn, working in the yard, so that she hardly ever saw him.

But her prediction had been right: the scrawny, fidgeting boy grew into a young man with a strong, trim build, wavy brown hair that he kept neat...but his shoulders were always a little stooped, and every time he returned, his eyes were more scared, more hollow, and he himself grew more and more still, like an animal crouched in the back of a cage, just out of arms' reach. When he turned eighteen, he cut off all contact with their parents, and by extension, since she still lived at home, her. She didn't see him or hear from him for another year.

When she was nineteen, their parents were killed in a car accident so mundane that it didn't even make the evening news.

She hadn't heard from her brother since before their last birthday; they saw each other for the first time in more than a year at the funeral parlor. Their parents had left Christopher nothing and willed the property and all their personal effects to her. She had found their paperwork in a safe beneath their bed and read how Christopher had been shipped from one in-treatment facility to the next to receive treatment for schizophrenia until he was eighteen. She discovered letters of correspondence from the last facility to her mother and gleaned that Christopher had struggled for a few months until he was able to successfully get himself discharged, but no further information was provided, as he was an adult and they could no longer share medical information. How he had lived, what he had endured during the last years of his childhood in those facilities, was a mystery.

Caroline hired a lawyer to split the estate and the life insurance policies so that he received half of everything they left her. It embarrassed her to do so.

She was ashamed of what her parents had done.

"I'm glad they at least left one of us something," he had said. It was his version of 'hello,' caustic and sarcastic...but there was a new self-assurance to his tone that left her feeling comforted. They stood in the cemetery, staring down at the fresh plots, the rich smell of upturned dirt redolent in the air. "At least you'll have a place to stay."

She had turned to him and fought against tears. The time for crying had long passed. "Where will you go?" and "Where have you been?" and "What happened to you?" all came out at once.

He looked at her in silence, and without answering, drew her into an embrace. It was warm, and he was solid now. Her skinny, wide-eyed brother had grown into a young man in the last few years, and she hadn't been permitted to be a part of that journey. He smelled clean, like fresh wood, and Caroline felt the bitter knife of lost time cutting into her heart.

He sighed.

"I can't stay here," he said.

"Are you okay?"

He shook his head 'no.' She was going to protest then, but his expression stopped the words: he was calm, certain. He took her hands and explained that he was seeking treatment, not running from it: a persistent, kind doctor had found the right dosage of an antipsychotic drug that helped. His psychiatrist listened to him in his twice-weekly therapy sessions and, for the first time, he felt no judgement, and a new hope that he could live a life of his choosing. "I can't talk the visions away," he explained, "but she's teaching me strategies for reality-testing and for coping when I experience hallucinations, so I know when an episode is building or if there's a problem with the medication." For the first time in years, he said, he could see and think clearly. He could *sleep*. He had a sense of who he was supposed to be, not what his illness had twisted him into, and he even had a part-time job...but this was a long process. This would take time. He would be alright in the end.

And...he was sorry for how he had made her suffer, he said. It wasn't something he could control.

She had helped him hide bruises and beatings for *years*, and *he* was sorry.

At last she broke; she sobbed into his shoulder and told him that it wasn't his fault, that she was sorry for what she had said that day, but he still shook his head. She had seen the scars on his forearms; he made no effort to hide them. She begged him to stay, but he pushed her away, resolute in his decision. He told her, over and over, that he had to do what was best for him now, for his own mental health.

And that meant that he had to go. This place wasn't good for him.

He stayed for a week to help her box their parents' things up, donate them to people who needed them, sign papers for the bank.

He had his own car, used and old, but *his*. That had shocked her more than anything else; it was like the symbol of an entire life he had built for himself, fragile though it must have been, away from her, someplace else, and he'd managed to cobble it together in a year, all on his own.

"You're the strongest person I've ever met, Christopher," she whispered. She felt as though she didn't deserve to be part of his life – she was part of the misery and abuse he had endured.

Their lives should have been intertwined, but instead, a blank page of time that had been lost held no answers. Why had he bought *that* car? When did he get his license? Who taught him how to drive? What job did he have – how did he make money for gas? What sort of music did he listen to when he drove? All the questions she should have asked, all of the insipid details that comprise a life, that a sister should have known about a brother, weren't there.

Christopher didn't know what to say to that. At last, he managed, "I love you, Caroline. Stay safe. I'll visit when I can."

She closed the driver's door and leaned in the open window, hugging him, then watched him drive away.

Across from Kuro, Caroline closed her eyes. "That was a while ago," she whispered. "I've seen him since them, every couple of months...

he'd drive up here, tell me a little bit more about what he was doing, how he was living. I know...I hurt him, badly. After a few visits, he told me a little bit about the places our parents had sent him to, and not all of it was good. Actually...most of it was awful. But I thought he was doing really well until the last time he showed up, and it was like...he'd lost a lot of ground in his treatment. He said I needed to be careful. He said there were demons in the woods. That's what he used to say when we were kids..." Her voice stumbled to a halt. "That's why I was angry that day, when you told me he was haunted. He thinks he's mentally ill. What if all this time...he wasn't?"

Kuro reached tentatively with his foot and touched the edge of her shoe under the table. She looked up at him, and he could see that she was fighting against tears, blinking with a rapid anger at herself. He collected his thoughts and tried to express himself as best as he could.

"It doesn't have to be one or the other," he said. "He could be mentally ill....*and* haunted. If he was haunted, it would have only made things worse. I didn't mean to – to downplay his illness, or explain it away. I don't know much about it, but... it sounds like he's genuinely ill, or medication wouldn't have done anything."

"I realized that too, later." She reached up and tucked a strand of hair behind her ears. "I wonder what he would think of you, if he met you...if he knew that demons were real."

That night, as Kuro slept alone in the barn in order to escape the ghost of a living boy, he hoped he'd never find out.

FIVE

October remained fairly dry at first, the weather good and bright. The mundane elements of daily life became amazing to him, having never witnessed them before. He heard a great commotion one day coming from Caroline's room – she was yanking out a clear, flat container from under her bed, swapping out sweaters that had been tucked away with tank tops and blouses in her closet. She still wore her dirty overalls to work outside, but now a long-sleeved shirt accompanied them, and thick, wool blankets had appeared on the couch and armchair.

At last, the autumn storms returned after their dry spell. One rainy morning he watched her peep through the kitchen window; the colors were especially vibrant in the early drizzle.

"I always feel a little bit of sadness in the fall, like the whole world has gone into mourning...but also relief. It's a strange feeling." He hadn't replied. He watched the water slip down the glass pane and thought about how it was a good thing to be dry in a wet season. Maybe that's what she meant.

At last, Jaden began to visit. Kuro could always sense him at the edge of the forest when he approached, long before he spotted him. The hairs on the back of his neck stood on end; a feeling like the buzzing of electricity moved down his spine, and his heart began to beat rapidly, his mouth going dry.

There was no rhythm or pattern to when he appeared; Kuro thought the unpredictability was intentional. Sometimes, he smiled cheerfully from the doorway, inviting himself to breakfast. Other times, he appeared mid-afternoon to laze in the garden and enjoy a cup of tea if the rain paused. More often than not he interrupted dinner, and Caroline had taken to baking desserts on the off chance he stopped by. He wanted to tell her not to bother; Jaden didn't care for sweets, but he ate them with relish, grinning at Kuro and complimenting her, ever the actor.

A hot flare of jealousy, something he had never known before, leapt up in Kuro whenever he saw the way Caroline's eyes lit up when she spotted him. She'd give a short exclamation and invite him in, and he was always gracious, affable, and neatly dressed, the perfect houseguest who never overstayed his welcome, made her laugh, and complimented every aspect of her cooking and home, then leaving before he could ever be considered an intruder or a bore.

One afternoon in mid-October he stopped by sporting a gray peacoat over black trousers. Caroline had picked up a jug of fresh apple cider from a harvest festival, and together the three of them sat in the garden drinking the cider and eating cinnamon sugar donuts, the world wet and rich around them with the autumn colors. She had asked him to come along with her to the festival, but Kuro had declined, nervous and unsure of himself, and she had gone alone.

He deeply regretted it; he could have walked by her side, could have spent the day with her...but no.

The food and drink reminded him of what he had missed out on, and he sat sipping, sullen and spiteful, as Jaden chatted amicably with her. In the beginning, she had tried to ask him about himself again, about *kitsune,* but he had such a disarming way of chuckling and waving away her questions, redirecting her to other things: art, culture, and the less interesting aspects of human life. Once, Kuro had sat unspeaking for an hour while he pressed her about the tax system, listening carefully to her explanation of how the government was structured.

Kuro had been bored to death.

She got up to go and get more cider from the house. Jaden watched her leave, and Kuro saw the way his eyes followed the sway of her hair down by her hips. When Jaden turned to him, the light of friendly openness was gone, and Kuro saw him as he really was.

The narrowed disapproval in Kuro's expression made Jaden smirk. "Are you about to accuse me of something?"

"I saw the way you were looking at her."

"And you never look at her that way, I assume. You just sleep here every night in perfect chastity."

Kuro didn't take the bait; he knew Jaden had looked at her like that just to get a rise from him, and he certainly had no intention of informing him that he slept mostly in the barn now. His voice was a low warning. "Don't interfere with her. If you're thinking something, let it go."

He sneered. "Oh, touch me not so near, Kuro." Seeing Kuro's blank expression, he rolled his eyes. "Shakespeare. Forget it."

He stopped by at least twice a week, but never more than for a few hours. His interest in Caroline remained polite and distant, but friendly, and he had taken Kuro's warning to heart: from questioning Caroline, Kuro learned that Jaden never came by when he wasn't there, on the rare occasions he left to run through the forest, to take some time alone to think.

"You shouldn't be jealous," she said one night over dinner. She had bought a duck from the market and fried the breasts in a pan until the fat had melted, soft as butter, the skin crisp. He had never had duck *cooked* before, and the unctuousness of the rendered fat had left him in ecstasy. His thoughts had turned to where to get more ducks, a certain pond not far from here, but he looked up mid-bite, caught off guard.

"What?"

"Of Jaden." She pushed a carrot on her plate. "He's your friend, but when he's here…you look angry, almost. Jealous."

"I'm not jealous of him."

He answered too quickly and furiously to have any shot at being convincing. She was still pushing the carrot around on her plate, not meeting his hardened gaze. "I don't necessarily mean that you're jealous of him, but maybe…jealous of *us.*"

He put his fork down, staring at her now. She wilted under the weight of his gaze and finally lifted her eyes.

"What do you mean?"

"You're very different from one another, and I think…" She spoke in a measured, hesitant tone. "I think that you think I like him better than you."

"Why would it matter to me if you did?"

She winced at the ice in his voice. "I'm not implying anything, it's just…you don't have to worry about that."

"I'm not worried about it." But he was, and the knowledge that he was so openly lying to both himself and her only made him angrier. "I get it – he's smarter than me. 'Sophisticated,'" he mocked. It was a word Jaden had once said he aspired to be, some time ago. He looked well on his way now. His clothes changed every time he saw him, and on each occasion they fit better, looked newer, *easier,* like he was no longer pretending but *becoming,* and now, no doubt, he was sophisticated enough to never own up to the desire of *wanting* to be sophisticated in the first place. He didn't look like a man who ought to be sitting in the field of a hobby farm in North Carolina. He looked somehow beyond all that now. "He can talk to you about all kinds of things I can't."

Her smile quirked with amusement. "Like what?"

"Like...*Shakespeare*," he suddenly hit upon. The word sounded like a curse. "I don't know what that is."

"Not what – who."

"Exactly," he snapped.

But she laughed. "Kuro, he may be smarter than you – I don't know. I can tell you he's smarter than *me*. There's no shame in admitting if someone is more clever than you are. We're not all created equally, and that's alright. Not all of us are going to go to college or be scientists; some of us are designed for simpler things, like...filing paperwork in a police station." She gave a small, self-deprecating laugh and shrugged. "And that's okay. I graduated high school, and that's all. The thing is, we all have different parts of ourselves that shine in different ways, different things going for us, and those parts of you speak loudly."

He didn't believe her. She saw him scoff and protested, "It's true!"

"Like what? What do I have 'going for me' that he doesn't?"

She took a sip of water, thinking. Her brow furrowed, and Kuro reached out a little, nipping at her soul just to see what was going on; she was deep in thought, and the current was hard to read. Calm, but moving in a forceful direction.

"You're *sincere*." She hit upon the word and held on to it. "There's no mask to you. Your feelings, your words...they just come through, and you don't try to change them or polish them. I like Jaden a lot," she said, and she smiled abashedly as if to apologize for admitting it. "He's clever, quick...charming, if I had to find a good word. But...and maybe this is just my perception, you could tell me if I'm wrong....but I don't know how many times he's been over now, and I don't feel like I know *him* at all. I feel like the real him is hidden under layers and layers of other things, and I don't think *any* of it's real." She came to a halt and glanced up, anxious. "I'm sorry if that sounds like I'm insulting your friend. I don't mean it to sound like a criticism at all. I just don't know how to quite express myself here."

"...No." He picked back up his utensils and returned to slicing the duck. He wanted to give himself a reason to not have to talk, and a mouthful of food seemed a practical excuse. "...I know what you mean." But he said no more.

The thought had stuck with him though, and he watched Jaden closely when he stopped by. Whenever Caroline stepped away, the friendliness in his eyes dimmed, and his smile fell away. Kuro noticed that he had been growing more and more silent around him, and he recognized the expression: he was brooding.

It wasn't just his outward appearance that had shifted. Something inside of Jaden was pulling his attention inward, and it was changing him. All of his sharp edges were being carefully smoothed away by his devotion to his new goal. The bouts of anger, the impulsivity was all gone; something had captured his attention so wholly that it had begun to transform him, and when Kuro squinted, he thought he could catch a glimpse down into those still, lightless waters of the person Jaden had always wanted to be...the person he had at last become. The corners of Jaden's mouth were downturned into a slight, permanent frown, and when he spoke, there was the sense that he was now measuring his words more carefully, that his mind never, ever stopped thinking. He was burying his true self even deeper, growing refined and controlled in a way he had never quite managed before. He would never kill a human just because he was moved to do so, Kuro realized now. It would take a force of will to shake this demon from his course, to stir him to rash action.

Understanding dawned on him: Jaden operated by calculation now. He seemed to take no action, say no word that wasn't designed to advance him toward whatever it was he wanted. His intellect funneled every behavior, every word and action through the narrow needle of his singular desires. It was a strange, strangled, self-mutilating way to live, Kuro thought.

They were on their own one afternoon, having a coffee in the city. Caroline was at work when Jaden stopped by, and rather than remain alone, waiting, Kuro had joined him on a trip into Asheville proper for the afternoon. It would be good to spend some time together again; as flawed as Jaden was, he missed him terribly.

Kuro studied him for a long minute before asking bluntly, "What's wrong with you?"

Jaden looked up from his drink, his blue eyes dim with malcontent. Kuro wondered how much longer he would have to use contacts.

"You know what's wrong."

"Jacqueline?"

He nodded and sipped.

Kuro huffed. "You spend your days just following along on the edge of her life – have you seen her in-person again?"

Jaden took another sip. "No, but she can sense me when I'm near. I make *sure* she can."

Kuro stared at him, demanding more. Jaden set his drink down, and with a heavy sigh, Kuro listened as he spoke, his face disconcertingly blank.

"I look at her, and she makes me feel like something is broken inside of me."

Kuro pressed him to explain. There was a moment – fleeting, brief – when Jaden looked almost as though he were in pain. He reached up involuntarily to his head, his fingertips trembling, then recalled himself, lowering his hand; it was so different from the day that he had paced in front of Kuro, madness in his eyes. Now, only the smallest action betrayed his true feelings, and it was mastered in the next instant, his voice carefully flat. "Sometimes I hear a roaring, like water...or wind. I look at her, and I want her so badly that it feels like my head is splitting open. Like something is tearing me apart. It's not *her*," he whispered. "There's nothing special about *her* as a person. And yet...it *is* her," he finished.

Kuro didn't know what to say. They drank in silence, each lost in their own thoughts.

A few days later, Jaden had returned when Caroline was out.

"Come with me, Kuro," he said, and Kuro felt his heart slow; he had said those same words the night that he was shot...and it was no coincidence. Jaden's memory was impeccable. "I want to show her to you."

He froze at the gate to the garden, his very bones grinding to a halt. "Jaden, I don't want to hurt her," he started, but Jaden was already striding away, waving away his anxiety.

"I just want you to see her," he called over his shoulder.

Kuro swallowed his fear, and followed.

Jacqueline was outside of a grocery store, examining the pumpkins; Jaden pointed her out. Kuro glanced at her, then back at Jaden, just to make sure it was the right girl. The demon nodded.

He wasn't sure what he was expecting, but he was thoroughly unimpressed. She was a tiny thing with long, dark brown hair, so dark it was practically black, and that was the fullest extent of what made her memorable. She looked so wholly unimpressive that Kuro had to keep himself from blurting out "*Her?*" She was pretty in the unremarkable way that every young woman is pretty, though her stature made her look childish, and when she turned, Kuro could see in her eyes what Jaden had told him earlier: she was haunted, clear as day. Why any being – angel, demon, *thing* – would attach itself to her was inexplicable.

Kuro couldn't fathom why Jaden was obsessed, *fixated* on her, to the point of feeling 'broken.'

"What do you think?"

Kuro opened his mouth to speak and closed it. The first thought that came to mind was how different she was from Caroline. Caroline was tall, strong, tanned, with easy laughter and sparkling eyes. She was everything this girl was not. But he looked again, and harder...and he could give Jacqueline this: there was a *gravity* to her that Caroline did not possess, a certain seriousness in the tilt of her mouth, the very gleam of her eyes. Even from this distance he could make out a dangerous, sharp intelligence, a wariness and maturity that Caroline did not possess.

The best he could manage was a non-committal, "She's...pretty."

"Don't patronize me, Kuro," Jaden sighed. "I know she doesn't look like much. She *isn't*. But I can't explain it...all I can think of is a trite image, a cliché: a *magnet*." He sounded disgusted for having to fall back on such a tired comparison. "I feel *pulled* to her."

It might have been romantic from another man, but Kuro had seen the look in his eyes: rage, and a mix of hatred at the notion.

"...What are you going to do, Jaden?"

His stomach churned while he waited for an answer. He didn't want another person to die; the thought made his very blood freeze in his veins. He didn't think he'd be able to look at him again knowing he had taken another life...and whatever specifics he was planning for this girl, Kuro doubted it would be quick. This wasn't vengeance or boredom...obsession was eating at the demon, reshaping him into someone Kuro hardly recognized any more. He had thought Jaden was dangerous before, but he had been naïve then.

Now, he was cunning...and that was so much worse.

You know what he's going to do, he reminded himself. *He's going to eat her soul, then kill her, and drag the 'angel' that's attached itself to her out into the open...and probably kill it, too. And you've agreed to let it happen.*

Because the longer Jaden remained fixated on Jacqueline, the less he cared what Kuro did...and the longer he could remain by Caroline's side...and he would die without her soul.

And even still, every day, he was growing weaker.

But Jaden didn't know that, and Kuro was afraid of what he would do if he ever found out.

"I plan to act soon," he said. "I don't think I can resist her any longer. But, if you were to help me...I think things could go a lot more quickly. I want to be free of *this*, whatever this...*hold* is."

He was staring at him from the corner of his eyes. Kuro stiffened, swallowing.

"*No.*"

"You said that before," Jaden said; there was no anger, no accusation, just a slightly impatient thoughtfulness, and he wasn't even looking at him anymore. His eyes crawled over Jacqueline as she walked toward her car. "I wonder how many more times you're going to repeat that until you finally change your answer."

"I'm not changing my mind –"

"Not your *mind*, Kuro; your *answer*." He turned to him, his eyes narrowed. "What you *think*, what you *feel*, and what you *do* are all separate things."

"Maybe for you," Kuro argued, and he had no doubt it was the truth. "But not for me."

"Oh? Consider Caroline, and the lies you tell her, to understand the concept."

Kuro tensed. Jaden was glaring at him with pointed insinuation now. "Can you imagine what she would do if she ever learned the truth?"

Kuro took a moment to draw in one, hissing breath. "...Are you threatening me?"

Jaden actually quirked a brow, exasperated. "No. Have I ever? *You are my friend*. I'm merely asking for your *help*."

Kuro refused him again, and Jaden let the conversation drop.

He was naïve enough to think the matter was at last concluded.

A week passed before he saw him again, and Kuro had been left to languish in the October foliage alone, bored. It used to be that the whole world was enough to fulfill him and provide him with endless entertainment, but now it was empty, a long game of waiting for someone you wanted to see come home.

This isn't my home, he reminded himself.

But it was beginning to feel like it.

He realized how empty his life was. What did he have? Beyond the day-to-day functions of living and breathing, what had he filled his life with? For the first time, he could finally understand Jaden's perspective: the world and all its forests *weren't* enough. Jaden had lived in this boredom for *years;* after just a few weeks, it was driving Kuro insane. Jaden sought out the cities in order to fill that hunger for things to populate the emptiness: he devoured art, consumed culture, studied people. Kuro grew ashamed of himself; he understood now that Jaden didn't stay only for a few hours because he was being polite.

It was because Kuro was a bore.

A lump grew in his throat, painful and raw, and he realized how much Jaden valued his friendship; he had chained himself to a corpse he had to drag around, an intellectual inferior with nothing to offer, and continued to remain chained to him after all this time. He felt almost guilty about refusing him assistance with the girl.

"I think I always took you for granted," Kuro told him later, as October was coming to a close. The sweet smell of corn drifted everywhere in the air, traveling from long distances and farms not far away. Harvest was in full swing.

Jaden looked up, surprised. They were leaning against the barn, watching as Caroline brushed down the mare at the far end of the pasture. Molly had grown used to Kuro, but she had shown a spirit unparalleled in her youth when she first saw Jaden, rearing and screaming. Caroline had had to drag her by the bit through the dirt to the end of the pasture, as far as she could get from the two demons.

"Is that so?"

Kuro nodded. "Any problem we had, you solved. After all this time...I'm just holding you back."

"You've never held me back. You know what I promised you." Jaden stared at him harder. His eyes narrowed, and Kuro could feel him examining him from top to bottom like he had never seen him before, his gaze sharp and penetrating in its exacting scrutiny. "...You don't look so good, Kuro."

Kuro knew it. He looked like a person suffering with pneumonia. He hadn't lost weight, but his eyes were sunken with dark circles, and he stood now on shaky feet and spent most of the day lying down, weak. In the end, they had never figured out how to get Caroline's soul to let go of him, and all their efforts seemed to have only made it worse. He was starving to death and hiding it from her as best as he could, which was fool-ish: she cared for him. If she knew how much he was suffering, she, too, would suffer, and he could feed on that in order to survive.

Or he used to be able to; the acrid bitterness, like burnt food at the bottom of a pot, had spread into all her negative feelings, and even what should have fueled him had become almost impossible to eat. He fed on those emotions gingerly while cringing. He was certain something in *her* hadn't changed.

It was him, but he didn't know why.

Not that it mattered, really; he didn't want her to suffer, and more importantly, he didn't want to be the cause of that suffering. When he thought about that, as he often did late in the evenings, alone, the thought spun around in his mind until he grew dizzy with it, unable to understand what that meant. He kept chasing it at night, trying to grasp its meaning, but it eluded him, and every day it grew harder and harder to rise in the morning.

He wondered how many more weeks he could survive like this.

He didn't think he'd live to see the winter.

"Kuro? Did you hear me?"

"I heard you."

"You look sick...and you're acting strangely."

That day, Jaden stayed longer than he usually did, and Kuro could feel his eyes on him, studying him, seeking out some secret, but Kuro was unbothered.

He had accepted he would probably die on this farm, and he had hidden that belief from Caroline for weeks now, and the practice allowed him to hide it with equal success from Jaden.

He was again contemplating his fate when Caroline's truck pulled up two days before Halloween. She had told him she'd probably have to work over the coming weekend, since kids had a way of getting up to no good in the late hours of the night. She'd been working long hours all week in prep for the holiday, and the sound of her car door slamming startled him. She normally wouldn't have been home for a few hours more.

He sat up in the garden, the reds and oranges of fall spinning momentarily. Whatever rock bottom was, he was approaching it. He called to her, but she ignored him, striding into the house. The screen door slammed shut behind her.

Kuro reached out with the *holy dark,* feeling for her soul, and pulled back, burned.

She was enraged.

Hesitant steps brought him to the front door, then into the kitchen. She was standing at the sink, gripping the edges with her fingers, and her body was taunt and shaking with anger.

"Caroline...?"

She rounded on him, pointing at the kitchen table. A folder

was open, and in it lay a few sheets of paper, a paperclip holding them together.

"How do you explain that?"

"What?"

Her voice was like a whip. "How do you explain that, Kuro!?"

He made his way to the table and picked up the folder, the paper shaking in his hands.

It was an incident report, taken a month earlier, from an adult male named Kenneth McMahon. Kuro's heartbeat slowed as he read Kenneth's description of the night they had attacked him: two animals, one maroon, one black with a bad leg, and people with them... The scene played in his head as he read the officer's shorthand version of Kenneth's statement, and suddenly he felt sick. He reached for the edge of a chair and managed to sit down, reeling.

"Do you see what it says at the end?"

He swallowed. He did.

"Read what it says, Kuro."

"Caroline –"

"*Read what it says!*"

The officer, at the end of Kenneth's statement, had written his own notes. "'McMahon is under the impression that the people who attacked him are linked to the Buncombe case, and the murder of Floyd and Rios.'"

Caroline's eyes were shining with tears. "You lied to me."

"I didn't lie to you."

"*Tell me that's not you.*"

Blood was roaring in his ears. Her fists were clenched, her arms shaking, and the color had drained away from her face.

"You think I killed those people just because this boy –"

"Kuro." Her voice came out in a whisper, and the note of betrayal in her words pierced him through. "Is that you?"

"...It's me." He dropped the papers on the table, desperate.

"But I had nothing to do with the murders. That's not why we were there –"

"Was that you and Jaden?"

He stopped speaking. She filled the silence by walking over and opening the folder again, pointing at some other paper. "They found maroon, unidentified hair at two of the crime scenes, and they found your hair at McMahon's house. McMahon describes the other animal as *maroon*. Is that Jaden, Kuro? Because *you both* told me he came here *later*. Did you both attack him...and kill those people?"

There was a trembling feeling in all that rage, a terror of being right and a *desperate* hope that somehow, someway, she was wrong. He grabbed hold of that feeling, deep in the furnace of her anger, and willed it to grow, sick at himself for exploiting her trust. She didn't want to believe the simple, correct explanation, he could feel; she desperately wanted him to explain this away. His mind raced. If she really thought him a murderer, would she have come home to confront him? No, he thought; surely she wouldn't. She'd fear for her own life. He took a deep breath; Jaden would think his way out of this, find a way to lie –

"You said they found my fur at Kenneth's house?"

She nodded, her soul heavy and sick with revulsion. He pushed back against that, holding on to her hope. "But they didn't find maroon hair at his house. They found that at the crime scenes. But not at his house," he emphasized. Luck was always on Jaden's side, *always*, Kuro thought, bitter.

A hope flickered in her soul. She nodded.

He swallowed, steadying himself for the lie, repulsed by what he had to do.

"Look at my hair, Caroline." He stood up and crossed to her, gently placing his hands on her shoulders, forcing her to face him. She had beat back the angry tears in her eyes, and she stared at him, desperate, longing to be convinced, and didn't pull away. "It's *black*."

"I can see that, Kuro. I'm not stupid."

"What color is Jaden's hair?"

"What?"

"What *color* is Jaden's hair?"

"...Brown."

Even as he spoke, he felt like a man cutting himself in two, and the heaviness of the lie settled in the pit of his stomach, spread, and poisoned him like lead. "You've seen my true form. Our fur matches our hair, exactly. Jaden is *brown*."

She stepped back from him, brushing his hands off.

"McMahon described a *maroon* –"

"He's *wrong*." He said it forcefully, convincingly enough to fool even himself in the moment. "I don't know why he said that. It was dark, so it's possible he just thought Jaden was a different color. Yes, we *did* attack him, but it had nothing to do with the murders. It was because he took my photo, and then they published a second one the next day. We went there to warn him and scare him into not publishing anymore, because if people thought we were connected to the killings, we'd be hunted. We wouldn't be able to go home, back to the mountains. We didn't even hurt him. And Jaden left afterwards; he came back later, like he said." The truth and the lies were all jumbled together; Kuro had no idea how he would keep any of it straight. He felt ill. "I didn't kill anyone, Caroline," he finished, pleading, and that much was true; she could hear the sincere veracity in that, at least.

She rested her back against the refrigerator and sighed, her hands coming up to rub her eyes. The rage in her soul sagged and smoldered away into quiet embers that soon went out; the hope he had held onto flowered, but embarrassment and confusion shoved it aside. He had forced her to make a choice: to believe him that, against all odds, that through some extraordinary coincidence, Kenneth McMahon had described the second animal with as specific a color as *maroon,* the same color later found at the crime scene, and was mistaken...or believe that Kuro himself was a liar.

"I didn't want to believe..." she began, but stopped. He could feel her soul shifting, surging rapidly, settling. Something very powerful, something he couldn't quite touch, was strong enough to blind her to the truth. She looked up at him, and the look in her eyes of clear, visible relief made him hate himself all the more. "I'm sorry," she started again. "I just thought – what if you were lying? What if all this time..."

"We didn't kill those people," he repeated, but he felt numb now. There was no triumph in convincing her, no relief: only the painful, searing discovery that he had betrayed her by convincing her that he had not, in fact, betrayed her, and the irony of that cut him to the core. "And we never went back to Kenneth's house."

She sighed again. "The maroon fur from the crime scene matches the type of fur they found at McMahon's home – *kitsune.* They don't know that, of course; they just know it's a match. There's another *kitsune* out there then, isn't there?"

Her logic was sound, even if the conclusion was wrong. He nodded, but words would not come.

She gestured at the folder on the table and shook her head. "No one has gotten anywhere on these cases – life has been moving on, and there hasn't been any more killings. Buncombe County and Marion County finally came to an agreement and decided to share their files with each other, now that the FBI is involved. I was copying them today in prep for delivery, uploading them into the database...Kenneth gave his statement twice. That's Buncombe County's statement. The one he gave to Marion County was almost identical."

The way she hesitated made his skin prickle. "...Almost?"

Caroline looked at him piercingly, searching his face. "He told the Marion County officer that one of the people who attacked him looked 'almost exactly like him.' According to the timestamp, that was the first interview he gave. He omitted that detail to the Buncombe officer he later spoke with."

Kuro didn't respond. Caroline continued to fix her eyes on him. "Kuro, if I called Kenneth down to the station, would it look like you walked through the door?"

He nodded, nauseous. Something crumbled in her face again. "Why?"

"...It's complicated." No, he thought, it really wasn't: he simply lacked imagination and stole some boy's form, but he didn't think he could speak to her about *anything* just now without blurting out the truth about all the rest of it. He needed time to be alone, to process his thoughts, to sort through his lies and commit them to memory. He had no idea how to fix this, make any of it right anymore.

Her smile was sad. "More complicated than all this?" When he didn't reply, her face lifted to the window, staring out into the autumn sunset. "Can you feel the other *kitsune?* Does...does the *holy dark* sense it? Do *you?*"

He shook his head again.

She was crestfallen. "It's been some time since the murders... maybe it moved on."

He walked to the door on weak legs, his back to her. "I'm going to go outside for a bit," he told the doorframe, unwilling to turn and face her again. "Just in the garden. I'm not leaving, but I...I want to be alone for a while."

He waited for a response, but hearing none, he left, slipping out into the safety of solitude.

Six

Jacqueline had broken into a sweat by the time she set up the third bear trap in the woods.

They were much heavier than she expected them to be, old and rusted – 'vintage,' the online listing described them as, *for décor purposes only,* the seller had underscored. The seller met her in the parking lot of the nearest grocery store; the man was in his seventies, and he stood behind her with his hands shoved into the front of his puffer jacket as she peered into his trunk, satisfied by what she saw.

Nine of them, with jaws more than sixteen inches wide, their cruel spikes rusted from age and weather.

He repeated twice that they were illegal for trapping nowadays, but the collection belonged to his grandfather, who was a trapper in Minnesota in the late 1800s. Jacqueline had nodded, only half listening, and interrupted to ask him to show her how the release mechanism worked.

He had eyed her up for a moment at that, but she stared back, steadily challenging his suspicions. She was a petite girl dressed in fall boots and an oversized scarf: nothing about her suggested she was going to be hunting bears.

And she wasn't.

She had far more dangerous prey in mind.

He demonstrated how to load and release the jaws; the slamming clang of the metal pleased her. She nodded, handed him two thousand in cash, and asked for assistance loading them into her car.

She waited two more days for a break in the rain before beginning the process of setting them up; it was hard enough to carry them out one-by-one into the woods, and she didn't want to complicate the process further by adding in slick leaves and slippery metal. Back on her kitchen counter, a print-out of a satellite map now lay, with nine circles carefully marked out where she intended to place the traps.

They filled the woods between her house and Caroline Lahey's.

Caroline was a police secretary with a pleasant smile and long hair that fell in loose curls that looked as though they could use a good brushing. She was friendly, helpful, a little distracted, and utterly forgettable, and Jacqueline was certain she was Eric's ex-girlfriend.

It had to be her; the other secretary was pushing past sixty (not impossible, but unlikely), and the third was a middle-aged man.

Which left Caroline as the one potentially harboring the demons.

Jacqueline had not heard the angel speak since leaving her house three days ago, and even when she approached the secretary at the counter, no supernatural force tried to stop her. She was once again on her own.

She had gone to the police station under the pretense of meeting someone online to sell her cell phone to; the station had a place in the lobby for anyone who wanted a secure spot for people to meet up with strangers to trade and barter, and here she was able to sit for ten minutes, casting anxious glances behind the counter toward where Carline sat, busily inputting information into a computer. A large stack of folders stood at her elbow, demanding her attention.

She was a few years older than Jacqueline, and a certain self-possession exuded from her. If she was harboring demons, she certainly didn't seem like it. Jacqueline had expected to see someone nervous, shifty, a woman terrified with a hidden secret stamped across her face. Someone who looked a little like *she* did these days, with dark circles under her eyes and cheeks beginning to hollow with fatigue.

Instead, she watched a woman carefully sorting through paperwork, eyes narrowed in concentration at her computer, fully absorbed in her tasks. Jacqueline looked down at her phone, checking her name on the property records, dragging her thumb across the screen to better understand the map: if you were to cut through the woods, Caroline lived about twenty, thirty minutes from her own home, Jacqueline estimated.

When she squinted, she could piece together a working theory: the demons had attacked Kenneth in his home, then returned to the woods. From there, the maroon one had attacked her, as she had been walking toward Kenneth's house...

But the black-haired one, Kenneth's not-quite-doppelganger, hadn't been there...because he had been at Caroline's house a few hours later, when Eric showed up.

It wouldn't have been a long walk.

Depending on when the maroon *kitsune* killed those other two people, the black *kitsune* may or may not have been with him, looking on at the carnage with perhaps indifference or approval. Or, maybe he had been at Caroline's the entire time. Not that it mattered; Jacqueline knew they would have been together since the Brittany Alice murder. The black one was no innocent.

Jacqueline was tempted to approach Caroline and show her a picture of Kenneth: she had even come up with a weak but plausible scenario in which to do so. She could walk up to the counter, hold up her phone, and say, 'This is the guy I was supposed to meet – can I leave my number and have someone call me if he shows up?'

And then she could gauge Caroline's reaction.

But no; it was tempting, but she had to resist. She needed to maintain the element of surprise, and if indeed Caroline was harboring the demons, she would surely be shocked by the photo and mention it to them.

After making a show of shrugging off no one showing up to buy her phone, Jacqueline had left. Caroline nodded absently, but did not look up as she exited.

Jacqueline covered the seventh trap with clumps of leaves and pine needles, satisfied when it was hidden. Near each trap, she had carved a small but visible 'X' into the two nearest trees. She'd know what to look for, where to find them again.

She was aware of the danger she was creating, first and foremost for herself: she kept glancing up, her eyes sweeping through the forest, senses straining for the hint of a blood-red demon passing through the underbrush...but fall was steadily thinning all the trees but the pines, and it would have been far harder for any large animal to go unseen. She had chosen to work swiftly during the brightest part of the day (even though that certainly wouldn't have stopped the demon, if he chose to attack), and she was eager to be done and safe behind closed doors.

Well, not quite *safe*; she wouldn't be safe again until a bear trap closed, and a gun fired.

She felt guilty about the potential for harm to other creatures, though; it was unlikely people would go walking through these woods, but other animals surely would, and the thought of a deer haphazardly stepping into a trap and findings it leg broken or bone pulverized caused her to cringe with regret.

She hoped she'd capture her quarry before some other innocent animal was harmed.

"Jacqueline!"

Her head snapped up, her breath stopping in her lungs.

"Jacqueline!" The voice came closer now, and in the distance, a head of black hair was visible, staggering up the incline toward her.

She was on her feet in the next instant, waving to him. "Kenneth – stay where you are! Don't move!" She raced to him; he had come to a halt twenty feet away from one of the traps.

He looked her up and down in steadily growing alarm. "Jacqueline, your front door was unlocked...you're all dirty. What are you doing out here? I was worried..."

Her hands and knees were covered in wet mud; Jacqueline wiped her hands on her jeans and lied smoothly, "Just going for a walk."

Kenneth looked at her in flat disbelief. "Then why are there two bear traps in your trunk?"

"...Shit." The trunk was popped open in her driveway. Of course he'd seen them.

"Jacqueline...what's going on?" There was fear in his voice, and steadily growing alarm.

She sighed and braced herself for the argument to come.

"Kenneth, I'm going to give you the choice: you can walk

away from this, because you're not going to like what I have to say. Or you can listen, but you can't try to stop me."

He paled and nearly drew back, then stepped forward on a second impulse, grabbing her by the shoulders. "Are you okay? Is everything alright?" His hands were shaking.

She reached up and steadied him, shaking her head. "No. No, I'm not okay, and everything is not alright. Come with me back to the house – let's sit down, okay?"

It was a tense walk; Jacqueline made a point of shutting her car's trunk before they went inside, then locked the door behind her. She steered Kenneth toward her living room, not bothering with her soiled clothes before sitting on the couch.

She figured this conversation was about to go badly, but it was going to happen, regardless, so better to simply get on with it. "I don't think the killers have left...or killer, actually. I *know* they haven't, because one of them – the maroon one – is stalking me."

Kenneth jolted at the news; he began to pepper her with questions for details, and had she called the police, was she safe – it was her turn to grab him by the shoulders and say, "Kenneth. *Kenneth,*" until he stopped, his breathing rapid, and waited.

She shook her head, her shoulders set. "No, Kenneth, I haven't called the police," she said slowly, keeping her voice calm and firm, annunciating each word. "Because they're not people. They are shapeshifters, and one of them intends to kill me."

She waited for Kenneth to protest, to offer *some* sort of reply, but he was stunned into total silence. When it was clear that he had lost the ability to speak, she sighed and continued.

"Remember how you told me Eric met someone who looked just like you at his friend's place? I found her." She adopted a distant, almost paternal tone, explaining the details of who Caroline was and where her property lay in relation to theirs, tracing the timeline she had come to believe in. When he still remained mute, she figured she might as well go all in, since she didn't think she could shock him any further: at last she revealed her encounter with the maroon demon at the library, how he was stalking the edges of her life now, waiting to kill her when he was done toying with her.

A flash of pain echoed across his expression. "You didn't tell me – all this time..." But he held himself in check, cutting off his words, and lowered his eyes.

"No," she whispered. "I didn't...but I'm telling you now. Are you willing to hear more?"

He nodded, somber.

She told him of an angel who spoke to her, who fought it off, who later whispered that the demon would never, ever stop wanting her.

She told him she would not wait around for it to satisfy its want.

"They must be *somewhere*. I think the first place to look would be Caroline's house; there must have been a reason the black-haired one went there when he was injured, and she cared enough to call Eric. Either she's helping them, which makes her an accomplice, or they were threatening her for aid, and she needs our help."

The 'our' had slipped out; she didn't think Kenneth would offer her any assistance, but with him here, beside her, even in a state of shock, it had felt like the natural thing to say.

Kenneth was opening and closing his mouth; some sort of response was struggling to come out. She waited, patient, and at last he managed, "What are you planning?"

She took a deep breath for this one. "I want to go her home and see if they're there, and if they are, I plan to lure them into the woods, to follow me. I've set up almost all of the bear traps; I have two to go. I know where they're at. I plan to catch them, and shoot them."

It sounded elegantly, foolishly simple.

Kenneth at last found his voice, though it was heavy with horror. "Jacqueline, *if* they're there, they're *dangerous.* If you really believe those people are still around, you should go to the police, because if they are, and you antagonize them...they could hurt you. They could *kill* you. And you – you're talking about... about *shooting* them..."

She knew what he was really saying: she was willing to become a killer herself. She had thought about it in great detail.

And she had considered the angel's revelation that only one of the demons was a murderer; it hadn't confirmed which one, but she knew. Oh, she knew...

But even if the black-haired one hadn't killed anyone himself, he had helped the other, and he too might become a killer if given the chance.

They both needed to be destroyed.

Kenneth stared at her in helpless dismay. "I can't change your mind, can I?"

She shook her head. "You could call the police, have me put on a psych hold, but no...even then, you wouldn't change my mind, and I'd hate you for it."

"Jacqueline..." She could tell he was struggling to speak. "But...the police..."

"Kenneth, *these people are not humans.*" He flinched, but she plunged on, adamant now. "These are demons – *kitsune,* fox shapeshifters, and no police officer is going to catch and arrest them, let alone believe what they really are." Her voice softened, but there was an accusing edge to it. "You saw them yourself, and even *you* don't believe what was right before your eyes."

He tried shaking his head, but the movement was an ineffectual denial.

"Kenneth," she tried, coming at it from a different route. "The maroon one...Sometimes, I feel him in the night...it's like he's just outside my windows, watching, reaching for me through the walls." Kenneth sat up straighter, his breath catching. "It's like a feeling on the back of my neck," she explained. "It's stupid and cliché to say, but the hairs stand up. It's this creeping, quiet feeling...and when it comes, I feel like I'm being pulled down into memories, thoughts I don't want to think about...They're demons, Kenneth. The police won't catch them."

Kenneth leaned forward, taking her hands. His voice was a frightened whisper. "Why are you telling me this? What do you want me to do? Jacqueline..." He looked down at his hand over hers, working his jaw as he decided what to say. "Do you want me to talk you out of this, or help you with whatever you're planning? You know I don't...I don't believe in things the way you do," he said. He closed his eyes for a moment, swallowing, and she felt the tremor in his arms still with the resolve of his decision. "But I won't let you do this alone, if you're determined to do it. I wish you wouldn't. I wish you'd just call the police, but...I'll do whatever you need. Whatever you want."

Her hands were so small in his. *This is love,* she thought suddenly, stupefied. She felt it in every part of his being, felt it move from him to her, saw it deep in his eyes when they at last opened and looked at her with the clarity of someone incapable of disguise or subterfuge. *He thinks I'm out of my mind and he doesn't care. All he knows is that he loves me, and that's enough for him, even in the face of this insanity.*

In that moment, she felt the sudden need to finally say, "I love you," but no; her own soul held her back. The words were too simple, meaningless. Kenneth was telling her *I love you* all over again right now, in this very moment, by staring down what must have felt like a long tunnel of madness to him, seeing her on the other side, and nevertheless finding the will to walk through it, to join her, so that she wouldn't be alone. She could see he was bewildered, terrified even: from his perspective, she was talking about confronting a serial killer who was stalking her and killing him herself.

And still, he was willing to stand at her side.

She stared at him, words simply not enough. He had said he loved her, and now he was proving it. She didn't know how to show her own feelings in return.

Love would have been going into a dark bedroom to hold a dying hand, to heed the call of a fading, desperate voice.

Her heart grew heavy at the waiting, expectant look on his face. *I don't know how to love without fear,* she thought. *I don't know if I'm capable of that...*

And if she wasn't, could she ever love him the way he deserved to be loved?

But Kenneth didn't believe he deserved to be loved, she knew. Kenneth didn't believe he deserved anything – least of all, her. Her mom would probably agree with him. Jacqueline didn't feel that way; she didn't think that what we did or didn't deserve factored much into how we loved someone or who we loved.

What did they *deserve,* anyways? What did she *want?*

A world where she wasn't afraid; a world where she could love him freely without fearing for their lives. A world without demons who invaded their hearts.

She had failed to act for her father. She had been called; she had done nothing, paralyzed by fear.

She would do better for Kenneth. She would be stronger. They had attacked him, too; she didn't believe for a moment they had truly left him alone, either.

"Jacqueline." He squeezed her hands, waiting.

She opened her palms and pressed them flat against his, as though they were one body knelt in prayer. She memorized the feeling of his fingertips, the smoothness of his inner palm, the heat at the beginning of his wrist, and when she was done, she leaned in and kissed him, slowly and sweetly, on the mouth. He stared back at her in numbed amazement as she pulled away and told him what she thought they should do.

For a long while, he said nothing, and then at last he let out a wearied sigh and nodded. "Okay," he whispered. "Okay, but...I think we should tell Eric what we're planning."

"Why?" Her hackles were up at once. "So he can try to convince me not to do it? Tell me how I'm crazy? Call the police on me?"

"No, Jacqueline – stop, don't look at me like that. It's just..." He struggled for a moment under the weight of what they were about to do. "If you're right about the...the killers being there, then that woman is in danger. He cares about her...about Caroline."

"Eric doesn't care about anyone besides himself." It came out harsher than she meant it; she cared about Eric almost as much as she loved Kenneth, but there was something fundamentally missing from Eric's interior world. She hadn't meant it as a criticism: she had only meant it as a statement of fact.

Kenneth shot her a skeptical look. "I think you're wrong. He cares. He was willing to risk his job by helping her...that means something to Eric."

She considered this for a moment, nodded, then gave him some quick advice on how to treat the topic when they spoke, what not to mention so that Eric himself didn't call the police on them...though she thought that was unlikely. They knew Eric had provided illegal medical aid to one of the demons, and although he was her friend, Jacqueline would tell the police in a heartbeat if Eric called the cops on *her*.

And Eric was smart enough to know that.

"I'm not going over there with you," she said. "If you want to talk to Eric, you'll have to do it alone."

"...I will. Later."

"Later?"

He was already at her front door, turning the handle. "We've still got two traps to set up."

In the evening, Kenneth faced Eric in his living room. They hadn't seen much of each other in the last few weeks, but Eric was always reliable: Kenneth had texted that it was urgent they meet, and Eric had immediately replied with a time.

And now that he was here, he didn't know how to begin. He put his head down and blundered forward without so much as asking how Eric's week had been.

"Was the girl who called you in September named Caroline Lahey?"

Kenneth regretted speaking the moment the words were out of his mouth. Eric's eyes had narrowed. His mouth pulled down into an angry frown, and when he didn't speak, Kenneth tried again, his voice unsteady.

"Am I right?"

Eric's response was nothing short of cold, simmering anger. "*Yes.*"

He followed Jacqueline's coaching on how to approach the subject. "Have you talked to her recently?"

A muscle twitched above Eric's eye. "*Why?*"

"Because..." He searched the room for something to settle his gaze on, a harbor away from Eric's frigid anger. Finding none, he looked apologetically back at his friend and cringed. "I think she might still be helping those guys. The ones who attacked me. The...possible murderers."

"Have they done something to you?"

"No, but –"

"And where did you get her name?"

Kenneth gave up and decided it was easier to look down at the floor. "Jacqueline went to the police station."

"*Why?*"

"She thinks one of the guys is stalking her."

"And I assume she has proof of that?"

"No..." The thought hadn't occurred to him. He hadn't asked her for proof. He had just listened as she explained what she wanted to do, and why, thinking all the while that no matter how ludicrous the words coming out of her mouth were, he didn't want to disappoint her again. She deserved someone who would stand by her, and no matter what, he would never let anyone hurt her.

He would not abandon her again.

"What does she plan to do about it?"

"We're going to go over there – to Caroline's house. We're going to see if they're there."

Eric scoffed. "And do *what*, exactly? Have a fist fight? Talk it out?"

Kenneth steadied himself for what he was about to say. "We're going to lure them out into the forest between Jacqueline's house and Caroline's property, then catch them in one of the bear traps that we set up this afternoon."

Eric stared at him, unblinking, and when he saw that Kenneth looked back at him in perfect sincerity, he stood up, took three angry steps away, and whirled on him.

"Are you fucking *kidding* me? Are you fucking *insane?*"

"Eric –"

"You're a goddamn idiot. That's *assault*. A bear trap – a fucking *bear trap?* That's assault *with a deadly weapon*. You're a *fucking idiot*," he spat. Kenneth watched, half ashamed, half astonished; he had never seen Eric so animated, so emotional before. "So Jacqueline thinks she's being stalked, and that's enough for you to endanger yourself like this? She's not *rational*. A rational human being puts up motion-activated night cameras around the property, or even the woods. A rational person installs some new lights, changes the locks, goes down to the station, and *files a goddamn police report*. I don't even need to ask if she's tried going to the police yet; I know her – she hasn't. A rational person doesn't convince someone to do something as *stupid* as this, unless they're *irrational* as well. And what happens if you can't get them to follow you, or you do and they *don't* end up in a bear trap? A fucking *bear trap*," he repeated, still unable to come to grips with it. "What *then?*"

Kenneth's mouth was dry. "You gave me a gun."

"Oh *Jesus Christ*, Kenneth, I gave you a gun in case you were attacked in your home and you needed to defend yourself. You're talking about pre-meditated *murder*."

"They're murderers themselves –"

"*You don't know that.* First, you don't even know if they're *there*, and anyways, what are you, a fucking vigilante superhero? Are you fucked in the head? If you're so goddamned convinced about this, *call the police.* Let *them* go raid the place and arrest them." He was shouting now, his hands curled into fists. "And you're an asshole enough to show up here and implicate me in this bullshit? You know that now that I know what you're planning to do, I'm an accessory to murder if you go through with this and I don't try to stop you, or report you? You're implicating me in *pre-mediated murder? You?* You're not going to fucking kill anyone," he finished, sneering. "Jacqueline might, but not you. You're pathetic."

He had flung the last words with all the venom of the insult it was. Kenneth let it go; he agreed with him. "I'm telling you this so that you can get Caroline out of her house. That's why I came here, Eric – not to ask your opinion or your permission or even your help. I came here because I think she means *something* to you, and I'm giving you the chance to protect her, in case any number of things go wrong, or in case they're threatening her."

Eric's shoulders rose with the heaving of his rage, and he stared at Kenneth now in open hatred.

"*What?*"

"We're starting tomorrow, Eric. I'm going to watch from the tree line, see if I can spot them. If they're not there, I'll try again the next day, and the day after that. If I spot them, I'll call you, and if you can contact Caroline, that would be best. Maybe you'll call the police after I leave here and stop us: you have all night to do it, if you want. But..." He swallowed, guilt overcoming him as he played his one and only card, "But if you do, I'll tell them about your going over there and treating the guy. I'm sorry. I really am." He hung his head and sighed. "If you feel anything for her, this is your chance to get her out of there. That's why I came here to tell you this."

Something brief and painful twisted across his face. "She doesn't care about me. We haven't talked since that night I went over. I doubt she'd pick up the phone." Eric sat down and wiped a sheen of sweat away from his forehead.

Kenneth tried to sound less meek than he felt. "...Jacqueline doesn't think she knows anything about them...anything about who they really are, or what they've done."

"'Anything,'" he mocked, but the spite was gone from his words. "I don't even want to know what insane bullshit Jacqueline believes now."

Kenneth sighed. "She's afraid, Eric. She doesn't think going to the police will help, and I believe her when she says we have to do something, or she's in danger."

Eric shook his head. "I don't know, Kenneth. I don't know if I can let you do this. This is dangerous, illegal – I think Jacqueline's fucking crazy, you could *kill* someone, or at the very least, maim them..."

"We can trap them and then call the police," he lied. "You're right: I don't want to be a murderer, and neither does Jacqueline. She doesn't think there's any chance the police could catch them on their own, but...if they were after *her*...we could catch them first."

"You're going to call the police *after* you assault them?" Eric shook his head. "Holy shit, you're the dumbest fucking person on the face of the earth. You'll go to *jail*. Just *call the police* now!"

"If we did that, they'd just get away."

Eric scoffed in disgust. "Then let them run. Who cares? Murders go unsolved every day. There's no such thing as justice, Kenneth."

Kenneth's hands slowly curled into fists. "I don't believe that, Eric," he whispered. "And it's not just about justice. Jacqueline is convinced her life is in danger. This is about *protecting* her. All I need you to do, if I text you that they're there, is call Caroline and ask her to come see you, just for an hour."

A bitter, hollow laugh escaped him. "Unless you're prepared to shoot me, Kenneth, I'm not going to let you do this. This has gone far enough. I'm going to call the police myself. I think you need medical help, an evaluation." He stood up. Kenneth watched as he walked toward his phone.

He took a deep breath, closed his eyes, and tried one last time.

"She stopped calling you when he showed up, didn't she?"

Eric's hand hovered over his phone. He didn't turn around.

"The guy – the one who looks like me. That's when she stopped calling you. Except for the night when she needed you."

Eric turned, slowly. All of the passion from the past few minutes had fallen away, and his face had become an expressionless mask of cold, empty detachment. *This* was the Eric he knew, the Eric he could rationalize with.

"Don't call the police or a hospital, Eric. Please...just talk to me."

Eric moved deliberately, purposefully, with almost predatory control back into the living room, his eyes narrowed. He sat, his arms crossed over his chest, waiting. Kenneth opened his mouth to ask about Caroline again, but he looked at that expression – pointed, *furious,* an inhuman snarl held just in check in lips curling back over teeth, and the words that came out were all wrong.

"...Do you resent me?"

Eric didn't reply for a long time. His gray eyes were cold, inscrutable as a thick autumn fog, but for a moment they cleared, and Kenneth saw down into the depths that it was indeed as he suspected: a hatred lived here. The fog returned, concealing it, but Eric answered him truthfully.

"Yes."

Kenneth sighed. It was almost relieving to hear him admit it.

"I think you've known that, though."

Kenneth nodded.

"You've had everything I've always wanted." Eric wet his lips, his teeth gnashing. "Two parents who love you, who raised you with wealth and warmth. You told me they bought your way into an excellent college, and you threw that opportunity away. You had summers to spend across the country with a relative who left you a small inheritance of property, not that you need it. Anything you need, you would only have to lift up a phone and your parents would provide it for you. You can afford to blunder your way through life, talentless, drifting, and fail your way through school without any real consequences, because you have multiple forms of security to fall back on. And you have Jacqueline," he finished. The flatness had broken, and a deep bitterness had invaded the syllables of her name. "You have someone who loves you, despite the fact that you cut her out of your life because you were too selfish to focus on anything other than yourself. You knew you could do that because she'd always be there for you, *waiting* for you." No, he wanted to protest, it hadn't been like that *at all* – he didn't think Jacqueline would wait for him; he thought she would move on, discard him, because he wasn't worth waiting for, but Eric continued. "And you have me," he added, rolling his eyes. "A friend who has even hated you, but still cares about you. A friend you could discard for two years, then pick back up when you needed me, because I had no one else. And that man...he looks like you." Eric bit out the last words, his eyes flashing, and Kenneth understood how cold that knife must have felt when it slipped inside of Eric, to know that Caroline had ignored him in favor of a man who looked like *him*.

Kenneth's gaze fell away from Eric's, back down to the floor. He couldn't lift it again.

Every word he said was true.

Eric pressed on. "Your life has been one of privilege and ease, and you've never been happy with it. Sometimes – a lot of times – I've hated you for that." Eric took a shaking breath. "I hated you the most when you came back here, when the door to Jacqueline's house opened, and there *you* were."

"I've hated myself, too." Kenneth tried to speak again, to tell Eric that he was completely right, but that there was something else that he possessed, in addition to all the things Eric had catalogued, something he *hadn't* chosen or wanted to have.

It was a heavy, coiling thing that he felt he had been born with; it had wrapped around his heart, squeezing. He carried that weight all his life even as it dragged him down into himself, crushing his spirit, so that some days it was an effort just to breathe, a victory just to get out of bed... How, *how* could he have ever spoken to Jacqueline when that *thing* was suffocating him? How could he have ever managed to even call *him*?

He didn't dare tell Eric that. Eric would have sneered and told him to be grateful that he could lay there, wallowing until the end of time, if he wanted; his parents could afford to give him everything he needed in life. Mental illness would never chase *him* into the streets, oh no; he was privileged enough that he could just mope around in bed without the terror of losing his house, without the burden of having to earn money to eat, regardless of what he was struggling with. If he was brave enough to just face what was wrong with him, his parents could have bought him the best therapy that money could buy, cutting-edge treatments in some resort by the sea. He could hear Eric in his mind, so clearly, as though he were speaking the words right this very moment: so he was *sad* some days? *Fuck off.*

Kenneth sunk down into wordless, despairing self-loathing.

"When I think about those things, in that moment, I resent you," Eric said. His voice had grown quiet, and the anger had cooled into a temperate, matter-of-fact tone almost close to pity. "But I know that the reason you can't take advantage of any of it isn't because you're selfish, or vain, or even an idiot. I know you're not purposefully throwing away all that you've been given – money, an education, my friendship...even Jacqueline's love. You don't have to say anything, Kenneth. I know what you're thinking. I know that what you've been fighting against is stronger than you."

His vision blurred; he hadn't expected Eric to understand.

"Eric," he said, his voice breaking. "Am I going to win?"

"...Against those guys?"

"No. Not them." Kenneth's eyes had welled up. He looked down at his hands, but the details were lost behind the tears.

"...I don't know, Kenneth." And then, quietly, "...No. I don't think so."

Kenneth sat in silence; he blinked, and the sharp, stinging sensation of the tears slipping down his face pushed him to regain control of himself. He heard Eric shift his weight uncomfortably.

"...I'll call her."

He scrubbed his face and looked up, surprised. If he had

expected to see sympathy in Eric's expression, he was wrong: Eric's gaze was unflinching, demanding. "There's no guarantee she'll pick up, and if she does, no guarantee she'll come over. There's no guarantee your idiotic plan will work, either, and that if it does, that you won't get hurt. And if they *are* there... whether or not they assaulted you, those are two people who, if you succeed in trapping them, will be seriously hurt. And if you *do* succeed, and you call the police, there are a lot of consequences you're going to face. Is it worth it to protect Jacqueline? For the possibility of facing serious jail time? This is a step past self-defense. And if something goes wrong – really wrong, and you need to use the gun – and you kill someone, can you live with that? And what then – will you call the police, or will you hide the body? Dispose of it? *How*?"

Kenneth shook his head. "The police, Eric. I'll call the police as soon as we catch them."

Eric eyed him with skepticism. "And what will you tell them when you do? Do you know?"

"Not yet, I –"

"You better figure all that shit out. What will you do if you go there and only one of them is there, the one who looks like you? If you attack him, or 'lure him out,' to use your language, you'll be alerting the other one that you're putting your chips on the table now. *He'll* call the police."

"No, Eric; I won't text you unless both of them are there. It's too dangerous to attack just one."

"...Then do something for me, for all the trouble you've pulled me into."

"What?"

Eric stared at him, merciless, and his voice came out through clenched teeth.

"If you catch him – the black-haired one – *shoot him*."

Kenneth couldn't hold that stare. If something heavy and

hurting had wound its way around his own heart, Kenneth thought, then just what was it that lived inside of Eric? He looked away and gave a weak nod.

His friend rose, went to the kitchen, and returned, shoving a glass into his hand. "Drink up," Eric said. "You're going to need it."

SEVEN

There was no way to balance the equation, Kuro thought. His fur was warm with the late afternoon sun, but the light was sinking now, and with it came the cold of an autumn night. He lay in the middle of the garden, his thoughts painful, his mind reeling upon itself. There was no way to make it all disappear seamlessly; the lies, Jaden, Caroline...and even that other girl, Jacqueline, lurked at the edges of his guilt. How long would it be until a police report came across Caroline's desk, detailing that girl's death? What would he say *then?*

He felt as though he stood in the middle of this storm, and all around him whirled these people and his lies, but he could not make them stay still long enough to somehow offer him a solution to escaping this net he was ensnared within. He would have to learn to live with these untruths.

And the lie about the murders...it kept cutting at him, sharper every time he replayed it in his mind. Why was it so painful? He kept turning it over, looking at it from new directions, trying to justify to himself why he had needed to lie in the first place. *I have to protect Jaden,* he thought. But no, that wasn't even the half of it;

if Caroline found out he was lying and protecting a murderer, she wouldn't forgive *him* – and that was important, at the heart of all the pain, somehow, but he couldn't see *why*. He kept reaching further inward, trying to understand this feeling inside of him that was tight, painful, and electric, but it had no name, no familiar distinction for him to pin it down.

He had tried to pace at one point but collapsed, heavy and winded. The *holy dark* stirred in feeble need, desperately hungry, dying. If he told her the truth, she would hate him – and maybe that hate would feed him, and he wouldn't have to suffer like this...

I don't want her to hate me... The thought brought him close to the mystery of the emotions he was puzzling over, but his mind pushed it away. He had realized he would have to keep the lie indefinitely while simultaneously relying on Jaden to never hurt anyone again here in Asheville, which would not happen, so why delay the inevitable, why delay her finding out the truth...?

That throbbing feeling inside him responded with a painful ache.

"Kuro."

He lifted his head and shifted forms, pushing himself up into a seated position. Caroline stood at the gate of the garden, a line of worry across her forehead.

"You've been out here for almost an hour. It's getting dark..."

He couldn't find the words to reply. His eyes drunk in her image, the way her fingers curled over the edge of the gate, the way the wind lifted the ends of her hair. She was barefoot, and she didn't care. Her soul reached out to him almost shyly, questioning, and he felt that it was afraid.

"What is it?"

"I just wanted to know...if you wanted to come inside."

Confusion swept in now. In his fog, he thought he had spoken directly to her soul, but it was her voice that had replied. He shook his head and tried again. "That feeling. Just now…" He felt her fear sharpen as she looked at him, and his heart plunged, sinking. It felt like a weight was pushing him down, crushing him. *She's afraid I'm lying, that I had something to do with those murders…* He lifted his gaze to hers, imagining what she saw when she looked at him, and for a moment he could almost see himself through her eyes.

Her fear spiked again as she suddenly took two steps forward.

He hated himself then more than any other time, and the puzzle inside him that he had been working on for so long merged into a suddenly clear picture. The understanding struck him, and with it, a despair he had never known before.

He didn't want to be hated, or feared.

He wanted her to love him, because somehow, new and painful as it was, he had already begun to love her.

"Kuro." Her voice cracked. Another tentative step brought her closer. He couldn't bring himself to look at her eyes, to feel any further; surely revulsion and hate would follow behind her fear, and that would break him.

"Please don't leave."

Her words were barely whispered, but the wind carried them to him. He watched as she drew near, his gaze lowered to her feet, the spongy grass between her toes, up her legs, and then to the hands that were reaching down, the fingers that were pressing themselves between his, pulling him up. Even standing, he could not bring himself to look at her face. Her arms moved and circled him, hugging him closely.

"Please don't leave me," she whispered. "There's something in your face…I'm afraid you're going to go, and you won't come back."

He hesitated before he allowed his body to answer hers, his arms circling around her back, burying his face in her hair, the scent of her lost in the cool, crisp autumn twilight. Her soul moved around him; he felt the fear in her again, but under it, propelling it, was an emotion that swelled like the tide, surging forward. It left him hollowed, burning.

The words left him in a rush. "Do you hate me?"

"How could I hate you?"

He thought of so many reasons why and said none of them aloud, and in the silence there came only their breaths. She helped him to walk, and together, they moved toward the house, exhausted and somehow embarrassed. He couldn't meet her gaze; she spoke only to offer him dinner in a hushed voice, and he declined, retreating to the living room as the darkness outside deepened.

She paused in the doorway, her mouth open. Their eyes met for a moment, but too much passed between them, and Caroline turned away, retreating down the hall.

He tried to slow his breathing, to mull over the sick pit of misery in his gut, but a need – oppressive, overwhelming – was crushing him. He felt like he was suffocating with the desire to feel her arms again, to look into her eyes and experience the heat from her body. He had almost lost her today, and he was acutely aware that all her trust in him was built upon a foundation of lies.

Kuro made his decision.

He stood and walked down the hall, his heart pounding, and knocked at her door with a trembling hand. She called, and he entered.

The rosary was on her nightstand. *She's been praying,* he thought. He leaned in the doorway, unsure if he should enter.

She looked up at him and gave a tentative smile, but a touch of melancholy lingered in the curve of her lips. "What is it, Kuro?"

He looked around the room, unsure of what to say. He was going to tell her the truth, he *wanted* to; he wasn't a creature built for deception – his heart wasn't made for this...but then he looked at her upturned face, open and waiting, and when he opened his mouth to speak, a different truth – raw and unguarded – emerged.

"I'm lonely."

Surprise flashed across her face for only a moment, and then she gestured toward the bed. He sighed and entered the room, and to his surprise, she moved, resting on her side with her head against her pillow. He mimicked her and lay down, facing her. She had her hands cupped under her head, and her eyes were sad.

"What are you thinking about?"

A shadow moved behind her gaze. She bit her bottom lip and shook her head just a bit. "Nothing," she said. It was a bold, artless lie. He could feel that something was occupying all of her soul, something straining against her heart. Until today, he hadn't known that feeling.

He wanted to forget the lie he had told her, somehow distract them both, even though he had come to her room to tell her the truth. Now that he had reached the threshold of confession, he couldn't do it after all, not with her looking at him like that. He wanted to forget the feelings inside of him. If she wouldn't speak, he would, but of other, inconsequential things.

"You remember when you asked me earlier if you saw Kenneth, if you would see me?"

For a moment she didn't respond, confused, but the gambit worked: clarity came back to her eyes, and he saw that he had successfully lifted her out of her thoughts and in the process distracted himself. She nodded.

"I thought, maybe...you'd want to know why."

Her eyes lit up. "Would you tell me?"

He lay next to her in her bed, and without stopping to think about it, he reached forward and began to tangle her hair in his fingers, their heads on opposite pillows. She didn't stop him or comment on the motion, and after a few moments of gathering his thoughts, he spoke.

The two *kitsune* had been watching humans for years after the *holy dark* moved in them; Kuro did not find people particularly interesting. They came to the mountains, then left. Jaden was endlessly fascinated by people, but there was a hateful jealousy in the way he watched them from the shadows.

They discovered their human forms during a sweltering, bloated afternoon in the heart of a summer heatwave. They had gone to a spot by the river earlier in the day, near one of the popular waterfalls, and from up high, far from any jumpers, they had watched groups of people attempting to cool themselves. Kuro had sunk into a panting nap. When he awoke, Jaden was still staring hungrily at the people below, his gaze rarely blinking and his teeth always bared.

Look at them, he said. *It must be nice – they have their whole history stretched out before them. They can look at thousands of years of records and understand who they are, where they come from, what their purpose is in the world. They have clothes and cars that carry them anywhere they want to go...and us? What role do WE play, Kuro? To hunt and live like the rest of these animals out here?*

It was no use talking to him when he got into such moods; he simply couldn't follow him down those paths. Kuro sat up dreamily from his nap, shaking his head. He'd heard some manner of this monologue before and knew that Jaden required no response from him in his turn.

When the afternoon was spent and the swimmers departed, they followed the sound of water through the mountains without speaking, another mile trek above the large cascade to a series of smaller crests in the river. Here, the water flowed gently into a tranquil, lazy stream, speckled with shimmering pebbles on the river floor, before it traveled farther along and joined with a second river to form the falls that the humans enjoyed. But this spot, too high and inaccessible for hikers, was secret and untouched. It was a spot they often visited, and now they dipped their snouts into the water greedily before jumping into the river to cool off as the first, early fireflies tested their wings in the late sunset.

Jaden climbed up on top of an algae-dappled rock, shaking the water from his fur. Kuro heaved himself up onto a drier rock and shook himself fiercely, spraying water all over the other *kitsune*. Jaden rolled his red eyes and looked up into the sky, deep in thought.

What would it be like to be human? He asked. He had undoubtedly thought the question to himself for a long time, but it was the first Kuro had ever heard him speak it out loud.

Kuro had leaned down and caught a fish in between his paws, and he looked up between a mouthful of scales to answer him with an enlightening *I don't know.*

I wonder what it feels like to sleep in a bed at night, Jaden went on.

Kuro had never heard him sound so wistful, and it unsettled him.

I wonder what it's like to not have to DEAL with the rain – to just stay indoors, Jaden continued. Kuro had found the flaky flesh and crunched through the pin bones, watching him.

I wonder what it's like to have hands that can hold things...

You'd miss your claws, Kuro said.

But then something peculiar happened; Jaden turned to Kuro, and his snout pulled up in a mixture of concentration and puzzlement, his long tail swinging out behind him, trembling –

– And then Jaden was gone.

Or, at least, Jaden as Kuro knew him was gone. The fish carcass fell out of the black *kitsune's* jaws as he jumped to his feet, horrified.

JADEN!

But Kuro stopped, stunned into silence.

There, reflected in the water, was Jaden as the young man he imagined he could be. It was the image he had longed for, the

picture of a reality he had dared to wonder at – and his first
moment of change had happened upon the mere solidification of
the thought. Kuro's eyes lifted from the reflection to the body that
produced it and found the mirror-image standing upright. The
process of shifting into the new form was like fading out one
image – the giant fox – and fading in the next so fast it was nearly
imperceptible, and Kuro had missed it.

And yet, it had happened.

Jaden swayed as he tested out his two human legs. Without a
tail to balance himself with, he nearly stumbled and fell into the
water, but his body was strong, and his vanity had made him
expertly crafted and handsome. He stood, naked and grinning, on
two long legs that led up to a strong torso, where two arms – with
no claws, Kuro saw – stretched out with open palms as he turned
around slowly and watched all the muscles ripple across his body,
no longer obscured by a pelt of fur as they moved and twisted in
new, undiscovered ways. He was lean and muscular, athletically
sculpted in the refined way of a marble statue. He stared down at
his reflection in the water, and his face grew radiant with joy.

"Kuro." His incredulous voice cracked on unused vocal cords.
He swallowed and tried again. "Kuro, *look.*" Better: deep and
smooth. And then, "Listen! I'm *speaking!*" He paused, fascinated
with his discovery before talking again.

"With my *mouth!*"

His voice was new to him. When the *kitsune* spoke, they could
hear each other, but it was as if the words were already in their
souls. This new way of communicating required the breath of life;
Jaden inhaled the mountain air and reveled in the way his chest,
gleaming with mist, expanded as he breathed in. He spoke again.

"Are you alright?" He asked.

Kuro had sat down heavily, panting, and gaped at his friend.
Are YOU alright? What happened to you?

"The greatest thing in the entire world!" He threw his head

back and laughed in a way Kuro had never heard before – it was a laughter filled with the ringing of unadulterated happiness.

It was the only time Jaden had ever laughed like that in his entire life, and Kuro had never heard it since.

But Kuro watched with a heavy heart as Jaden, fulfilled by achieving his wildest dream, continued to laugh with pleasure in his new body. So that was it, then – Jaden would leave him, go live as a human, and Kuro would be alone, abandoned to the wilderness. One moment Jaden had been a *kitsune* – and the next, with a solitary blink, he was a human.

So now you're going to leave me. Kuro was suddenly, acutely miserable. Jaden looked at him; the sinewy muscles of his neck stretched elegantly as he cocked his head to the side, smirking.

"I'm not going to leave you, Kuro," he said. "We're friends."

Kuro slumped. He didn't believe him. *You're going to abandon me. I know it.*

Jaden laughed again and put his hands on his hips. "Kuro, don't look like that – we're all we have. We understand each other. We *need* each other."

Kuro looked up at him, uncertain; did Jaden really *need* him? *Promise?*

"Promise what?"

They both reacted to the word with cold suspicion; the *holy dark* told them both that a promise was *more* than a promise, and a promise couldn't be broken without painful consequences.

Promise you won't abandon me.

Jaden looked at Kuro and smiled; he sighed, shook his head, and laughed again. "What would we do without one another?"

Kuro narrowed his eyes. *Then* promise.

The smile fell away from Jaden's face, and they stared at each other in silence until Jaden nodded slowly.

"I promise," he said. "I promise I will not abandon you."

Kuro was satisfied; he settled back and began to study Jaden and found himself fascinated; he circled him in slow wonder, observing him from all directions.

*You might look like a human…*he decided, finally. *But you're not.*

Jaden's delight returned, impervious to reality. "Who cares? If you look like one, that counts enough!"

But you don't *look like one.* Kuro couldn't stop himself; he began to laugh, filling the air with his foxlike barking.

Jaden looked up sharply, his face pulling down into an angry scowl.

"Why are you laughing!?"

Kuro continued to bark with amusement.

"What's so funny, Kuro?" His eyes flashed now.

Kuro had never seen Jaden behave this way. He seemed genuinely angry at him, and so Kuro wheezed and inhaled, stifling his laughter to appease his friend.

Your hair. He said, his black eyes glinting. *And your eyes.*

Jaden looked down sharply at the river. He was well-built, powerful. *Human.*

Perfect.

He looked back up at Kuro and quirked an eyebrow, confused. He reached up and touched his eyebrow after it moved, having not noticed it before. How funny! He could make all sorts of facial expressions – he could even smile! And yet…it seemed all he could do now was frown.

Don't you see? Kuro asked.

Jaden was beginning to grow annoyed; Kuro grinned.

Your hair is red! He snorted. *And not like HUMAN red, that orange color – it's the color of blood, just like your fur! There must be a word for it, but it's so…dark! There's no such thing as a human with that color hair – and especially not your eyes.* They'd seen every natural hair color and blend that existed, but not one living being had the deep, bloody maroon belonging to Jaden. The hair was one thing; he could get away with it, though it would attract unwanted attention, but the *eyes*...no human would willingly look into eyes that looked like *that*.

Kuro's amusement faded immediately as he realized what this meant for his friend. For all Jaden had dreamed, as much as he yearned to live among humans, he would never be able to walk open and unnoticed among them, not entirely...not as *himself*. He would always have to hide this part of who he was.

It was a small thing, really, and there were probably any number of simple solutions to hiding his hair and eye color...but he would never truly, *completely* belong.

Jaden snapped his head back down at the water. His jaw clenched as his hand flew up to his face, clutching it in disbelief. It looked bizarre, terrifying; his irises were indeed the same, deep maroon of his pelt, and so too was his hair.

Jaden's wrath escaped his mouth in a wordless scream of rage. When he was done, his chest heaving, eyes blazing, he turned to Kuro in a fury.

"Let me see what *you* look like!" He snarled. For a fleeting moment, it looked to Kuro as if Jaden had been between forms – it was horrifying, even to the *kitsune*. Jaden, a human, had suddenly had the demonic fangs and features of the *kitsune* – the whipping tail, the hands that ended in claws – but it came and went so quickly that Kuro forgot it before he could even fully understand what he saw.

Jaden remained standing, his fists clenched; Kuro could see that his nails were cutting deeply into the palms – thick drops of blood, the dark blood of a demon, were dripping down onto the rock and causing splotches of brown, dead moss.

"Do it, Kuro." Jaden's voice was shaking as he struggled for control. "I want to see what *you* look like."

Kuro backed away, nervous, and thought hard. He wasn't particularly intelligent, nor was he by any stretch of the imagination creative. Kuro could no more imagine himself as a human than he could imagine himself a rabbit, something he knew extraordinarily far more about. He thought hard, desperate to please him, searching for an image, unsure of how to even change.

Then a thought came to him.

It was a memory from a year or so ago. They had come to the same river he had tried to kill himself in, back when he felt the *holy dark* for the first time in his heart. In the summer, the water flowed soft and shallow after the gushing bursts of the spring thaw.

A boy had been there, startling him. He had waded across the river. A patch of wildflowers grew right on the other bank; he was moving toward them with a purpose. From up on the incline, Kuro watched him: it was the longest he had ever looked at a single person with any interest.

And then for one clear, brief moment, the boy had looked up and locked eyes with Kuro. They had seen each other. Kuro had turned and fled back to where Jaden was, a half mile away.

He had never forgotten that boy. The boy had seen him, Kuro was sure of it – but he was only a child. Children imagined they saw a good deal many things in the shadows of the forest.

Kuro gave up trying to imagine himself as a human. Instead, he wondered what that little boy would look like now, grown up.

Before he realized that the rock he was sitting on felt rough against his human flesh, Kuro had transformed into a strongly built adolescent with two dark eyes like chipped onyx and matching black hair. He was more solid, more muscular than Jaden, he could tell; they were of the same height and similar build, but he could see at a glance that Jaden would be able to hide the strength of his cruel frame under clothes. Kuro would not; there was an imposing quality in the set of his shoulders, the firm arc of his neck as he studied himself, eyes narrowed. Kuro *looked* like he could kill a man with his bare hands; Jaden actually *could.*

He had no way of knowing that he was taller than Kenneth McMahon would ever be, or that he possessed fifty pounds of more muscle than Kenneth would ever have, but in a certain light, he could *almost* pass for a twin, certainly a brother, and definitely a cousin of the young man he had never known. He thought he had done a passable job of picturing what that boy might look like grown up, and the *holy dark* had reworked the thought into something better suited for violence and desire.

In a deep voice, husky with disuse, he asked "How do I look?" He offered Jaden a lopsided smile.

Jaden muttered a curse and looked away.

EIGHT

"So you just imagined what that boy would look like grown up...and you became a human?"

Kuro had stopped toying with her hair, but he continued to let the strands lay flat in his palm, and nodded. The version of the story he had told her had left out many details, almost all of them about Jaden. Halfway through the telling, he had come to realize that lying by omission was still a form of lying.

"And that boy was Kenneth?"

He nodded again. "But I didn't realize that until later, when he took a photo of me on the Parkway. That's how he got the photo – I wanted to see if it was him again. I was certain it was."

Her voice was quiet. "It seems fate brought you together." A shy, amused smile played upon her lips. "Maybe I should thank him." She chuckled at his sudden expression. "Don't look so offended. If he hadn't taken a photo of you...we would have never met."

Maybe it would have been better if we hadn't, he thought, but he swallowed it down, unwilling to contemplate a world where they hadn't come to know each other. He regretted so much –

things he had done, things he *hadn't* done, the things he had left unsaid...but he didn't regret meeting her. They fell silent again, and the look from earlier returned to her eyes. She drew a deep, heavy breath.

"...There's something I want to tell you, too."

He looked up, waiting, but she wouldn't meet his gaze.

"I lied to you about something."

He was glad she wasn't looking at him; she would have seen the shock come and go as he wrestled for control. He made himself as still as possible, waiting. A shudder passed through her whole body as she spoke.

"When I told you about Christopher, about what happened before they sent him away...I told you that I couldn't really remember everything I said to him." She looked up then. Her eyes were dry, but the pain was there, raw and fresh as the day it had first come to live in her heart. Kuro felt the regret in her surge again, and with it, the self-loathing that he hadn't understood that day that she had stood, crying, and fled from her living room. "That was a lie. I remember exactly what I said."

He waited for her to go on, and when she did, he had to strain to hear her speak, even this close beside her.

"I told him all the things I told you I said, but there was more...He still had the tool in his hand, the razor he was using to carve the feathers. I looked at it – I remember that, that I *looked* at it and really knew how sharp it was – and I told him...I told him he should kill himself. Not in those exact words...but that's what he heard." She took a deep, shuddering breath, her eyelids pressing shut. "I told him our lives would be so much easier if he didn't exist. I told him I wished he was dead. And I looked at that tool in his hand...and he saw me look at it...and that's when I left him. Do you understand?" She opened her eyes, and Kuro felt all the pain in her rush into him, aching. "*He saw me look at it.* I walked away *on purpose*, so I wouldn't have to see, because he would have done anything for me – even *that...*"

There was no sob, no tears; the time for that had left her. Now there was only a shaking, a shuddering, at the confession of the horrific thing she had done.

"You told me I should forgive myself – I've tried. I've tried to look back at that moment and rationalize it to myself that I was in pain, I was a child, I was stupid and I was selfish, I was horrible... and even though all of that is true, it doesn't change how I feel about it now, or then. I left him alone for a whole minute, Kuro...I knew what he was going to do. For a minute of my life, I was the worst version of myself that I have ever been. I knew the moment I turned and walked out of that door what would happen. I'm not a good person." She looked up at him, her eyes moving across his face, searching for some sort of reaction from him. "I didn't tell you because...I didn't want you to know. Because I'm ashamed. I can't forgive myself for that. I've tried, and I don't think I ever will. I don't deserve it."

He reached out and touched the edge of her arm, searched for something to say, and found he had become an inarticulate fool. "But you love him," he tried, and stopped.

Her mouth twisted into a bitter smile. "And I loved him then, too. We hurt the people we love. It's because we love them that we can hurt them at all."

Her soul moved all around him; he could feel the door in her soul, sealed and locked, rattling with the agony of this memory: the darkness on the other side would never stop testing her resolve, would never stop pushing against the hinges. Maybe someday it would succeed, and she would be haunted by this; he understood that even if he wanted to lift away her regret, he could never do that – it had cut so deeply into the core of her being that it had become integral to who she was and how she lived her life. She had deliberately done a terrible thing as a child, and now, as an adult, she was forced to face it every day and atone. Deep, deep down in her heart, he could almost see the belief that no matter how she lived her life, she could never make that right again, never balance the scales in her favor against what she had done to her brother...but she wasn't haunted. Not yet. Her brother had lived, and that, he knew, had made all the difference.

"Why did you tell me this?"

She sighed, and the heaviness of it settled into her bones. "You've told me so much about you, and I...I didn't want to carry a secret in my heart. I didn't want to hide that from you. I want you to understand who I really am. Do you know what I mean?"

She looked up into his eyes, and the feeling nearly devoured him. He wanted to tell her that yes, he knew so deeply now what it meant to keep a secret that it was like hiding a knife inside of you while it worked to cut its way out, that it *hurt* and mutilated the heart. He reached out and pulled her hands toward him, gripping them, and he felt her warmth again, her soul flowing into his.

He closed his eyes against it; he couldn't tell her about Jaden. *I can't,* he thought, *I can't,* but her soul filled him, deep inside his very core, and her feelings toward him – care, concern, empathy, and even something else, something very bright and impossible for him to quite recognize – moved in him.

Jaden's words floated in his mind. *She makes me feel broken,* he had said of Jacqueline.

Caroline didn't make him feel that way; he had felt broken at one point, yes, but it felt now like all the pieces of him had been reassembled in some new, better way.

She made him feel whole.

"I want to tell you something." Not the truth, no; he was still too much of a coward to risk her love. But this...there was something else he could give her, something of equal weight and value. The words came out of him in a breathless rush. He didn't want to think about what he was about to do, didn't want to look into her eyes again.

Her voice was close. "What is it?"

"My name." He tried to control his breathing, to calm himself, but he was shivering now, frightened and exhilarated all at once. "It's not... my name isn't Kuro," he said, and before he could stop himself, he pushed forward, desperate to give her *this* truth, at the very least, the truest part of him. His voice dropped to a whisper. "My name is Kurobushko."

"Kurobushko." She said the name slowly, and before she could say more, he groaned with the pleasure of it and felt everything inside of him release. He closed his eyes and felt his entire body relax against the bed as he gave himself over to the feeling, melting. It felt like he had been making some sort of journey, he thought, through a tunnel that grew increasingly narrow and dark, all the oxygen sucked away...and he had emerged just then, at last, on the other side, exhausted and resigned to his defeat.

He rolled forward and buried his face against the softest part of her throat, breathing in the scent of her skin, and there was no hesitation before she moved her hand around him, lifted it, and stroked his hair.

He fell asleep with the cadence of his name whispered from her lips, over and over, their arms wrapped around one another.

He woke up to the sound of Caroline screaming.

She scrambled from the bed, shouting. He tried to get up and found himself tangled in the blanket she had at some point dragged on top of them.

With a thump, he fell to the floor.

The wood scratched under his claws. He tried to cry out, but the blanket had tumbled down with him, and he was trapped in it.

She was still shouting from across the room, but he was confused. A high-pitched bark came out of him, foreign even to his ears.

The blanket was suddenly jerked away, sending him sprawling into the closet. He knocked against the wood and stared up at it, bewildered.

Everything had become too big, *tall,* and the colors were...*muted.*

"*Kuro!*"

He turned, searching. Why did the bed loom so high above him? He ducked and came around the corner of it, his heart hammering in his chest.

Caroline stood in the doorway, pointing at him. She seemed like a giant...and she was pointing *down.*

"Kuro...you're..." But she was sputtering. She suddenly shut her mouth, took a steadying breath, strode over to him, leaned down, and *scooped him up.* Stunned, he allowed himself to be carried into the bathroom and there, in front of the mirror, he stared at his reflection.

Caroline stood, disheveled and wide-eyed, holding an actual fox at arm's length.

And the fox was *him.*

He gawked. He was solid black, but not the perfect, single, unvarying shade of a *kitsune*; there was a hint of white, like a layer of frost, across his face, ruff, and back, and his tail ended in the white-tip of a true bottlebrush, so different from the flowing tail of the *kitsune*. Although the pupil remained the same slit of deep black, his irises now were a rich, maple-hued amber. He looked like a perfectly normal animal, though having seen foxes in the wild, he could tell he was unusually large for his size.

"You're a silver fox," she said, awestruck. "A *big* one. You're *at least* twenty pounds. And..." Her nose crinkled up. "You smell bad."

He let out a screech and flailed, falling to the ground.

Kuro fled back into her room and leapt onto her bed.

Think! He told himself. How had this happened?

Caroline came in the room sat beside him, her arms open. He crept into her lap and pressed against her, her arms wrapping around him as he fought against panic.

"Has this ever happened before?"

He gave a shake of his head.

"Okay, try to stay calm..." She took a deep breath and pulled him up again, holding him under his front legs as though he were a cat, rotating his body so that they stared at one another. "Just... picture yourself."

Picture myself. To his surprise, the first image that came to mind was not that of a *kitsune;* instead, he saw his hair, his arms, his human legs...

"Oh!"

Caroline toppled backwards as he shifted forms, suddenly sprawled on top of her. He hoisted himself up with his arms and burst into uncontrollable, joyful laughter.

"What the *fuck*?" He gasped.

She laughed beneath him, her soul spreading with relief. He felt it all flow into him and lift him, her happiness expanding with her smile.

"Kuro – what in the *world?*"

He stopped, staring down at her. Her hair puddled around her head; he wanted to brush the loose strands out of her eyes. "I don't know."

She was still laughing, her eyes crinkled, and her soul was bubbling with the delight of it, filling him from head to toe with its buoyant, sparkling joy.

He could feel it.

Really feel it.

She saw his eyes go wide, her laughter gone. "Kuro – what is it? What's going on?"

"I don't know," he repeated, slower now, his heart racing again. "I need you to – to think of something good. Be happy for a moment."

"*What?*"

"Think about – anything. Think about something you love," he said.

But she was sitting up, growing concerned. He sat back, giving her room. He could feel her worrying about his reaction, and her worry was unsettling. He wanted to shove that away, grab again for the joy and let it lift him into weightless wonder.

"Kuro, I – "

His hands darted forward and grasped hers. "Please, just do it. Ask me questions later."

She opened her mouth and then closed it, shaking her head. She grew quiet, then a feeling – warm and unfolding, like a picnic blanket spreading over the ground on a perfect summer's day – fluttered open inside of her. He felt it and gasped. She saw a light come into his eyes and broke into another confused smile, and joy, unlike anything he had ever felt, filled him. A newfound sense of lightness spread, lifting his heart, like being small and fast, and floating –

He shifted again, back to the true fox form. He leapt high into the feeling as Caroline laughed, his tail brushing against her as he jumped into the air. He tested his vocal cords, and a yipping bark erupted before shattering into the fox gekker.

"Oh my god, what an *awful* sound." She laughed again and he rolled on the bed, shivering with pleasure in the delight of her sparkling joy.

It was so new, and seemed so...*impossible*. He didn't care to understand it, didn't yet seek for an explanation. Instead, he settled back, human again, his chest light, eyes shining.

"I can feel it," he whispered. "It doesn't hurt."

"What doesn't? The form?"

"No – your soul."

"My *soul* doesn't hurt you?"

"The parts of it that used to burn," he said. "I can...I can *feel* it..."

More than *feel;* he could *feed,* and her soul filled him up and erased the empty, gnawing hunger. The pain and the fatigue, the agony, like seeping poison, was all leaving him, swept away by this strong, palatable current that flowed into him...and the deeper he fed, the more he filled himself with it, the more it grew in her, intensifying as her own eyes lit up with excited happiness and... and *hope,* so bright and light that he gasped. *This* was hope? This shining, ephemeral feeling that left his limbs feeling as light as air? He had tasted it before, and it had burned and prickled at him, raking his insides...and now it warmed him with a comfort that told him anything was possible, *all* was possible – even this.

"Is it the *holy dark?*" She asked. "Is it gone?"

He shook his head 'no.' It was growing, feeding even now; he could feel strength inside him, building for the first time in weeks. "It's just...different. Something's changed."

"No kidding." She laughed again, and he loved the sound. He never wanted it to stop. "I woke up and thought I had a heart attack. There was a *fox* curled up next to me. A *real* one. Have you ever been able to do that before?"

"No. *Never.* I didn't even know that could happen..."

"Can Jaden do that?"

He wanted to push Jaden as far out of his thoughts as possible, but he was certain of the answer, though he didn't know why. "No."

"Was it because you told me your name?"

He considered this for a moment, then shook his head slowly. "No."

But she was curious about something, her eyes squinting. "Are you allowed to tell me Jaden's real name?"

He stared back at her, a sinking feeling in his gut, and suddenly felt foolish – so, so foolish.

"...He never told me."

Caroline reached forward and touched his cheek gently, the tips of her fingers brushing against his skin.

"Forget I asked. Let's not talk about him." With the movement of her hand came a warm wave that stole away his sheepishness and drew him away from a hard fact he didn't want to face right now: Jaden had never trusted him enough to give him his name. The sting of that melted away at her touch. He leaned into it.

"Look, can you...can you keep feeling...all this?" He didn't have words to describe it, but he managed an inarticulate gesture. "I don't want to think about anything else right now. I don't want to think about him. I just want to feel...whatever this is."

She smiled. "I can try."

They sank back down onto the pillows, and the wonder of the newness filled him. He refused to let go of her hands, but his eyes closed, drinking it all in. He'd spent so long avoiding touching these emotions that now he felt like he had years of discovery to catch up on; joy and happiness, he felt, were *not* the same – one felt bubbly, bright, and the other was woven with gold and made of stronger stuff. And relief was so *light*, like drinking air and floating...the other half of the human heart had opened up to him for discovery, and he wanted to know and touch it all...and there was that feeling again, the one with no name, that moved with so many hues that he felt dizzy trying to squint at it in his mind's eye. It felt familiar; he had touched this before, he knew, but his entire understanding of the landscape of her soul had changed, like realizing he had been studying a map upside down all this time. He couldn't recognize the shape of things, unfamiliar now in their accessible newness.

"What *is* that?" He was breathless. He touched the feeling

again, trying to trace it, but sunbeams had more substance. He tried again and felt it, his brow furrowing: it was *familiar*, and warm, changing and shifting, diffusive of itself, but solid and true...

Caroline's voice was hushed. "That's love, Kuro."

He opened his eyes to look at her and found that she had grown very still. He hadn't been able to feel it before, not the way it did now. When he'd felt it on the night they met, it had felt like touching pure, molten fire, all burning and agony... but now it was soft, new, and when it flowed into him, it left him radiant.

"You're thinking of your brother," he said. "I felt that before... the very first night we met."

But she shook her head. "No, Kuro," she whispered. "...I'm thinking of you."

His heart clenched within his chest. He didn't know how to respond, and so he lay there, still and too frightened to speak. He wasn't sure he'd even heard her right, and he stared back at her, nearly pleading with his heart to believe that he hadn't imagined it.

He rolled onto his back, staring at the ceiling now, and felt like a stranger to the world. Next to him, she drew closer, and he closed his eyes, feeling the pressure of her body beside him.

It felt like the first time she had touched him in her living room, soft and wondrous. Kuro lay flat and still, the only movement the quickened rise and fall of his chest, his eyes shut almost painfully tight as she reached out to touch him. He flinched at the first contact; she paused, waiting for some sign to continue, and he relaxed almost imperceptibly, willing himself to a calmness he didn't truly feel. Her hands began at the top of his head, fingers gliding up through dark hair, nails raking his scalp and sending waves of shivers jolting through him. He kept his eyes squeezed shut, his heart leaping in his chest, frightened but yearning.

Caroline leaned in close and breathed deeply, her hair brushing against his shoulder. Her hands slid down to the hem of his shirt, gently tugging it up. He lifted his arms, felt the fabric glide up and off of him, and then her hands were flat on his chest, sliding over the muscles there.

She leaned down and kissed the hollow of his throat; he gasped at the sensation of her lips against his bare skin, his hands coming up to her waist.

"You're beautiful," she whispered against him. "You're beautiful, Kurobushko."

There was no stifling the groan of pleasure at the sound of his name, whispered against his lips. Their mouths found one another, her hands working now at the button on his pants, insistent fingers sliding along the groove of his hips, down to his groin.

He sucked in his breath as her flat palm glided across his inner thigh. He raised his hips just enough for her to pull his pants off in a firm tug, and then in one, swift movement she had climbed on top of him, kissing him again, his body stiffening beneath her under the fabric of his boxers.

"Caroline," he tried, his voice hoarse as she reached down, her fingers ghosting over the fabric and the hardness there. He hadn't been this scared since he thought he was going to die, bleeding to death in her barn.

"What is it? Is this okay...?"

It was, it was *ecstasy*, but it was too fast; he was almost dizzy with apprehension. She saw the look on his face and drew back, sliding off of him, gently pulling him toward her. Her fingers caught his, guiding them up the flat of her torso.

"There's no rush," she whispered. "We can slow down."

He let out a sigh of relief as she closed her eyes, leaning back into his touch. He understood the invitation and followed her example, lifting the shirt from her body. He marveled at the soft lines of her hips, the gentle grooves of her toned core, and gave himself over to the desire to taste the sweetness of her skin. He kissed her first at her naval, amazed at the way she responded to him with a slight bucking movement, her breath hitching, drawing up over ribs he now brushed gently. He moved upward slowly, tasting each part of her inch by inch until he came to the curve of her bare breasts. He leaned back and hesitated for only a moment, and that was enough for her to reach down and run her fingers through his hair, drawing him back toward her. His mouth found her right breast, his body electrified by the impossible softness of it. It yielded to his touch as he cupped it more firmly.

She made a sound above him, a quiet, half-stifled gasp, her fingers clenching in his hair. A sharp heat pierced his core, and experimentally, eagerly, he moved his tongue in a slow, cautious stroke; when he was reworded by the sudden curving of her lower back, the dragging intake of her breath, his tongue moved in a languid circle of liquid pleasure, selfish in its insistence and delight, until Caroline's nails *raked* against him in burning need.

He mis-interpreted her desire and transferred his attentions to her other breast; she gasped and whispered something, an incoherent word of pure desire, and grabbed at his right hand, lacing his fingers through hers, and guided it down to her thigh.

He hesitated, nervous, but she was beneath him, her soul golden in its molten want, and lost to its haze, Kuro stilled his breath and let his fingers slide under the elastic band of her under-wear, seeking.

A tight, soft warmth answered him as he slipped his fingers inside her; she pushed up and wrapped her arms around his shoulders, drawing him down, moaning against his shoulder. He nearly couldn't breathe; already he had pulled back, her legs pushing up against his hips, inviting him, *wanting* him. She moved his hand for him until he understood what to do, thrusting with his fingers in a slow, tortuous, curling drag, then plunging back in, his thumb sliding upward by pure happenstance and electrifying her with melting pleasure.

"Caroline," he whispered. "I don't know what to do," he rasped, his voice thick with longing, his face flushing with the heat of embarrassment, "But....please..."

Liquid eyes opened to stare at him...and then she nodded, kissing him, and gently pushed him down onto his back.

This time, he let out a ragged exhale as she drew his boxers off, touching him. He closed his eyes and focused only on the sensation of her body as she pressed her weight against him, at the whisper of her lips along his inner earlobe as she asked, "Can I...?"

There was nothing she could ask that he wouldn't have said yes to in that moment. He would have laid his head across a block for her, if only she desired his blood. He tried to answer and succeeded only at a guttural, half-choked sound in the back of his throat, then a nod. She took his hands, gently placed his shaking arms on her waist, and propping herself on her knees, guided him into her.

She moved on top of him slowly with a gentle, coaxing rhythm until he felt comfortable enough to open his eyes, to look up at the beautiful woman who pressed her flat palms against his chest, her head thrown back in sheer delight. The heat of her around him left him insensible to anything else than the pure, all-encompassing pleasure of her body; nothing had ever felt this *good* and perfect. She opened her eyes, saw him staring, and smiled, and Kuro felt everything in him loosen and relax.

He acted on instinct, freed from inhibition, and moved at once, wrapping his arms around her as he shifted their positions, rolling on top of her. A pleasant, laughing sound of surprise transformed into a sharp exclamation as he reached down and pulled her leg up, his hips rolling into her with the full heat of his needful thrusts, his lips crushed against hers as he drove into her, deeper, faster, until she was breaking free and gasping, sharp and shaking with pleasure against him, her soul burning like fire with the heady satisfaction of this, and an answering fire built in him and released all at once, collapsing them both.

He lay on top of her, spent and sweating, his chest heaving. A final, pulsing vibration shuddered through his body.

No awkward embarrassment moved into the silence, no regret; it was comfortable, this quiet, with only the sound of their panting threaded through it. They fit together in perfect harmony, their legs entwined, content and waiting.

"...Kuro," she whispered after a few minutes. "Should we clean ourselves up...?"

"No." His answer was immediate; he reared up on his forearms, reaching for her breast again with new confidence and curiosity; he palmed it and watched the nipple tighten as his thumb slid over the edge of it, once, twice, and then leaned down, tracing it again with his tongue. She jolted beneath him, her breath catching in surprise at the commanding hunger in his voice, the sudden, forceful power in his limbs that touched her now with the fresh desire to ravage her, caging her beneath him. *"Again."*

They stayed entwined together as the morning crept on, a starving pair with no end to their appetite. His initial fear and embarrassment gave way entirely to desire. His hands and lips explored her body in open amazement, a penitent at the altar, eager to worship and adore, to please her in every way that could be uncovered. In the early morning hours he found the places of her that were softest, most secret, and he discovered that if he was gentle and patient, she would make sounds that left him reeling with the drunkenness of sensation, but it was nothing compared to the way *she* made him feel. Other times patience was forgotten, and their bodies collided with almost panicked intensity, legs tangled with frantic need, and in those moments he looked down at her through clouded eyes and saw a woman so beautiful that it was maddening, and she responded by stifling her cries against him until she could no longer restrain herself, lost to the pleasure they shared.

He wrapped her in his arms, their bodies slick with sweat; they fell asleep at last to the gentle rhythm of each other's breathing.

The afternoon sun filled the room with a gentle glow, and she kissed his brow and murmured his name into his ear, lifting his bangs off his forehead. He sighed and leaned into her touch, drinking deeply the emotions that poured freely from her soul: happiness, contentment, satisfaction...*love*. Greater than everything else, he wrapped himself in it, and her soul held him to itself in an embrace that warmed him to the marrow of his bones.

At last, she disentangled herself and pushed out of the bed. He reached for her, desperate, but she put his hand back gently, smiling at him.

"Stay," she said, "and I'll make us lunch."

He sank back into her pillow, his eyes closing.

He would stay, for as long as she would have him.

NINE

For a week, their evenings were spent entwined together.

Kuro was an eager lover; he reveled in the touch of hands gliding over his body; he burned with a yearning heat, enthusiastic to learn and know, experience and please. He was tireless in his appetite, catching at her the moment she parked in the driveway after work.

He marveled at the feel of her and the peals of laughter he could steal. When she came home, he stood and lifted her, spinning, as she threw her arms around his neck and kissed him. He had never known such love and happiness before; he had thought it had to be such a complicated thing, but it wasn't: it was simple. Love was listening for the sound of tires on gravel, the quiet breathing of a body in the night, the feeling of fingertips reaching out to brush you, just to affirm that you were there. Love was a sugar jar set out next to his cup of coffee in the morning before she left.

Love was wrapping his arms around her waist in the stable at sunset, pulling her down into the hay, and not emerging again until well into the night, even if the dog was barking outside the barn door.

For a week, he felt giddy and newborn, and then Jaden arrived.

The moment they heard Feral begin to bark from the barn, they looked up, expectant. Kuro realized in that instant that he hadn't seen Jaden all week, and only now did he think of him at all.

A knock came at the door. Caroline rose, opened it, and gasped.

Kuro looked up just as he came into the room. He walked wearily to the chair and collapsed, his hair dull, face gaunt. An unnatural, feverish glint was in his eyes.

Caroline's whisper was worried. "Kuro, quick – let's get him to the spare room."

Kuro moved to help him stand, but Jaden waved his hand away, annoyed. He had said nothing to either of them as he followed Caroline down the hall. Emotions warred in Kuro's mind: fear at the way his friend looked, haggard and starved; anger at the entitled way he had interrupted Kuro's tranquility, intruding on their private world...and anxiety, all-encompassing, that he would do or say something now that would ruin everything.

Caroline held the door open to Christopher's room; he walked inside, collapsing on the bed.

"I'll get him something to drink," she said in a hushed voice, leaving them.

Kuro looked down at him. Jaden had thrown an arm over his eyes, his mouth set in a grimace. "Jaden..."

"Whose room is this?"

Kuro hesitated. "It's just a spare."

"The feeling in here..." Jaden shuddered. "It's like when sickness lingers after a death." He moved his arm from his eyes, frowning. "Is this where you sleep?"

"...No. This isn't where I sleep."

They held each other's gaze, the silence communicating everything that Kuro didn't need to say. Jaden's lips pressed tightly together until they were a thin, white line of distaste. "I see." His mouth turned up into a half-smirk, bitter and caustic, and he rolled onto his side. "Leave me alone, Kuro."

"...I'll come back later."

Jaden said nothing in reply.

He slept for nearly fourteen hours before rising to eat in silence. When he returned to the bedroom to lay down again, Caroline whispered to him in a hushed tone. "What's wrong with him?"

Kuro shook his head. He'd never seen him this way, and although he was worried, another feeling was upon him: distress. He wanted Jaden to leave, and was ashamed of it; it felt like betrayal.

"Let's give him space," she whispered.

It wasn't until the next morning that Jaden spoke to him again. Kuro had followed Caroline out into the morning light, watching her with his back pressed again the barn. Soon, the front door of the house opened, and Jaden emerged. He walked over to where Kuro sat in the dirt, his gaze off on the woods.

Kuro cleared his throat. "You look like you haven't been eating..."

"I ate yesterday with you, Kuro," he replied flatly.

"I didn't mean food."

"Do I look that bad?" Jaden sat beside him, his hands limp at his side. In the pasture, Caroline exercised Molly by her lead.

"...You don't look so good," he allowed, nervous. "Has something happened?"

"...I want her, Kuro."

He was about to ask who when he stopped himself. He knew who he meant; he knew what girl had driven that mad light into his eyes.

When Jaden spoke again, his voice was strained. "I want her so badly. I keep pulling away, leaving her...but I've never wanted anything so *much* before. It's not like anything else. It's not normal. There's no comparison. I don't even want to feed on anyone except for her. I could kill her...I *want* to. But the satisfaction would be...fleeting. Meaningless. I want her soul."

Kuro did not reply; they had had this conversation before.

Jaden's eyes slid over to him, unblinking in the silence. "Help me to have her."

Kuro shuddered; Jaden spoke with an intensity that disturbed him, and within him, he felt the *holy dark* shiver and move, responding.

"Jaden...I can't..."

"Why?"

It's wrong, he thought, and the words nearly left his mouth. His teeth clamped down on them, holding them back.

Instead, he tried for a reasoned, level tone. "We said no more killing..."

Jaden sneered. "You've become so squeamish, Kuro...and I don't need your help to kill her."

Kuro's mind worked quickly in a selfish direction: if Jaden were to sate himself on the girl, there would be nothing keeping him here. Jacqueline had kept him occupied, pulled him away from Kuro, and in return...his days and nights had been filled by another. The moment Jacqueline was gone, Jaden would want to leave this place, and Jaden wouldn't want to leave him...and Kuro, too, did not want to lose his only friend. But what would Caroline think, when they found that girl's body?

At last, the words broke free of his thoughts. "Jaden, we can't...it's...it's not *right*..."

Jaden stared at him hard. "Would you say it lacks...justice?"

Kuro winced. "I don't know what you mean."

Jaden's gaze moved from him out to where Caroline stood. Kuro watched him observing her and saw the way his hard stare studied her movements, crawled along the contours of her body up from her legs to her hips, lingered on her breasts, and finally, puzzled over her face.

His voice was indifferent when he spoke again. "It must be cramped in her bed."

His spine stiffened, his blood flowing more quickly; a spike of adrenaline set his heart beating much too fast. He could sense where this was going by the too casual, knife-edge tone of Jaden's words. *He's going to threaten her,* he thought. *He's going to force me to help him, and he'll threaten Caroline if I don't help him –*

Jaden turned back toward him, waiting for him to say something.

Kuro's thoughts raced wildly under the scrutiny. "What about the angel?" He tried. He wanted to sound calmly rational, disinterested even, and knew that he was failing by the slight tremble in his words. "It'll kill you if you attack her."

Jaden's eyes narrowed. "I think if it could, it would have done that already." Kuro squirmed; Jaden had returned his gaze to Caroline, and his eyes followed her with a sense of calculation. "But regardless, I think the two of us could be enough to defeat it...and rip her soul out."

Kuro swallowed. "I can't help you, Jaden," he said; he wanted to sound firm, wanted the matter over and done with...but he could hear how he was nearly begging without even realizing it. "I can't help you get what you want. I won't do it."

Caroline playfully kicked up some dust, laughing. Jaden's frown deepened as he watched her. "Because you'd have to look at her after you did it, and she'd see what you did reflected in your eyes. You're transparent, Kuro. Every thought you think is right there, in those black irises of yours." He turned back to him, and Jaden's face was impenetrable. "Even the things you think about me."

Kuro shook his head. "I don't think –"

"Don't ever lie to me. Not again."

Kuro stopped talking. Jaden rose to his feet, dusting his pants off. He was weak, but his hunger cast a wild look upon him, his movements slow, deliberate.

"How long does the average human live for, do you know?"

Kuro's pulse began to race. "No," he said. He could feel himself tensing. "I don't."

"About eighty years, for females. She's...what, in her 20s?"

"Jaden." Kuro rose beside him, his voice low with warning. The muscles in his arms bunched, the *holy dark* building within him, the power rolling like the deep building of an ocean wave. He knew Jaden would be able to feel it; he didn't care.

He didn't like where this conversation was going.

The demon continued to watch Caroline, his gaze thoughtful now. "If the books are right, then we live for a thousand years, Kuro. She has, most likely, a little less than sixty of those thousand left."

Kuro stepped forward, teeth clenched and ready to fight.

But Jaden's easy posture hadn't changed, and he didn't even deign to glance at him or acknowledge his anxiety. "Help me to have to her, Kuro," Jaden repeated. "If you help me, the next sixty, seventy years are yours to spend with her. We'll stay here, together. Help me to have *her*, and you can have us *both*."

It was like a rubber band had snapped back upon him. He stood, dumbfounded, waiting for the threat that hadn't come...yet.

His mind was already racing ahead. "...And if I say no? What happens to Caroline?"

Jaden sighed. He turned at last to Kuro and frowned, his

shoulders sagging at the look of bracing caution on Kuro's face. "Whatever life has in store for her. I know what you were thinking; I always have. You think I would threaten her, to force your hand. And then what, Kuro? You would hate me."

He said the last sentence so simply, with so much plaintive sorrow that Kuro felt a wave of guilt wash over him. And yet...

He's a liar.

He had always been a liar. He lied easily to everyone about everything, and he did it with a smile, a wink, a shrug – or with a look of sadness so close to genuine ache that Kuro found doubt creeping round his heart. Was this real, this defeated man before him? Or was this just another manipulation? Did he think of Kuro truly as his friend, or merely a tool whose feelings he could mold or else disregard altogether?

And he never told you his true name...

"I made a promise to you that I wouldn't abandon you, Kuro. I won't. But I can't go on like this..."

"Jaden." Kuro swallowed and risked meeting his eyes, willing himself not to blink and look away. If he could extract one single truth from him, *one true thing,* then maybe all the rest of it could be believed...but he knew, even before he asked, that he would not be given even that much. "I'll help you...if you tell me one thing."

They stared at one another, the expectant silence hovering with tense anticipation.

"You never told me your name. Your *real* name."

Jaden looked at him for only a moment longer; something flickered in the depths of his eyes, and then he turned away, gazing out to the tree line and beyond. "No." A breeze picked up, bringing the smell of the damp autumn forest on the wind. "I didn't."

Without another word, he strode toward the house, the door swinging shut behind him.

It was late in the afternoon when Caroline's phone rang; the earliest rays of sunset had begun, heavy and quiet in the November air. Sunsets had grown rare – more often than not, gray clouds had choked away the twilight and muffled the barrier between night and day.

Jaden was reclining on the couch, reading a book. Kuro sat in the armchair, listening as Caroline did the dishes, lost in his own thoughts. Neither had spoken to each other since their conversation outside, and Kuro found it impossible to swallow his anxieties. Jaden would not let this go, he knew.

He's asking you to hurt that girl...

I can't do it.

You have to.

He didn't threaten Caroline, he thought, *he said he wouldn't.*

And you believe him?

He tried not to stare at Jaden; he tried to focus on the small of Caroline's back as she stood at the sink, scrubbing a pan. He could argue with himself for hours if need be, but he wouldn't get anywhere. It was too heavy; it felt like a weight settling upon his shoulders, crushing him. There had to be other choices in the world, there had to be more options than this false dilemma he could see no way around. There had to be some other exit, some other *way*...and yet, his mind could only see a few clear paths, and all else was obscured in shadow.

And temptation loomed.

If you help him to get what he wants, you can stay with Caroline for the rest of her life, and Jaden will stay here, too...

That was assuming Jaden wasn't lying, which he undoubtedly was...but his heart strained against logic, desperate to believe him.

If you don't help him, he says he won't hurt Caroline, won't force you...

But no, that couldn't be right either; there was a lie somewhere in the center of each choice, and it poisoned its way outward, making each version look equally unattractive. If only he could *see* it, know the lie, see its rotten core –

I promise I won't abandon you, Jaden had said, all those years ago. Kuro had asked him to make the promise. *Abandon* had so many meanings...what had *he* meant when he spoke those words and made that promise? They weren't physically compelled to remain together, so it *was* possible for Kuro to refuse, to stay here, and for Jaden to leave...

And if he succeeds in killing that girl, and Caroline finds out about it – which she will – are you prepared to look her in the eyes every day, for the rest of her life, knowing that you could have stopped it?

It's not my responsibility to stop him, he thought. A flash of anger flared up in him; who was Jacqueline to *him? I don't give a shit about her! I don't care what happens to her! He can have her, for all I care!*

The phone rang a second, insistent time, cutting through his internal argument. He heard Caroline answer and caught every third word over the sound of running water, his thoughts occupying his attention.

A few minutes later she hung up and came into the living room, wringing a towel in her hands. She seemed troubled.

"Listen, I have to run out..."

Her soul was anxious, unsettled with confusion. He looked up sharply, searching her face. Bewilderment prowled the edges of her soul, her tone nervous. "Everything okay?"

"Yes, it's just a friend who needs to see me...now. He was very insistent."

Jaden put the book down but said nothing. His expression was carefully neutral.

Instinct prickled Kuro's skin; her anxiety was peppering him. "What about?"

"I don't know. It was... odd. I'm a little worried. I should be back within the hour, though."

"I'll come with you." He was on his feet at once, but she shook her head, firm in her decision.

"No, you stay here. Everything is fine; I'll be back."

She disappeared into the kitchen; he stood there awkwardly, watching her go, and in another minute, the low rumble of the truck engine grew faint as it clamored down the road.

Jaden returned to reading.

He tried to sit back down at first, then gave up. He began to pace from the kitchen to the living room, clenching and unclenching his fists. *Something's not right.* Instinct had yet to abandon him, and a deep feeling of unease kept him on his feet, the *holy dark* moving within him.

Jaden sighed and closed the book at last, his eyes trained on him as Kuro paced.

A quarter of an hour passed.

"Kuro." Jaden sat up suddenly, his face drawn and puzzled. "Do you feel that?"

He stopped at once, a cold sweat breaking out on his forehead. "Feel what?"

Jaden was on his feet in an instant, striding to the kitchen. He lifted the curtain next to the door, peering outside. "*Her.*"

"*What?*" If Caroline was back, he would have felt –

"And *him.*" The words escaped in a low hiss.

Kuro joined him at the window, squinting.

At the far edge of the forest line, two humans stood limned in the last of the sunset. Their eyes locked, and the demons stared full-on into the faces of Kenneth McMahon and Jacqueline Beirioux.

Then the humans turned, and fled.

Kenneth hoped that they wouldn't be there, that Jacqueline was mistaken in her deduction. He'd made the same walk through the woods for days now, hiding out in the forest with a pair of Albert's old bird-watching binoculars, scanning, hoping she was wrong.

She wasn't.

He'd seen both of them in the morning, outside by the barn. The eerie feeling of staring at not-himself, even from this distance, left him rattled and stumbling the entire walk back to Jacqueline's. He hadn't even had to say anything; Jacqueline took one look at his face when he came through the door, saw his pallor, the sweat despite the chill, and knew.

"This afternoon," she had whispered. "We'll do it today."

There was always the chance they'd be gone by then; Kenneth half hoped they would be.

Their lives hung in the balance.

"How should we get their attention?" There was no need to whisper, but his voice was hushed, all the same.

"If they're there, he'll know I'm out here." Jacqueline had drawn a steadying breath. "And if so...he'll come for me."

They had mapped the route and practiced running it twice; as long as they were fast and sure-footed, they could get to the traps first. He hoped it would work: there would be the spring, the catch...and then they could follow through on the lie he'd sold to Eric, that they would call the police, have them arrested, and face whatever consequences came from that.

Or he could shoot them.

The more frightening and very real possibility was that they would only catch *one* and not the other. He didn't know what he would do in that case; he considered Eric's words and felt sick. He didn't know if he could shoot and kill someone, especially someone who looked almost exactly like himself.

Or worse: what if he *could?*

He would have to find the courage to do it; he had a sinking, leaden certainty in his gut that he would need to put a bullet in one or both of the...*the shapeshifters,* Jacqueline had said. *The murderers,* he knew.

He could do that much for Jacqueline. He didn't want her to become a killer.

They came to the edge of the tree line, not far from a rotted slat fence, and waited.

In less than a minute, two pairs of eyes were looking at them from Caroline's front window.

There was no mistake: it was *them.* For an instant, the shock of seeing *almost* himself in the window froze his limbs.

Then Jacqueline grabbed his palms and yanked him forward. Standing on the tips of her toes, her mouth pressed against his in a frantic kiss. Everything seemed to dissolve; the forest, its colors, its smell, the panic in his heart.

There was only her.

She broke away, tugging him forward. *"Run."*

Jaden had looked at Kuro – a single, commanding wordless look of *need* and anger that cut him right to his core, and then they were out the front door, shifting their forms.

They had spent years hunting together; there was no need to speak, only to look and listen, and *run.*

The seasons were against the humans: the forest floor was matted with the thick debris of fallen, wet leaves, the bark slick and black in the last of the sunlight. It would be hard to run in shoes, and the dense forest had lost all its leaves spare those of the pines. Once, he had run through these very woods on a night with a full moon, in the heat of summer, heading the way he was running from now...

He shook the thought away.

Jaden came to a halt and lifted his head high, peering into the forest. *They had a good head start. It doesn't matter. We'll get them.*

Jaden, why were they here? His mind was reeling; what on earth had brought them to Caroline's house? Had they come there looking for them? And if so, *why?*

That phone call was no coincidence, Jaden growled. *I don't know what they did, but they got Caroline out of the way. This could be a trap.*

Kuro's stomach turned over. *Let's turn back. Leave them, Jaden!*

Jaden's teeth gleamed. *I think not.*

He surged forward. Kuro gave chase, a blackberry vine tearing at his ankles. He stumbled forward and paused, squinting. He could make out two figures, indistinct but nevertheless human, running in the distance into a small grove of mostly bare trees bordered by pines.

Jaden came to a halt, his ears flattening backwards. *There they are.*

Kuro knew there was no chance of talking any sense into Jaden; the mad light was back in his eyes, his fur on end. He found himself at the crossroads of choice: he could clamp his jaws around Jaden's legs and try to physically drag him back to the house, do nothing and turn away, letting Jaden wander into whatever trap these humans had planned...

Or stay with him, and see this through to the end.

Jaden had promised not to abandon him.

Kuro would do the same.

He was sickened by himself, his heart already cringing away from what was to come as he asked *what do you want me to do?*

"Get the boy away from her." Kuro turned to him; Jaden had switched his form and was closing and unclosing his human palms slowly, staring down into them, studying his fingertips. "I want you to head out quickly toward the far right, then circle back toward them. Drive Jacqueline back toward me and chase Kenneth away."

How?

His eyes were cold, devoid even of menace or anger. Here stood the calculating demon of calm exactitude. His need was laid bare, singular and demanding. Kuro shivered. "Any way possible."

What if he attacks us?

Jaden snorted. "He won't. He's a coward. Didn't you touch his soul?"

Kuro blundered for an answer. Jaden didn't wait for a response; he gazed off toward the retreating figures. "Melancholia, wound throughout him. Like a *weed*, choking him, eating his soul. He's a coward – he'll run."

He tried to swallow, to nod, but something was still creeping up his spine, something that Jaden's desire had chased away from him, a primeval sense of warning, danger, telling him to run.

If he's a coward, he asked, *...then what is he doing here?*

Jaden's eyes narrowed at the humans in the distance. "It doesn't matter," he hissed. "Just *go*."

Kuro obeyed.

TEN

They had nearly come upon the first marked tree when the black beast came leaping over the underbrush. It landed, fur bristling, and turned, swiping the air at her. Jacqueline cried out and stumbled backward in shock. Kenneth looked at Jacqueline, then at the animal, and turned to run in the opposite direction with the clear intention of luring him away.

He's got it all backwards, Kuro thought, almost with pity.

The demon followed, leaping over a downed pine and crashing into a pile of leaves. About two hundred yards ahead, Kenneth turned and looked back at him, eyes-wide, then took off again, veering to the left.

But something wasn't quite right – no matter what, Kenneth kept turning, doggedly trying to scramble back to the path that Kuro was chasing him from. If he was trying to lure Kuro away from the girl, why keep running back toward her...? He couldn't drive Jacqueline *toward* Jaden and Kenneth *away* at the same time. It should have been easier than this.

He's leading me somewhere, he realized, and his instinct

warned him again to beware, the animal-sense dulled from days spent living as a human.

Kuro gathered his strength, dug his claws in, and leapt.

He collided with Kenneth and slammed the boy down into the leaves, one paw slashing out and connecting with his chest. The boy gritted his teeth and struck out, slamming a fist against his skull. Kuro fell backwards and landed on his hands as a human, his head ringing. He cursed, rubbing at his head, his anger roused.

Before he could move again, Kenneth had stood on shaking legs. He was fumbling for something in his pocket, but his hands were trembling. Some weapon, no doubt. Kuro looked up slowly and fought the urge to snarl at the pathetic attempt at heroism. The boy's eyes were terrified.

A mean, furious spark in his gut reminded him that *this* was the boy who had published *multiple* photographs of him.

"Jaden was right about you," he snarled, and the *holy dark* moved in him, summoning fox fire. He looked at the ground beneath the boy's feet, and there it sprung into a blaze that swallowed him whole.

There was the single second of an agonized scream, shattering the quiet of the forest, and in the next moment, Kuro snapped back to himself and ceased the fire.

Where Kenneth had stood, now he lay on the ground, panting and clutching his chest.

Kuro stood and walked over to him, staring down at the boy.

He didn't want to think about how Caroline had said that he had Kenneth to thank for bringing them together; he didn't want to consider how fate or coincidence had pulled them both into this moment again, how *he* had made the boy scream in terrible pain.

He didn't want to think about what Jaden would do to the boy, short of killing him. That at least was a promise he couldn't break.

It would still be a mercy to cut his throat right now, he thought. Kuro didn't know what Kenneth's relationship to Jacqueline was, but if he tried to stand in the way of Jaden...

The boy had rolled over and was struggling on all fours, gasping. Kuro walked up to him, grabbed him by the collar, and hauled him against a tree.

With all the force that he had, he punched him in the temple, and the boy slumped, unconscious. Kuro tossed his body down and stared at it. The chest rose, up and down; not dead, then.

But asleep.

He won't have to watch what happens to her, he thought. That was good enough; it was the most mercy he could extend. He wished he could spare himself the same thing. Regret, and with it, a hot shame, spread inside of him. Kuro closed his eyes tight against it, against the body laying at his feet, and waited.

The boy – a coward, maybe. But the girl? He'd caught sight of her eyes, for just a moment.

There was fear there, yes...but also unconquerable, stalwart determination.

He looked up sharply, scanning, listening; something was moving frantically toward him, running.

He emerged from behind a pine and came to a halt, colliding with the source of the sound. He wished he had had the good sense to hide.

She might never have found him otherwise.

———

Jacqueline ran, backtracking, following the sound of the commotion ahead; the animal had chased Kenneth on a winding path, but always, it righted itself, heading back the way they had come, and then she'd lost sight of them both. She threw herself to the left as soon as she spotted a tree marked with the jagged 'X' carving, narrowly avoiding one of the traps.

Jacqueline stumbled, calling for him, and felt the sensation of something *behind* her now, something coming and closing in –

Kenneth was there.

"*Kenneth!*"

She ran to him and grabbed his arm, tugging him around. Too late, she saw the twin body in the leaves in front of him.

He turned, his arm already pulling out of her grasp, and stared down at her with unfamiliar black eyes, eyes that nearly lacked depth in the dim fall twilight. She peered up into a face familiar yet strange, at a form too tall, and tried to pull away.

He was fast, huge and solid. He seized her by the elbow and jerked her forward, grabbing her, her head barely mid-chest. One hand came up around her mouth, muffling her scream. The other forced itself through her arms, twisting them behind her. His body was all heat and muscle, and it pressed her to him, buckling her knees to the ground with no effort; he dropped with her, his grip unyielding. She tried to scream again, but the hand only pressed more firmly.

Panic overtook her. All her life, she had felt fearless, powerful, but now, confronted by his overwhelming strength, she struggled ineffectually against the man who looked like Kenneth and knew, with the cold certainty of a bird caught in quicklime, that she would have to tear her arms apart to escape this grasp. She wrenched hard and succeeded only in increasing the strength of his grip.

She heard the footfall in the underbrush up ahead before she saw him.

Her eyes lifted and watched as a familiar young man came forward, his gaze boring into her.

He walked with the stillness of a tiger in the forest, never blinking, until he stood right in front of them. Slowly, he knelt, and with one hand reached tenderly for her face. She recoiled back into the not-Kenneth, her scream stifled by his fingers, and his arm twisted through her own more tightly, holding her in place against him.

'Jake' slipped his fingers through her hair, pulling it past eyes wide with terror. He watched it fall through his hands with a curious detachment, his stare sliding over her with a sense of satisfaction.

"When you look at me, Jacqueline," he said, handling her name like a delicate possession, lingering on each syllable, "do you see a pale rider on a pale horse?"

She screamed again, and again, her lungs straining to burst with the effort, lips curling back from teeth to bite, but the hand was clamped too firmly against her, his body rigid and immovable.

A feeling of nausea hit her so suddenly that she froze all her struggles. A lashing pain suddenly whipped at her heart, then plunged inward with an intensity that robbed her even of breath. She moaned a little and strained feebly to her left, her legs caught between the legs of her captor, her knees sliding in the leaves, her body limp. Not-Kenneth held her up, and with his hand supporting her head now, the fingers still laced over her lips, she looked upward into the face of the man she believed would kill her.

He was smiling.

He was smiling, and his eyes were *red*.

She blinked. It had to have been a trick of the light, something she had imagined as the pain of being ripped apart overtook her again.

"Where is your angel, little one?" He cocked his head, amused. "Has it deserted you?"

It said it would try to protect me, Jacqueline thought, desperate. But it had also said it couldn't always be there...

I'm trying, she heard its voice whisper in her memory. *I'm failing.*

I am not yours.

"I'm disappointed," he mocked. "You have no idea how much I was looking forward to meeting that angel. Well, maybe it's just a matter of time. Maybe we can encourage it to join us."

Knives thrust into her soul, violating her. Her body went stiff with the force of it, pressing back against her captor, like a lover seeking shelter in his arms. She wanted to retreat as far as she could, disappear into his body if possible, and fade away from that feeling of claws prying, forcing open her very soul, of blades carving her apart from the inside. The not-Kenneth smelled of earth and sweat. She twisted back into him, desperate to escape the pain in her soul, her cheek pressed against the hollow of his throat.

The hand around her mouth slackened for only a moment. Her eyes rolled backward, neck craning, and with a gasping, desperate sob from between his fingers, she begged him, "*Please.*"

He flinched away from that word, but he held on.

The spasm of pain came again, and with it, a fresh scream.

"Kuro," 'Jake' spoke with a clinical detachment, all his attention focused on her. "Push her to the ground."

"Jaden –"

Jacqueline discovered in that single word that his voice was different from Kenneth's, *deeper*. She was startled by that; she had expected to hear him speak with Kenneth's voice, and the *manner* almost was the same in its pained, cringing plea...but the tone was entirely different.

Red eyes flashed again, and Kuro obeyed. He pushed her down flat into the damp leaves, his knees crushing the back of her legs; compared to her, he was huge, unstoppable. One hand held both of her wrists behind her, and the other pressed her head down, flat on the earth.

She screamed for only a moment before the tearing feeling

came again from inside her, choking off her air. It felt as though razors were cutting at her heart, trying to slice something away from her insides, and all the while a man who looked like Kenneth stared down at her while she endured this torture. Jaden gave a throaty laugh.

"Give up, Jacqueline," he whispered. He knelt and traced a knuckle along her cheek. "Give yourself up to me. Let *go*. You won't win this battle."

She probably wouldn't; despair moved in her like the creeping tendrils of ivy, choking away her resolve.

"Give up," he said again, coaxing now, and it was so tempting...

She closed her eyes, and in the darkness behind her eyelids, it was like being in her bedroom again, a blanket pulled over her head, her pillow crushed against her ears, stifling the feeble call of a voice slipping away.

A cold wind blew through a door in her soul.

No!

Jacqueline rallied and tried one final push against the demon he had called Kuro, but it was as useless as trying to hoist a brick wall. She panted, her eyes blurring.

Jaden leaned down and leered. "Are you going to cry?"

She snarled, a rasping, indignant sound that broke into a scream of anguish.

He cocked his head at her. "I'm curious about all this regret inside you," he said. She cried out as something cold penetrated a secret place in her heart, the very core of her hurt. "So much *guilt*. Kuro, what do you think?"

He didn't say anything immediately. Jaden looked up, frowning. "Try her," he said.

The voice above her answered in a whisper of barely disguised disgust. "She's yours."

"Oh, *I insist*. Go ahead," he urged. "Right...here."

She sucked in her breath as the cold, piercing feeling touched the rawest part of her soul. This was almost unendurable now; she would pass out if it continued. The wind inside her was howling, freezing her very heart, trying to call her through the door into some dark place of howling wind and sucking water –

"No, Jaden."

Jaden's expression darkened. "Kuro, *do it*."

His left hand curled harder around her wrists. The sharp pain brought her back from the brink of unconsciousness; she shrieked, and his grip loosened at once as though the sound had burned him. "...I can't."

"What?"

"*I can't!*" He snapped. "Just – finish this!"

Jaden's eyes narrowed, and when he spoke, the words sounded almost like a punishment. "Turn her over."

"What?"

"Put her on her back."

Jacqueline felt his hesitation more than she heard it in his voice. "Why?"

Jaden sneered, his lips lifting away from teeth that looked too sharp, utterly inhuman now. "What's the matter, Kuro – can't stand to look her in the eyes? It would be a gift to her; she can look into the face of someone she loves just before I kill her."

"Can't you just take her? You don't need my help." The demon's voice was nearly desperate now; she could feel the unwilling strain in his body.

Jaden's expression shifted into one of wry amusement. "I'm the one helping *you*, Kuro."

She tried to heave herself upward and managed to slip her head out from under his hand. A yank with both arms, and they were free, but before she could scramble out from under him, the pain hit her again from inside her heart, harder and more vicious than before. She lay prone under the demon, gasping as something dark forced itself into her, tearing now...

The pain was gone with a sudden severing, though the weight of the demon pinning her remained. She opened her eyes, shocked. Two people were grappling on the ground in front of her in a tussle of arms and legs and rage. The shorter one with the black hair was screaming, fists flailing, while Jaden kicked forward, sending him flying.

She twisted with renewed energy, and for one moment, the hand pinning her slipped. *"Kenneth!"*

Both of them looked up at her at once, two expressions: a joyful, emboldened smile, and a snarl of vicious rage.

And then Jaden disappeared.

Where he had been, a maroon *kitsune* now stood, its tail lashing behind it. Its ears flattened backward as it roared in fury, its jaws a bed of silver fangs.

Kurobushko – kill that boy!

The hands around her released immediately, like a trap springing open. Jacqueline looked up just in time to see Kuro leap at Kenneth. Like twins lost to one another in time, they fell into the grass, their fists colliding with each other's face. Kenneth's head snapped back with a heavy crack, but he took the blow and threw a fist into the shoulder of the other version of himself, and the demonic version of him stumbled backward. For a moment, Jacqueline saw the shadow of a black tail appear, as though it had balanced him.

The two men stood, staring at one another in equal hatred.

She was already scrambling to her feet, ready.

Kenneth turned to her; there was blood pouring down his neck from a wound on his head, his hair matted with the liquid.

She didn't hesitate; she grabbed him by the wrist, and together, they ran.

In a dim way, Kuro was aware that he did not want to kill Kenneth...but his true name had slipped around his throat like a collar, choking him, driving him from his senses, and the *holy dark* within him was no match to the similar power within Jaden. It answered the call of a greater power; he obeyed, struggle as he might against it. He had tried to fight the compulsion when Kenneth shoved him away, just before Jacqueline had grabbed the boy's arm...it gave them a moment's head start, but then the order slammed shut on his mind again, and he gave chase.

Kuro was faster. Only a hundred yards ahead, Kenneth turned and looked back at him. Kuro hissed and ran forward, expecting him to turn and run, but the boy's left arm shot out, shielding Jacqueline, pushing her away, as he turned to face him –

His right arm held up a gun.

Kuro whirled and threw himself down into the leaves, skidding. No gunshot came, but the threat was enough to force him below a rotted trunk, panting. He pushed onward, springing forward and running to the right, passing him, then looping back, rushing down now through the trees, forcing the boy to either run back the way he had come or stand and fight.

"Jacqueline – *run!*"

Kuro watched as the boy shoved her; two knobby knees struck out, stumbled, then carried her as she put her head down and ran.

Kuro snarled.

Kenneth raised the gun again, but Kuro didn't need to be able to feel his soul to know that the boy's finger – twitching and uncertain on the trigger – would never pull it.

"I tried to be merciful, earlier," he said. Kenneth blinked at him, surprised to see the human in front of him now. Kuro looked at the ground below him, the *holy dark* surging inside him as he prepared himself. "Let's do it your way."

The boy was plunged into an inferno.

It was everywhere, all around him, a shimmering, dancing sea of blue flame, and it *burned.*

He screamed and tried to stand up, but everywhere, the fire surrounded him. He fell again to his knees, a second scream tearing through him, wracking him. He collapsed once more, his hands clutching at the dead leaves, fistfuls of dirt between the knuckles.

Kenneth managed to raise his head and stare through the flame, out into the wavering form of a mirror image on the other side of it. The eyes were his own, and they hated him. The arm was outstretched, and inside the fire, Kenneth felt it consuming him from the inside out. This was what it was to be tortured, to be humiliated and shamed and laid prostrate at the feet of a man who would kill you. He opened his mouth to scream again, but all that came out was a gasping, rasping cry, and he sunk whimpering into the dirt.

The fire didn't stop.

There was no shielding himself from it. It burned away all of his defenses and forced him to look upon the painful, pitiful waste of his life. He was a fuck-up, a failure, and everything, *everything* in him burned with the shame and pain of it. It was burning his very soul, and if he remained here, trapped in this flame, it would destroy it. He would die.

It lifted with the suddenness of a spring rain. Kenneth convulsed and drew inward, forcing himself to look up and see his torturer.

His other self was gasping, sweat on his forehead from the exertion. He took a step backward, his chest heaving...and he clutched his head as though he were fighting a migraine, gnashing his teeth. His arm shot out suddenly, punching a tree; it splintered, and Kenneth watched as the demon's arm remained rigid against it, trembling, even as dark blood dripped down his knuckles.

The demon heaved and pulled back slowly, straightening. He looked like a caged animal straining against its chains; there was a wildness in his eyes, a battle he was fighting in his mind...and he was losing, Kenneth saw. He was fighting it with every passing second...but he could not win.

They stared at one another, each unable to move, neither capable of speech. Kenneth wanted to ask him what he had done to him, *why did he look like him*, why had they killed those people, why had he not moved forward to kill him now, but all he could manage was a sobbing, truncated, "*Why?*"

The too-dark eyes of the other version of him widened. He froze, and for a moment, Kenneth thought he was going to answer him...but he didn't.

"Stay *down*, you goddamn *fool!*" He snarled. "*I don't want to kill you!*"

And then, as though the effort cost him all his strength, the demon took off running.

He didn't know how long he could hold out against Jaden's order; it was terrifying to learn what he had always suspected (that he was weaker than Jaden) and sickened to know that Jaden would use that against him, compel him by the very use of his name to act as his agent of death.

He would resist it for as long as he could, even if it frayed the threads of his mind.

Kuro shifted and ran, streaking down the slope to rejoin Jaden, trying now to outrace the order. Behind him was shame –

behind him was a series of events that would have horrified Caroline, a scene that would have appalled her, and he was rushing headlong now to something even worse. *You can never tell her,* his mind whispered. *She can never know. She'll hate you if she knows what you've done – what you're going to do.*

Even if he had done it to protect her.

You can justify it a million ways, he told himself, *but she'll never forgive you if she knows.*

It sickened him, the knowing. He flattened his ears and ran faster, sprinting now. He could just make out the other *kitsune* up ahead, his shoulders hunched as he exploded through the underbrush, jaws gaping, eyes hungry, and Kuro was nearly parallel with him, just a body length behind as they closed in on the girl, one hundred feet – eighty feet – fifty feet now.

The girl was ahead of them, and a single, panicked cry tore from her lips as she ran faster, *faster –*

A scream suddenly wrenched from Jaden's jaws, high-pitched and shrieking. Kuro didn't understand what he was seeing: it was as though Jaden had suddenly been yanked backward by an invisible rope and then crashed down into the ground. Ahead of them, Jacqueline had stopped running. The girl had turned around, gasping for breath.

Jaden screamed again, flailing on the ground. His left leg was stretched oddly behind him, and Jaden kept jerking it forward, a metallic, clanking sound rising above the noise of something heavy being dragged through the leaves.

Kuro fell down on human knees next to him only to discover that his arms were shaking. A metal trap, wide and heavy, had clamped itself around Jaden's right leg, just above the paw, where a human ankle would be. Its rusted spikes had penetrated deep into his flesh in two large semi-circles, and blood was already staining the leaves.

Jaden screamed again, his eyes rolling back in inarticulate pain.

It's a weapon, Kuro thought, dumbly trying to understand – *and it's touching him.*

It was torturing him.

He looked up and found Jacqueline staring at him in triumphant disbelief.

"Please." The word slipped out of him, stupid and desperate, the plea of a child. Her mouth hung open in a small 'oh,' and she shook her head as she took a halting step backward.

Kuro looked away and took a deep breath, frightened of the pain to come. Lunging, he pressed down as heavily as he could on the trap's release lever, and a bolt of searing agony shot through his arms.

He fell backward, stunned and choking, frantically shaking his head to clear the fog. It had felt like fire, electrocution. Not the consciousness-snuffing obliteration of the gun touching him, but it was torture all the same. His heart was racing with panic; all the while, Jaden thrashed, his eyes senseless and rolled back to the whites, the high-pitched screaming of the *kitsune* growing in volume.

A sound stirred him to action. Kuro looked up at the way he had come.

Kenneth staggered forward, the gun in his hand. His shirt was soaked with blood from where Kuro had slashed him across the chest, and more poured down his neck from a wound on his head. There was a new rawness to his look, like skin peeled back in some invisible place, that left him grimacing with every step...and yet, he staggered forward once, twice, and stopped, his breath coming in heavy gasps.

Their gaze met in the mirror of each other's own eyes, and this time, when Kenneth raised the gun, his hands were no longer shaking. A new resolve had formed, visible in the firm press of his mouth as he aimed.

Before Kuro could move, tree bark exploded next to his face as the bullet shattered into the tree. He stared, dumbfounded, as Kenneth readjusted his aim, moving the gun an inch over.

A body slammed into Kuro, knocking the wind out of him just as the gun fired. He felt the demon on top of him, heavy and heaving, and breathed in the familiar scent, took in the maroon hair limp now across his chest.

Jaden spasmed against him, human in unconsciousness, his skin ashy white, and collapsed. Kuro's arms reached out to support him and felt liquid, hot and slick, on his fingers.

The bullet had grazed across the top of Jaden's left clavicle, burning through the flesh before colliding into the tree behind him. Kuro stared, his limbs shaking; the bullet would have found its mark in Kuro's chest had Jaden not fought his way through torture and shoved him down in time.

He had thought that Jaden would never protect someone other than himself, incapable of feeling anything but his own self-interest...that he was only a tool for Jaden's use...not truly his friend.

He had been wrong.

With Jaden's unconsciousness, the power of his true name evaporated; Kuro felt the lifting from his mind all at once...but now hate moved in him. He looked up at Kenneth, back toward the barrel of the gun, and saw that the creeping, scared thing from earlier had returned to his eyes.

"*You...*" The word came out in a snarl. An anger inside of him snapped like a chord pulled too tight, and the air grew charged around him as the *holy dark* surged, thunderous with his rage. His fingers ached with the weight of Jaden's body, the nails suddenly painful as he struggled to control his form, tensing to leap forward and tear out the boy's throat.

This was the humans' plan. They had hurt his friend...and they intended to kill them.

Jacqueline came to her senses first. "Kenneth – *shoot him!* The maroon one!"

Kuro roared in fury; around him, all of the fox fire he could summon leapt into the clearing, raging toward them.

Jacqueline screamed, turning to shield herself, as Kenneth threw himself in front of her.

A burst of painfully bright light slammed against the blue flame. Squinting, he tried to see and understand –

Fire, *real fire,* had unfurled in a sudden explosion like the petals of a spreading, tremendous flower, or the wings of some great bird. The blue fox fire had flowed against the wall of golden flame and fled upward, spent. In an instant, the twin fires had dissipated, plunging them into the inky hues of dusk.

The humans trembled, staring. Jacqueline reached out, hand shaking, and gripped Kenneth's wrist, reaching for the gun.

It loosened in his fingers. She lifted it slowly, took two steps forward, and with careful precision, aimed.

Kuro let Jaden slip to the ground. Seething, he stepped over him, a black *kitsune* with his tail coiled over the human beneath him, his snout pulled back in a snarl.

You'll have to kill me first, he warned.

She fired.

The recoil sent the gun whipping backward; she yelped just as a bullet whizzed past Kuro's left ear.

She raised it to shoot again, then gasped. Beneath her feet, the shadows were coiling, sliding over the ground, twisting around her legs, traveling up her body with fingers and claws. She screamed and fired wildly, shooting at the demons. Another branch erupted into a shower of splinters above Kuro's head, but still the shadows reared, opening jaws –

"Jacqueline, *stop!*" Kenneth grabbed her wrist, holding the gun above her head. "*Stop shooting!*"

The shadows had come together now, wrapping around the

two of them, hands reaching up to claw at their eyes. It was all illusion, but it had worked: they were screaming, trying to fight them off.

Kuro hissed again and drew all of the shadows toward him, plunging them deep into darkness. Jacqueline turned in desperation, screaming, and fired twice more.

The first bullet hit the ground, a foot from Jaden's head, peppering him with dirt.

The second time, all that came out was a dry, empty 'click.'

Kenneth shouted again, dragging her forward. Jacqueline stumbled once, twice, then found her feet, and with Kenneth still gripping her by the elbows, took off running up into the woods.

Kuro bared his teeth as they ran. He exhaled, exhausted, and the darkness, like spilling ink, melted away from him, back to where the shadows belonged. He stared once more at the bear trap and readied himself, his fury strengthening his resolve.

Jaden had managed to save his life despite enduring the worst agony of his life.

Kuro would have to, as well.

The iron felt as though it were branding him as he pushed it down, a scream tearing through his clenched teeth as it finally sprung open. He fell backward with the jolt of it, gasping and stunned, struggling to kick his legs out and gain his composure. His arms seized; he collapsed and rolled over, vomiting from the shock of it.

It took a minute of reeling white pain before he could see well enough to discern the fresh blood flowing from the open puncture wounds on Jaden's leg. Kuro swallowed and grappled in the slick leaves, his body still ringing from the shock of touching the trap, and hoisted one limp arm over his shoulders as he moved to pull Jaden up, struggling to stand. It was difficult work: Kuro's arms had gone completely numb.

One staggered step followed another. The cords in his neck

stood out as he strained his head backward with the effort of carrying him, and in his heart, a silent prayer had begun. *He's going to be okay,* he thought, over and over, *he's going to be alright.*

But Jaden didn't stir, even as dusk fell away into dark night. Kuro continued to drag first one foot, then another, digging deeper into himself for the strength to make it.

"Jaden," he kept trying, pleading, but his head hung down, unresponsive. The trail of blood left behind by the wounds in his leg had at first fallen with fat plops down onto the leaves, but as it slowed, the spill had grown to a trickle, then to drops. Kuro glanced down and saw that his own pants were covered with Jaden's blood from where his prone legs had dragged against him. The flesh was mangled; he prayed Jaden's bones hadn't been crushed.

The muscles in his shoulder blades were on fire by the time he saw Caroline's rotted fence. He didn't have the strength to lift Jaden over it, and there, at the edge of it, he collapsed, his breath emerging as small clouds in the cold night.

Her truck was back – and strangely, another car was next to it. He gulped in air and screamed for her, insensible and roaring. He paused only to suck in more air, his pitch rising.

A door opened and slammed, and even though he could see her running toward him, he screamed for her one last time until she was there right beside him, gripping his shoulders, asking him what was wrong, *what happened.*

"Caroline." His voice cracked on her name one last time, and the sharp terror of losing someone he loved sliced through him. *"Please...save him."*

She reached down to help him, and as they lifted him between them, Kuro looked up just as the front door opened again.

Eric Gallagher stood waiting in the doorway.

ELEVEN

"Eric," Caroline called, "get the door!"

In front of them, Eric stood rooted, his face white, eyes pinned, his gaze locked on Kuro.

Under the sound of his own gasping breath, Kuro heard the shocked whisper that escaped him, the same word he undoubtedly said the first time he'd seen him: *"Kenneth."*

"Eric!" Caroline repeated. *"Get the door!"*

He stumbled backward, hand fumbling for the latch, and recoiled from them as they staggered through the doorway, pressing himself as tightly against the frame as possible. Kuro could feel his eyes on the back of him, following them as they turned their bodies sideways to get Jaden down the hallway.

They laid him down on Christopher's bed. Kuro slumped to the floor beside it, panting.

"Save him." His mind was bereft of anything else. A steady chant of *save him save him please save him* drummed in his mind, and every time he opened his mouth, in between the gasps, it echoed in a frightened whisper.

Caroline whirled to get Eric, but stopped. He had followed them to the doorway where he stood frozen now, staring.

Kuro looked up, frantic. He remembered the look in Eric's eyes the last time they saw one another: surprise, but tempered by a strong belief in coincidence, and a final coldness. It was different now...the viciousness was gone, knocked out of place like a book off the shelf, tumbled under the humility of confronting something previously unknowable. He had changed since he'd seen him last; some new knowledge, some new *thought* had entered that young man's mind, wormed its way through the foundations of logic and reason, and set just enough cracks into the framework to let the first springs of water through.

And now, looking at the two of them together, the levee was breaking.

Eric's fists unclenched slowly, but his eyes still didn't blink. A glassy, pained quality had come over them.

Caroline stepped forward, reaching for him, then let her hand fall away. "Eric," she tried, her voice steady. "Are you okay? We need your help."

Something snapped; a tension released. He looked at her, sweat shining on his forehead, then back at Kuro.

"...I know you," he said slowly, as though in a dream. "I was unsure before, but..."

Kuro ground his teeth. They didn't have time for this.

Caroline stepped forward again, and this time, without hesitating, she grabbed for both of his hands, pulling them toward her. A brief flare of jealously shot through Kuro, gone in the instant it came.

Eric came back to himself, surprised by her touch. She squeezed his hands and looked at him with all the force of desperation that she had.

"*Please,* Eric," she begged. "I can explain later. I promise I will. I can't take him to a hospital. *Please* help him."

Eric looked down at her hands. He swallowed, nodded. She released him.

"My car," he said, the words thick, his voice choked. "There's a kit in the car..."

"I'll go with you." She took him by the hand and led him out again. Kuro listened to the footsteps, the front door, the sound of Caroline guiding him out and back.

When he returned, he looked more like a prisoner than a willing participant. There was a look in his eyes of something *moving,* but it was hard to pin down...like wind rushing through a crack in a doorway.

Eric shuffled past him, paused, looked down, then came to the end of the bed where Jaden's head rested on the pillow. Jaden's breathing had grown shallow and quiet – but he wasn't unconscious, couldn't be; his hair was brown. It would have turned back to its true color if he were unconscious, like when he had slumped against Kuro in the woods. When had he struggled upwards into enough awareness to change it back? He must have done it when he'd heard him screaming for Caroline; he must have realized what would have happened if Caroline had seen his true hair color.

Even clinging to consciousness, Jaden had found the strength to protect him, yet again.

Kuro remained at the end of the bed, watching him from the floor. Eric's eyes slid over Jaden, down to his mangled leg. The puncture wounds extended up his mid-calf, horrific to behold, and were still bleeding.

"Will he be okay?" Kuro rasped.

Eric glanced at him as though he'd forgotten he was there. "It seems like he's lost a lot of blood."

Kuro felt a dizzy, falling sensation taking hold of him. Before he could say anything, Eric gestured at the wounds.

"The pattern," he said. "Looks like... a bear trap."

Suspicion flared up in Kuro; the way he said it seemed as though he was trying to gloss over his certainty...but Kuro didn't have time to question it.

He managed a curt, sick nod.

"A bear trap..." Caroline leaned against the doorway, hugging herself. "Oh my god..."

"And a bullet." Eric pointed at the wound on the top of his shoulder, then leaned down and pressed the edges of it lightly. He looked up to find Kuro staring at him.

Their eyes met. Kuro bit back on the bile in his throat. "It missed the mark," he hissed.

"I'll get towels – and some water." Caroline left, her footsteps echoing down the hall.

Eric said nothing, turning to his bag. Kuro watched as he took something out – a vial, small, and a hypodermic needle. His left hand clutched the bottle tightly, the knuckles white, his other hand shaking as he withdrew the liquid. Seconds stretched and bloated as the needle continued to fill, drawing back toward its max.

The numbers, Kuro's mind raced, watching. *The numbers on the side...* They meant something, something important – what had Eric said to him that night? If one could calculate the precise location of the boundary between life and death, the numbers were somewhere on the edge of that needle, on the bottle Eric had slipped into a pocket as he leaned forward now, an unsteady hand pressing almost tenderly for a vein in Jaden's neck. Kuro felt like the world had slowed down; he turned to reach forward, to shout, but already Eric had pressed the needle against the skin, a plume of dark maroon invading its cylinder –

Jaden surged upward, eyes wild, the needle tip snapping off. His right hand had grabbed Eric by the collar and yanked him down. Eric had turned the sour whiteness of curdled milk; Kuro couldn't feel it himself, but he could sense that Jaden had used everything in him to *wrench* on Eric's soul.

He pulled Eric close.

"*If –*" he hissed into his ear, but the rest was lost to Kuro; he saw Jaden's mouth move as he whispered, saw Eric's eyes widen as he listened.

And then Jaden released him, collapsing back onto the bed, gasping in pain and exhaustion.

Eric stumbled backward like a man who had been snake-bitten, his eyes locked on the demon.

He looked sick.

Not sick... Kuro thought. Jaden's eyes seemed to glow with a feverish intensity, and all around him, Kuro felt the *holy dark* surge and pulse, aching in his bones. Jaden maintained Eric's gaze, jaw clenched, sweating. Kuro could feel Jaden using the *holy dark* to sustain himself, and he understood now the look in Eric's eyes: the wind had rushed through the door of his soul and blown it wide open, the gale winds coming through. Its locks had loosened when forced to confront the terrifying reality he could not comprehend and tried to run from, and all the door needed was a final shove, and the cold came through.

He was *haunted* now.

All at once, Kuro let out a breath he hadn't known he was holding. He relaxed against the wall and watched, pitiless, as Eric set the needle down in his bag, forgotten. The human's movements were harmless and pathetic now, his manner wholly changed; like a whipped dog, whatever Jaden had said to him, *done* to him with those words, the boy had been brought to heel. Jaden struggled to sit up, and Kuro watched as Eric, eyes downcast, cut away the pants, peeling them away from the blood, and began to clean the wounds with water squirted from a pipette. The boy jerked and winced every so often as he worked, and Kuro knew that if he could feel any other soul besides Caroline's, touching Eric's would be like touching a deer who lay supine on the ground, kicking in a frenzied, agonized terror as a wolf muzzle mauled deep into its intestines, working efficiently and ruthlessly to eat the animal alive from the inside out.

The demon was feasting on him.

It would take an enormous amount of effort to tear and eat away like that, to hold on with such frenzied insistence, but every effort was rewarded. Already the color had come back to Jaden's face, and although he winced and gripped the bedsheets in silent agony, the *holy dark* was *rallying, alive* in his eyes, shielding him from the torture of his leg.

"Do you need any help?"

Caroline's voice cut through his thoughts. He hadn't even noticed that she'd returned, a bucket of water and a stack of towels in one arm.

Eric looked up sharply at her, then quickly back away. He wouldn't lift his gaze to her again; his breathing had grown uneven. "No," he said. "If I need anything, I'll let you know." He glanced up at Jaden, then back to the leg where he was working. "...You all should go."

"I'm staying," Kuro said.

Eric didn't reply, but Jaden looked at him. That surging feeling of the *holy dark* hit him full force, suffocating him. "Kuro: *leave.*" He gasped and jerked his leg, then held it still. One hand came up, pressing against where the bullet had grazed the top of his shoulder, wincing. Eric's own face contorted into a grimace as something unseen twisted inside him.

"But –"

"I'll call for you," he said. There was no arguing with the look that followed. Kuro nodded, struggled to his feet, and with Caroline waiting for him, walked into the hall.

The last thing he saw as the door shut was Eric's eyes. He had looked up for just a moment, the furtive glance of some sneaking but small predator – no wolf now, but a weasel, perhaps – and had snatched one final glance, but not at him.

His eyes lingered on Caroline, and then the door shut on them both.

An hour slipped away, lost in a haze of movements he didn't register. Caroline spoke to him gently, helped him out of his bloody clothes, made him a hot tea. It sat on the edge of the kitchen table, the steam growing thinner until it disappeared entirely, untouched.

"Kuro, you've got to talk to me." Her hand pressed gently against his. He looked up to find her eyes, already forgiving but insistent, searching his face for answers. "What's going on? What's happened?"

The truth would be the easiest thing to tell, he thought, but that seemed like madness.

She loves you – she'll forgive you.

Did people always forgive those they loved? What if they didn't? What if he told her the truth – was it like the beginning of a rockslide? How much else would come tumbling out with it? Was a half truth worse than a lie?

"Kuro." Her fingers curled around his, reaching through his own in a gentle grip. She held him firmly, pulling him toward her. "Please. Let me in."

For a moment, he thought he would. He intended to say it all; he imagined the sheer relief of letting go of the lies and the guilt, and in a flash, he could even picture a world where Caroline would forgive him – and even possibly Jaden.

...But the moment came, and went. At his back, even from down the hallway, Kuro could feel the *holy dark* filling the house, moving around and through him. It sharpened everything, heightened every sensation, and clarity yanked him back from the precipice of speech.

"I can't tell you."

"Why?"

He looked down at their hands; they still held each other. They fit so well, and her skin...he knew the feeling of her palms, loved the coarseness of the callouses there, the edge of dirt around a fingernail. He shuddered.

"I don't want to hurt you."

She drew her hand away and stood up. Kuro watched as she took two steps toward the kitchen sink then turned back to him, her decision made.

"I deserve the truth." He found it difficult to look at her now, but he forced himself to do so anyways, to feel her soul that was moving now with steady resolve. "I won't accept this silence from you. This silence is a lie, Kuro."

"Caroline –"

"It's a lie by omission," she continued. "Something isn't right here. You're keeping something from me. Both of you... and I'm not going to live with that. I'm not okay with that. You don't get to choose to protect me from something that I deserve to know. I can see you thinking; I can see the worry and fear in your eyes. I can't do what you can do – I can't just reach out and *know* how a person feels – but when you love someone, Kuro..." Her voice trailed off. She closed her eyes and steadied herself. "When you love someone, you don't have to. You *know*. And it hurts both people. Jaden was caught in a bear trap – why?"

"It was in the woods...he ran into it."

"That's not what I'm asking." Her voice had an edge of anger to it now. "What were you doing? Why did you both leave the house? Do you think it was set up deliberately? And who shot at you – and why?"

The truth welled up inside of him again, and it was an ugly, hateful thing. *I can't tell her...*

He wasn't just protecting Caroline anymore.

"He saved my life." Kuro's voice was thin, strained. "Caroline, you weren't there. Jaden was caught in that trap, it was a weapon, he was *screaming,* and he still managed to push me out of the way of the bullet. I would have died."

They shared a long silence, his eyes pleading with her, insistent. Finally, she looked away, staring out toward the dark forest.

When she spoke, her voice rose just above a whisper. "I'll give you until tomorrow." She turned away completely. "You both are going to talk to me, then. You're going to give me the truth, or...."

"Okay." He stood up. He didn't want to hear the end of the sentence; it would have been too horrible, too much to handle. "Tomorrow."

She turned back to him and smiled. He'd never seen quite that look before – it was sad, almost cynical, and it twisted up into a single word that dropped the floor beneath him.

"Promise?"

He felt frozen to the spot, stunned. He swallowed, tried to speak, and finally managed to nod.

"What do you promise, Kuro?"

Oh Caroline, please don't do this to me – please not this way...

But her eyes...that look of tired, desperate longing held on to him, and he answered, defeated.

"I promise you'll know the truth."

She nodded.

All of a sudden he couldn't be in the same room with her; he turned away, shamefaced, and moved back down the hallway. Each step brought him deeper into the heart of the *holy dark,* like wading through an ever-thickening swamp, until he stood outside the door, pausing.

It was too quiet to understand the words, but Kuro could hear it...the whispers.

He pressed his ear against the frame, trying to make out the sounds. It was a steady stream of whispering in Jaden's voice, not rushed – insistent, creeping, inimical. Kuro shivered, and for the briefest moment, felt pity for the human behind that door. Jaden had been feasting on Eric for nearly two hours now with vicious abandon...tearing away at that haunted, poisoned soul, and whatever it was he was saying moved through the room and slid under the door like serpents, winding their way around that boy's mind.

He's a monster.

He's my friend, Kuro thought in reply to himself, opening the door.

Eric sat on the floor, slumped at the foot of the bed where Kuro had been hours before. He looked up when the door opened, his eyes wild, his skin a pallid gray. A pile of wet towels lay on the ground beside him, stained with blood so dark that in the dim light it looked nearly black. The cloying smell of antiseptic hung around the edges of the room.

Eric looked away, twisting to look back at Jaden with a nervous, questioning expression.

Jaden sat bolt upright in the bed, his back against the frame. He had an air of cool detachment now; the raw anger was gone from his eyes, but something else now possessed them...some sense of purpose and forward momentum, Kuro thought. The *holy dark* was so thick around him that he felt like a man walking against the wind of a snowstorm, each step arrested by the weight of being pushed back by the force of the cold. He didn't *glow,* exactly – the room was dim, though not dark – but Kuro could feel it, very nearly *see* it in some invisible way as the *holy dark* emanated from him, like electricity flowing from an exposed wire. To have amassed that much power so quickly, in such a time of need...*he's hasn't just been feeding on him,* Kuro thought. *He's been devouring him.*

Like a roiling lake calming, the *holy dark* began to disperse and melt away, retracting back toward the demon. The tight control in Jaden's expression relaxed just a fraction, and with a curt nod toward Eric, the human scrambled to his feet, gathered his bags, and pushed past Kuro without a glance or a word.

The door shut behind him.

Kuro sat on the edge of the bed, staring down at his leg. Eric had cleaned and stitched the puncture wounds then wrapped the leg, starting below the ankle and up to the calf, in tight white bandages.

"Six puncture wounds," Jaden said, gesturing toward his leg. "When it caught me, I tried to twist and pull away, so four of them are severely lacerated. He cleaned them out and applied stitches, along with some gauze and antibiotic ointment. It'll have to do for now. Two of the spikes hit bone; had I been a human when the trap closed, it would have probably crushed the bone entirely, and I would have lost this leg. Eric also gave me a tetanus shot, which was remarkably...unpleasant."

"Compared to being in the trap?"

Kuro's attempt at humor fell flat. Jaden only stared at him and then spoke slowly, each word measured. "I was in that trap for... how long would you say? Five minutes? Five minutes," he mused. "*Minutes.*" The word escaped in a long hiss. Kuro looked down at the leg, shuddering; once, Caroline had thrown a gun at his back. It had touched him for perhaps a *second.* He imagined the pain he felt, drawn out over that time...it would have driven him into madness, suicide.

Or murder.

Jaden's eyes rolled to him, baleful and narrowed. "I don't think I'm going to ever forget that, for as long as I live..." He licked his lips. "Comparatively, the bullet wound was not that bad. It only grazed me."

Kuro saw that a white, square bandage had been taped down across his clavicle, the adhesive traveling over his bare shoulder. "Two inches lower and it would have shattered the ball and socket of my arm, and I would have probably never been able to use it again. Two inches to the right and it would have hit my carotid artery, and one inch lower and it would have hit my subclavian artery. It skimmed clean flesh, which certainly *hurts,* but in the end, it would seem I have the devil's luck." His version of a snort came out as a dry, cruel sneer.

"How did you convince that boy to help you? It looked like he...he became..."

"Haunted? You saw it, then." Jaden's face became a mask of quiet thought. "I didn't know if you'd be able to tell or not."

"Why?"

His gaze was penetrating. "When I told you to feel Jacqueline's soul, you said *you can't.*"

A feeling of warning began to creep up his spine. Jaden wasn't threatening him, wasn't angry; he was preternaturally calm, even his breathing stilled. His eyes were searching though, looking for something in him. Kuro could feel them gazing deeper into his, scrutinizing his face as he sought some answer there, but what the question even was, he didn't know.

He tried to look back and failed, finding the floor suddenly arresting. "Yes."

"What do you mean by 'yes'?"

"I can't feel – or feed – from anyone else...except Caroline. I don't know why, either...we tried so many times to make it stop, or open up...I don't even know how to phrase it. To *let go.* It's like her soul is holding on to me, or maybe –"

"*We?*"

The word brought him to a halt. Kuro glanced up and found

Jaden's brow furrowed. "Yes. *We*. Caroline and I tried to...separate, I guess." His mind worked fast, trying to steer the conversation away. "But I can still feel the *holy dark* inside me, *outside* me, I can still sense some things, and with Eric...I saw him *become* haunted." He shuddered; it had felt like witnessing something dirty, private, *shameful*. "I always thought it was more of a gradual thing, but it happened in a moment. What did you say to him?"

Jaden waved the question away with a decisive gesture, signaling its unimportance. "I used the last remaining strength I had – everything in me – to grab onto his soul. It was like pulling a piece of furniture that was bolted to the ground right out of its mooring. He felt it, and the force of it was enough to haunt him. I think everything was a little too much for him to be confronted with all at once," he mused. "I gripped him, fangs and claws and all, metaphorically speaking, and held him fast. That's all."

Kuro hesitated. "I saw that, but I heard...whispers..."

Jaden ignored the comment. "Besides not being able to feed on anyone besides Caroline, what else is different?"

A sense of unease was stirring in the back of his mind, a warning perhaps; the first tug of a tide before being swept out to sea. He didn't understand the current or the destination, but he tried to swim against it. "Why does this matter, Jaden? We've got to figure out what to do about Kenneth and Jacqueline now...they *planned* that. They won't leave us alone." *Because* you *won't leave* her *alone,* he might have added, but there was no sense in arguing over that anymore. What's done was done.

"You were right," Jaden agreed. "It was a *trap*. They set up a number of bear traps in the woods with the intention of luring us out toward them, catching us, and shooting us." A sickly grin spread across his face. "Jacqueline decided to be proactive and make a move against me because she knows I won't ever let her go.

She decided to take matters into her own hands." He sounded almost *proud.*

Kuro was flabbergasted. "How – how do you know this?"

Jaden tilted his head toward the door. "The boy told me. Kenneth came to him and told him the plan. The boy's job was to lure Caroline away, which they succeeded in doing, but not for long – she didn't want to stay with him, despite his insistence. When he realized he couldn't stop her from leaving, he followed her back here in his car, just in case something were to happen. He said she was irritated by his presumption and told him she wouldn't let him in the house." He snorted. "Luckily for us, he nevertheless followed her; luckily for him, no key unlocks a door as quick as *need.*"

Kuro struggled to follow. "...And he told you....all this?"

Jaden nodded.

"*Why?*" He felt like he was trying to solve a puzzle, but the picture didn't quite match the pieces he was given, and no matter how he tried to fit it together, he found himself coming up short.

"I already *told* you, Kuro. I was feeding on his soul; it was nothing to get him to speak." There was a note of annoyance, but his tone softened. "Forget him. What does Caroline think about all...this?" He indicated his leg and the bloody towels.

"...Caroline..." Kuro swallowed, his mind sluggish, still puzzled at Eric's casual betrayal of his friends. *Why?* He kept asking himself. Jaden's explanation didn't make sense, but the demon was staring at him expectantly, waiting for an answer. "...I didn't tell her what happened. She wants to know, Jaden. She wants to know the *truth,* and I...I made her a promise..."

Jaden reached out to him, his hand resting on his shoulder. Kuro looked up, startled, and heard the rustling of the tape and bandage on the bullet wound that had been meant for him. "Kuro." He looked at him with level-headed composure, his voice low and soothing. "It's alright. I have everything taken care of; I know what we need to do. I just need to know anything else you haven't told me so that I can help us as best as possible, and resolve this...situation."

Could he trust him? The immediate answer was 'no,' and yet... *He took that bullet for you,* Kuro reminded himself. He stared into his friend's eyes and saw that it was true; dumb luck and gravity had saved Jaden from an instant, fatal shot to the neck, the loss of an arm, or a slow death by blood loss. Whatever lies and manipulations he had done in the past, even to the point of using his true name to compel him against his will, *that* had been no act; *he was willing to die for you.*

He'd been lying to Caroline, telling half-truths to Jaden...but at some point, he knew, he had to trust them both...and the time had come. Their lives were in the balance. Jaden was looking at him insistently, patient. A voice – Jaden's voice, younger yet every bit as sincere, spoke up in his memory.

I promise never to abandon you.

Kuro exhaled, and at last told him everything.

He hadn't meant to – at least, not at first – but it poured out of him, and the relief – *the sheer relief* – of telling someone the truth lifted him to a place of near peace and exhilaration. He started at the beginning, with that feeling of Caroline's soul reaching out to him, then told him how things had changed, slowly at first, but unmistakably.

Jaden interrupted him from time to time, holding up his hands as though to stop a runner.

"So she was the one who shot you?"

"I know, I said she wasn't – but I didn't think you'd understand, or forgive her, and I –"

A magnanimous gesture waved the comment away, as though this revelation was insignificant, and Kuro continued, his voice growing excited as he raced on about how even what he *could* feed on had changed. It still fueled the *holy dark,* fed the hunger inside of him, he tried to explain – *that* didn't feel any different, in fact, no *part* of him felt different at all... but whereas, say, sadness used to taste like melted butter on hot toast, now it was bitter, acrid to him; the world had turned upside down and reversed itself.

He told him about hiding the truth from Caroline, how he had done it to protect Jaden, but that he had made a promise that would have to be fulfilled tomorrow, and there was more...Before he knew he had said it, he told him about the form – the *new* one – that he could assume, and in the next moment, a silver fox stood on the bed, gazing up at Jaden.

He expected him to be surprised, shocked, or even horrified... but there was nothing. Jaden stared at him with perfect impassivity.

"...Can you talk?"

Yes, I can still talk.

Jaden's mouth cracked into a half-grimace, half-grin. "It's so different to see you like this...I imagine it takes some getting used to. Did you know that you can't snarl?"

What?

"Foxes can't snarl. They lack the muscles to do so. They make that horrible noise...*gekkering,* I think it's called." He settled back, conversational now, humored even. "Or that awful *screaming.*"

I haven't tried it. This is only the second time I've been like this.

"So it's still very new. I see." His humor fell away, his expression a mask that hid his thoughts. "I wonder what the utility of such a form is; it's weaker, small, fragile...what purpose does gaining such a form *serve?*" His voice trailed away, and then in a slow, exhaled whisper, he said, "*Aah.*"

What is it?

"...I can't feel you." His face was calm, almost serene...but there was a note very close to fear underneath all that calm. "I can't *sense* you...not even the *holy dark*...at all. It's like your presence is completely gone...masked." He blinked suddenly and forced an appreciative chuckle, but Kuro wasn't entirely convinced by his nonchalance. "Oh, well. I suppose you can't help what you are, Kuro."

Kuro looked up at him, confused. Jaden was regarding him with a mixture of disappointment, boredom, and just a slight revulsion.

What am I?

As though delivering the news of a death, Jaden answered with pity. "You're a *myobu*."

Kuro shifted back and felt the mattress sink beneath his human weight, unable to hide his own surprise.

"You know what this is? What's happened to me?"

His answering grin was playfully, almost kindly, mocking. "I told you about this *years* ago. Not too long ago, you were asking me about it again. And to think, if only you would have come to me sooner, I could have helped you...you wouldn't have had to suffer the way you have, to have starved..." His voice was pained.

"I'm fine now," Kuro said. "It passed. I think...I felt it the moment it happened." But *that* was too personal, too fresh to put into words; it was something he wanted to belong only to him. He pushed forward, anxious. "But now you know everything, and I... I promised Caroline I would tell her the truth, too."

Jaden's eyes glimmered, but the look was gone before Kuro could catch the hue of his mood. "That's not *precisely* what you promised her, but I understand the sentiment. Are you scared of what she's going to say when she finds out about us? ...And me? How do you think she'll react?"

Kuro fell into a thoughtful silence, searching for an answer. He pictured the scenario so many different ways, but in each one, disaster struck: betrayal, then abandon. Try as he might, hope as much as he dared, he could not imagine forgiveness. He hadn't realized the silence had stretched on too long until Jaden's voice broke into his thoughts.

"Everything is going to be alright."

Kuro looked up, eager to believe him. Jaden sat in perfect confidence, nodding. "I told you – I already have a solution worked out. I've had a few hours now to think...to plan. I want you to listen to me very carefully, and do what I tell you to do."

Kuro leaned forward, waiting.

"Outside, near the barn, at the edge of the horse pasture at the righthand corner of the fence, closest to the tree line, I've buried something. You remember the little box that held the contact lenses?" Kuro nodded. "Dig six inches, and you'll find it. Don't open it," he added, stern. "You're going to take that box to Kenneth's house. Do you remember how to get there?"

"Yes, but –"

"You'll take it there," Jaden continued, "and be careful if you go through the woods. There're more traps out there. Scan the trunks for an 'x' carved into them; the traps are set near those.

"If you can't get in the house and it looks safe enough to break into, do that, but don't make it obvious – no forced doors or shattered windows. If you *can't* get in, hide the container somewhere outside the house, somewhere safe but obvious and accessible...a drain gutter would work."

"Why?"

"It'll ensure that those humans never bother us again." Jaden's voice was kind, but his tone betrayed a hint of impatience. "He can rave about *kitsune* all he likes – no one will believe him...if he even believes it himself."

Kuro's confidence faltered. "...Caroline will."

But Jaden smiled a long, knowing smile. "Caroline loves you," he pronounced simply, as though that solved everything. Kuro's face burned; it felt new and vulnerable to hear that from another person's mouth. "I saw it the moment I met her, Kuro, even if you were too foolish to realize it at that point...but she does. Love blinds people," he said, and the feeling came back to

Kuro of creeping, icy doubt, of *wrongness,* but he couldn't figure out why or catch the thread of instinct. "She'll believe what her heart convinces her to believe in order to preserve her own happiness...and she won't have to know the truth about us."

About you, Kuro nearly corrected him, but stopped the words before they came. Instead, he said, "But I *promised* her the truth."

Jaden rolled his eyes. "The truth is relative, Kuro. You promised she'd know the truth – your *intention* means a lot when you make a promise, you know. What you were thinking of, how you interpreted the words within their *prescriptive* meaning. We can think our way around it."

He flushed. "I intended to tell her the *truth,* Jaden – I wasn't lying to her or playing some sort of mind game. I wasn't crafting a riddle," he argued. "I intended to tell her about *you.*"

Jaden's mouth twisted into a cruel smile. "The truth about *me* is all wrapped up with the truth about *you,*" he warned. "After all, *you* knew what *I* was doing. You could have stopped me. You even protected me. Do you intend to tell her that I and *I alone* killed those people?" He laughed, a deep, full-throated chuckle. "At the very least, you're an accessory, an accomplice. You're not innocent. And anyways, you can always break the promise – I doubt it will hurt very much, and if it does, presumably it won't last long. I wouldn't know," he added, his voice heavy with meaning. "I've never broken any of mine."

Kuro felt dirty all of a sudden. He stood up, turned away too quickly, and tried to relax his shoulders, but he was tense again. That current of unknowing was pulling him along, and this time, he knew he was trapped in it. Somehow, one little box would get rid of Kenneth...but what did he intend to do to Jacqueline?

He tried to speak, found his voice hoarse, and managed, "After I drop the box off at Kenneth's house – then what?"

"After you leave here, Eric is going to make a few phone calls.

He'll ensure that this is all taken care of. But there's no rush – get some sleep, Kuro."

Kuro glanced back at him; the *holy dark* was gathering around him again, growing thick. Jaden's smile lingered below empty eyes.

"I'll see you in the morning."

TWELVE

"How is he doing?"

Kuro looked up through his fingers. He sat on the edge of Caroline's bed, holding his head, deep in his own thoughts. She came into the bedroom and shut the door. Eric was staying the night, and she had set up the living room couch with sheets and a blanket for him before joining him. The house felt oddly crowded.

Caroline sat beside him.

"...He's going to be alright."

"I called my brother." She wasn't looking at him; the change of subject caught him off-guard. "I haven't seen him since September, right before I met you, and for some reason...I felt like I needed to."

"What did you say to him?"

"...A lot of things. Some of it selfish. I told him I was worried I might need him to come here."

Because she's expecting me to leave, he thought. He turned to face her, anticipating that she would ask him more, return to the same questions from earlier: what had happened? *Why* had it happened? What was he keeping from her? He glanced up, ready to protest, but she said nothing. He felt for her soul and discovered a sense of calm and trust; he had promised the truth to her.

She had faith it would come.

They didn't speak; she pulled him down toward her on the bed, drawing him close in an embrace. Her arms came around him, her fingers in his hair as she held him, breathing deeply.

"It's going to be alright," she whispered. "Whatever it is, it'll be alright."

He tried to suppress the shudder, but it came all the same. He felt the dreadful suspicion that the more people told him something would be alright, the less likely it would be.

Exhaustion set into his bones, heavy and leaden. He exhaled and brought his arms around her. Neither bothered to undress, to draw the blankets over them, to even turn the bedside lamp off. They lay clinging to one another, their pulses beating in rhythm, and slept.

He awoke when the first soft, bright rays of dawn touched the window. In the gray light, he watched the motes float, remembering a similar morning that felt like a lifetime ago, when he lay in the hay in her barn, waiting.

Caroline still slept. He gently disentangled himself from her and sat up, looking down at her sleeping form. She was all energy and strength, hope and joy, but sleep had brought a frozen grace to her. Her hair tumbled over the side of the bed, and without thinking, he reached out and gently touched the ends.

Her eyes opened, and somehow, she knew.

"You're leaving."

He offered a weak smile that fell away with the effort. "Not for very long – I'll be back. There's something I have to go do."

He expected a question again, but none came. She stretched slowly and drew herself up, sitting beside him. He watched as she reached to the bedside table and opened a small jewelry box.

Caroline turned to him and pressed the onyx rosary into his hand, curling his fingers over it.

"There's a look in your eyes...I can't explain it. For a moment, I wanted to ask you if what you're going to go do is right," she said, "...but I can't be your moral compass, Kuro. I don't even think I'm fit to judge you, anyways. But I want you to have this."

He looked down at the rosary in his palm and frowned.

"Caroline, I don't believe in this kind of thing..."

She offered him a half-smile. "Neither do I. But when I've needed to reflect, to look inside myself or just think and try to find answers...it's helped. I want you to take it with you, and if you find yourself needing to think – Kuro, if you find yourself...needing *something,* I don't know what, it'll be there. Just run your hands over the beads, try to still your thoughts and quiet your mind. If it helps, good. If not, oh well."

He slipped it into his pocket and took her hands in his. He leaned forward and breathed in deeply, his eyes closed. *Remember this,* his own voice told him. *Remember how she feels, right now.*

"Caroline," he whispered, "is there anything I could do that would make you stop loving me?"

He opened his eyes to find her wearing that same strange smile from the previous night. "I don't know," she answered truthfully. "The world is filled with horrible things, Kuro...many of them unforgivable. Try to avoid doing those things, okay?" She laughed, but it was forced; it stumbled and stopped. "I'm scared to ask why you asked me that, or what it is you're thinking of doing."

Don't ask, he pleaded in his heart.

She didn't.

She stood up, her arms wrapping around herself, and faced him. "I hope that whatever it is you're about to do doesn't hurt anyone – including yourself. I'm not going to beg you to stay, to stop... I won't do any of those things. That's not who I am. I'm not going to insist on coming with you, either, because I can see that you don't want me to. I think you're ashamed of something, Kuro, and I hope you'll unburden yourself of that. I hope that whatever is happening, whatever you've gotten mixed up in, can be settled. I hope you'll let me help, if you want me to, because I love you. My life is small, Kuro." She gestured toward her cramped bedroom. "But if you decide to come back here, I'd like to share it with you...but only if you're willing to share your life with me, openly...honestly."

He rose and took her in his arms again, tilting her head back with a kiss, threading his hands through her hair. They held on to one another until the room was fully lit by the sunrise, and only then did she pull away, staring into his eyes.

"I'll be back," he whispered. "Soon."

She nodded. "And when you do..."

"I'll keep my promise."

Caroline sat back down. When she looked at him, he could feel her faith in him. Her voice was quiet, but weighted with conviction. "I know you will."

He shut the door quietly behind him, his chest tight. In front of him stood another closed door, and behind it, he could feel Jaden, the *holy dark* pressing outward. He drew a deep, steady breath and walked on.

Kuro paused at the doorway to the living room. The light from the kitchen window had filtered in slightly, and in the gray atmosphere, he saw Eric.

The boy was sitting on the floor, his back against the armchair, hunched over. His eyes were narrowed and staring, the skin puffy around red rims. The blanket that Caroline had draped over the couch remained untouched.

For a moment, their eyes met, and then Kuro moved away as one would step gingerly from the corpse of some animal. Eric's eyes were *haunted*, and his stare…he shivered and stepped out into the morning, the front door closing behind him.

He shifted forms and heard a soft *thunk* beside him in the dirt. The rosary hadn't assimilated; he turned back into a human and picked it up, putting it on like a necklace. Caroline's spiritual imprint on it was too strong; for years she had clutched it in her hands, drawn its beads through her fingers: too much of her had been impressed upon it. He doubted it would ever assimilate, if she had meant for him to keep it. Absently, he decided to give it back to her when he returned.

The contact lens case was exactly where Jaden had said it would be. Kuro heard Feral give a few restless barks from inside of the barn when he approached, then settle down.

He shifted forms, clutched the case between his teeth, and ran into the woods.

Within the hour, he had arrived at the back of Kenneth's house. It looked exactly the same since the last time they were there, but this time, he found, all the doors were locked. The windows, too. He slunk around the outside, pressing himself between the bushes and the house, slipping up toward the front porch. There was no car in the driveway, either.

Not home, he thought. It was early yet. He was most likely with the girl.

A shrill cry startled him; he turned around to find a red-tailed hawk had swooped down to the ground. He expected to see a mouse or a small rabbit in its claws, but there was nothing; only its eye as it turned toward him, shrieked again, and beating the ground, took wing into the trees.

Kuro shifted forms and sat down on the front porch, staring

after the bird, thinking. He glanced down at the dirt and noticed that the car tracks seemed relatively fresh, slightly wet from rolling over morning dew. Had Kenneth come home, then left? It didn't matter, he thought...

Put it somewhere safe, Jaden had said. A drainpipe, maybe...a gutter? Perhaps behind the bushes?

The box had rattled the whole time he was carrying it in his jaws. He turned it over in his human hands. There was no lock, just a simple latch on the edge.

Don't open it.

Without realizing he had done it, he had flicked the latch. The plastic case opened.

A human tooth and nail fell into the dirt.

A feminine hand had scribbled Brittany Alice's name on the inside in blue, permanent marker.

Kuro stared down at the fragments, uncomprehending at first. They seemed curiously fake, plastic almost – movie props. He reached for the tooth slowly, picking it up by the end. In the morning light, he could make out the shining curves of it, the slight indents of the molar. He recoiled at the smell; the roots, long and pointed, had chunks of some pulpy, rotting matter still clinging to them, reeking almost sweetly of death.

He heard Jaden laughing in his memory, heard him talking about souls, and how hard it was to rip one out. He's described it like pulling teeth...

He dropped the tooth back to the ground, his stomach turning over. It fell next to the human nail, which was painted a bright pink, the underside caked with blood so dry, it looked like mud.

He could see Jaden now, jeering at him, hear him saying *you knew what I was doing. You could have stopped me,* and it was true...*I knew,* he thought. But he knew it in an abstract way, in a way that allowed him to not *really* know, not really lean down over the bed and check to see the shape of the monster in the shadows, not *really* see it, like a child pulling a blanket over his head, shivering in the dark, thinking *if it eats someone else, that's okay, just not me just not me just not –*

He jumped to his feet, the case clattering in the dirt. Mercifully, it fell on top of the human remains, hiding them. He kicked it away in anger, forcing himself to look, to really *see* and understand and *know*. He had known about Jaden in the way one *hears* about something horrible, pictures it, reads about it...he *knew* what he had done to those campers in Tennessee, but he hadn't *seen* or even *heard* him do it, not up close, not like the girl in the car, her eyes open and glassy and dead...

You knew about that one, he accused himself. *You saw it happen, right in front of you. And you were able to move on. What was your limit? Your line? You always knew what he was. You just chose to ignore it. To pretend.*

He didn't want me to look, he thought. *He didn't want me to see this...to know this...to understand who he really is.*

Or did he? He had pointed Kenneth out to him, in the mountains, then told him not to approach the boy. He had told him to dig up the case, but not to open it. The thought would have never crossed his mind if Jaden hadn't put it there.

Had he wanted him to see this...? And if so, *why?*

He forced himself to stare down at the remains until he was certain he had memorized their appearance, forced the bile back down his throat, and fought against the increasing coldness that was flooding his spine like ice water.

He never told you his true name, he thought suddenly. From the very beginning, Jaden hadn't trusted him.

Kuro should have done the same.

He swallowed and looked up at the house. That boy, *Kenneth,* he thought, lived here. He had been angry at him – had hated him, even...he had tortured him for a moment of time, burning him with his fox fire. He had fought against the power of his true name to stop himself from killing him, then would have killed him anyways for what he had done to Jaden.

But suddenly all of that was gone, replaced by an overwhelming sense of pity.

Kenneth was human, and weak, and Jaden had said there was melancholia inside him, and if that was true, Kuro was certain that if he could feel his soul, misery would have corroded the color of every corner of his life, distorting every joy into a shame from which to flee.

Kuro felt a sudden clarity: Kenneth was not his enemy.

He was a victim.

The boy was afraid, and he had struck back at them, but he was a cornered animal, not a hunter. He was only trying to protect himself...to protect that girl, Jacqueline.

Hadn't Kuro just been trying to do the same?

Kuro crouched in the dirt and put the tooth and nail back into the case, closing it. Perhaps Jaden thought him too slow to figure it out, but he understood to what end Jaden had sent him here on this task. He wouldn't do this to Kenneth; he wouldn't implicate that boy with Jaden's crimes, lock him away for the rest of his life, leave him to rave of demons in some psychiatric hospital somewhere, if the prison system felt compelled to send him away, until he found some method to kill himself before anyone noticed. Jaden had constructed an elegant, simple solution to do away with the boy, a cruel revenge that would hasten him to suicide. Kuro wanted no part of it.

He would leave him – and the girl – alone.

He turned to leave, then stopped. The red-tailed hawk was still looking at him from the tree line, the sun glaring from its yellow eye. That stare held him still, and the feeling of icy numbness returned. Without understanding why, his pulse began to beat faster, his senses growing heightened. Everything seemed brighter suddenly, sharper; he could even smell the pine needles crushed under his feet, the rot coming from the sagging wood on the front porch.

Eric's face floated up suddenly, that wild, haunted look from the living room, the sleeplessness of a waiting animal, and with it, he heard Jaden telling him, *"After you leave here, Eric is going to make a few phone calls. He'll ensure that this is taken care of."*

The feeling was stronger now, twisting his insides, cutting him up. Even if he didn't hide the remains here at Kenneth's house, presumably Eric was going to call the police, tell a few lies about his friend, and they would show up, anyways.

Why would he do that? Why would he do that for Jaden...?

And why had he helped the demon at all? He had seen the syringe, seen the panel on the side – Eric had recognized them, understood what they were, *he was going to kill Jaden –*

But then Jaden's eyes had snapped open; he had grabbed him, pulled him down, his lips had pulled back against his teeth, and he had whispered

(If)

And Eric's eyes had widened, and he had become *haunted.*

If? Kuro could see the memory now – he saw Jaden's mouth moving, but the words were still inaudible. Like watercolors, moments blossomed on the paper of his mind, their colors spreading, combining, connecting, the full picture slowly taking shape.

The awful whispers in the night. Convincing, pushing, wheedling into his mind, whittling away any resolve, like maggots moving through meat.

The look on Eric's face when Caroline pulled his hands toward her.

If.

He took one stumbling step forward, his breath hitching. The hawk shrieked at him, urging him on. The forest answered the predator's call with an unnatural stillness, the breathless quiet of small things hiding.

Kuro saw him again in his memory, saw Jaden grabbing the boy by the collar, and whispering, his mouth's movements visible now

(*If you give Jacqueline to me –*)

and he remembered the way Eric's eyes had lingered on Caroline when they left the room, how he had stayed behind with Jaden, the door closing on them, and there was the look in his eyes, the first time they met: it was like the hawk's eyes that were staring at him now, fierce, narrowed, *hunting.* It was the eyes of a person who would kill to get what they wanted. He had thought they were merely cold, then, but no: there was bitterness and jealousy and hatred there, just below the surface.

You look like someone I know, he had said. Eric knew Kenneth...and Kenneth had trusted him enough to tell him they had set up traps in the woods to catch demons...and Eric had told Jaden.

What would it take to convince the person behind those cold, gray eyes to betray a friend?

He didn't tell you what he said to Eric. He felt light-headed, the blood roaring in his ears. *You asked him twice, and he wouldn't tell you.* His hand was trembling as he reached up, gripping the end of the rosary where it dangled against his chest. He tried to calm himself, tried to think, but he kept replaying the same moment on loop, Jaden whispering into Eric's ear

(*If you give Jacqueline to me –*)

and his mind was racing too fast to keep up with it now, the picture melting and forming together. There was only one thing Jaden wanted: Jacqueline's soul. It had a grip on him he couldn't understand (*can't you?* His own mind mocked. *You can understand Caroline's grip on YOU – why is it so hard to understand this? This...opposite effect?*), and the lust for it had driven a madness into his eyes.

What would it take to convince someone to betray a friend? Kuro's throat was tightening.

Eric hadn't been the only betrayer.

Love blinds people, Jaden had told him.

Kuro had been blind for a long, long time

(*Don't look*)

and now, too late, he could see.

He didn't have air in his lungs to gasp; he hadn't been breathing. Instead, he went rigid, silent, his eyes widening as he understood.

(*If*)

(*If you give Jacqueline to me –*)

He could see it clearly now. In his memory, Jaden's lips twisted with cunning cruelty, and Eric listened, a weak human already poisoned and hurting, confronted by something too big for him to deny, lost to a temptation so enticing, so powerful and sudden that he had given in to it the moment it had fallen on his ears. The shock and shame of succumbing to it had immediately *haunted* him, and would until the day he died.

"*If you give Jacqueline to me,*" Jaden had said to him, and only now Kuro could remember how the demon's eyes had slithered over to where Caroline stood in the doorway, "*I'll give her to you.*"

He dropped the lens case and began to run.

THIRTEEN

Kenneth lay flat on Jacqueline's bed, his head resting on her pillow, eyes shut, shirt off, concentrating on the sound of his own breathing. Jacqueline had cleaned the blood off of him with a wet washcloth, then worked on the slashes across his stomach. The first aid kit sat next to his hand. His head throbbed, but the blood there had at least washed out easily and relatively painlessly; no bone had broken, only skin, although he had a terrible concussion. He was finding it hard to concentrate, and a persistent, muddled sleepiness was tempting him to close his eyes...

He sucked in his breath as she drew an antibiotic wipe across the wound. The sound of scissors cutting tape interrupted his thoughts, followed by the uncomfortable feeling of his skin being pulled closed by the adhesive.

"They're not deep," she said. She laid gauze over the wounds, then helped him to sit up enough to pull a bandage under his back, wrapping his chest. "Just a little wide, still bleeding a bit."

She looked up then, attempted a smile, and whispered, "We almost had them."

Kenneth fell back, silent.

Them.

They looked like people...or they had, for a moment.

And then they had *changed.*

Shapeshifters, she had called them, two months ago. He'd thought she was dreaming of impossible things.

Maybe they both were...but he couldn't pretend he hadn't seen what he saw. Not anymore.

*And the fire, and those shadows...*he shuddered.

She cleaned the supplies up and sat next to him on the bed. He sat up, suddenly embarrassed by his partial nakedness. "Kenneth... you believe me now, right?"

He didn't want to...but he nodded.

"...What do we do now?"

He looked up to the ceiling, pondering. The *kitsune,* as Jacqueline now called them, would either slip away to terrorize others...or else come back to kill them.

"...Do you think he's still in the bear trap? The maroon one."

Jacqueline considered for a long time before answering, "No. I don't think so. I think the other one – Kuro, I heard him called – would have found a way to free him by now."

"Then we run," he said. "We'll pack up tonight and get out of here, go somewhere...somewhere safe."

"No, Kenneth," she whispered. Jacqueline closed her eyes, her small frame slumping with weariness. "He'll never stop, the one he called Jaden...he'll never stop wanting me."

Kenneth tried to fight against the roiling dread in his stomach. "How can you be so certain...?"

"An angel told me."

He probably should have been stunned, but Kenneth was shocked to the point of almost numbness from everything else that he had experienced in the last few hours: his mind was already reeling, grappling, and coming up short. In contrast, Jacqueline was remarkably composed.

Kenneth was trying not to shatter.

Was she wrong, and Jaden was out there now, trapped and dying? Or had the other one, the one who looked like *him*, freed him? One or both of them would want revenge.

And what would they do, then? Everything had shifted now; there was no returning to the 'normal,' to routine.

So run. It seemed the most sensible option, but the enormity of it struck him like an unassailable mountain: *how?* It was impossible: sure, they could buy plane tickets, get across the country – but there'd be a paper trail. Okay, fine, use cars – pack up, hit the road, make themselves more difficult to track. Buy a tent, camp out instead of staying at hotels to save money...but eventually, they'd have to buy food, and money would run out. And what about their families? They would panic, call the police, file missing persons report to try and find them. Should they risk informing their families when they were up against *demons?* The *kitsune* were smart; they'd start their hunt *with* their family. No; they'd have to let them suffer in ignorance in order to protect themselves, and even then, beyond that cruelty of just disappearing and not letting them even know if they were alive or dead, there'd always be the time-bomb, the ticking in the background drawing closer to the moment when the demons finally found them again –

Kenneth reached for Jacqueline's hand.

"When my father was dying, I didn't go to him." He looked up to find her staring down at the plume of thick gray smoke that rose, twisting in the air, from the burning shell down on the floor, where she had lit sage a little while ago. "I couldn't stand the way he looked. I couldn't face it. I just wanted things to go back to the way they were; I had never imagined a future filled with *cancer* and...and death. But it was there. It was hideous. Everything about it – the smell, the misery, the pain...it was too awful to face. He hurt so much...I could hear him, crying and moaning. I covered my ears at night sometimes, pressing a pillow over my head. Sometimes, I still think I hear him. He would call for me...and I didn't go. In my own way, I was running. It wasn't that I thought that if I could avoid it, or avoid him, that it would change anything; it was just that I was afraid to meet it head on, because it was terrifying. It was *unfair,* as childish as that sounds. Eventually, he stopped calling for me. And then he died."

She had grown very still; a calm resolve had come over her. She wasn't unafraid, he saw, but there was a new steadiness in her voice. "There is no running from this, Kenneth."

No...no, there isn't... He wanted to have her resolve, but instead, all he felt was a dim sense of hopelessness.

"He's the one who killed those people. It's him."

There was nothing more that either of them could think to say. Kenneth reached forward and pulled her to him, and unbelievably, she relaxed into his arms. He winced as she settled closer to his side, the skin from the wounds pulling slightly; she propped herself up on her elbow, readjusted her body, and lay down beside him, their heads close together on the pillow.

He awoke in the morning to a buzzing in his pocket. Jacqueline was still asleep. He pushed himself away and gingerly stood up; for a moment, his head spun, dizzy, but then he found his footing and made his way into her kitchen, his skin itching from the bandages, the slashes stinging.

His phone stopped, then began again, insistent. Eric's number flashed on the screen.

"Hello?"

"Kenneth." Eric sounded almost breathless. "You're okay..."

Kenneth mumbled something, but Eric cut him off. "I need you to meet me at your house. Can you get there soon?"

His mind sharpened, waking up with a start. "How soon? And why? What's going on? Are you alright?"

Eric's words came out in a hurried rush. Kenneth had never heard him sound like this before, and fear, fresh and new as the day, struck him in the gut. "I'm okay, but we need to meet in person. It's about...it's about the demons."

The demons. Kenneth's heartbeat slowed to a near halt. He'd never thought he'd ever hear *Eric* say those words so...so matter-of-factly.

"What's happened?"

"I'll explain at your house. I want to talk in person. It's *important,*" he emphasized, and Kenneth found himself nodding to the empty air. "You didn't call the police, did you? Are you planning on calling them?"

"...No."

"Good. Where are you?"

"I'm at Jacqueline's."

"Is she with you?"

"She's sleeping. I'll get her, and we can be over there in –"

"No." Eric's finality cut him off mid-sentence. "Don't bring her – don't even wake her. Are you sure she's still sleeping?"

"Eric, what's going on?"

"Just you. Don't wake her up," he added again, his voice almost commanding...but then it softened. "Just let her rest. It won't take us long, and we can go get her afterwards. When can you leave?"

"...I'll go now."

"Good. I'll meet you there in ten minutes, okay? If you get there before me, just wait. Don't go anywhere."

"Okay."

"Kenneth?"

"Yea?"

"You'll wait?"

"Yea."

"And don't bring Jacqueline."

"I won't. Eric, what –"

But the call dropped.

He beat the dawn to his driveway, a hastily scribbled note left behind for when Jacqueline woke. Inside the house, he called Eric to let him know he was there, but it went straight to voicemail.

He decided to wait in the living room. The silence only made him more anxious. A cloud of dust rose off the couch when he sat on it.

He tried Eric's phone again; still no answer.

He should have been there by now.

His phone rang, startling him. He sucked in his breath and fumbled to get it out of his pocket, expecting Eric...and instead saw Matthew Langton's name.

"Hello?"

"Oh thank *Christ*, you're alright. What's going on?"

Kenneth sat up straight. "What do you mean?"

"I came in early, and I just heard the police scanner. Local patrols are in route to *your* house. I heard the address –"

"*What?*"

"Why are police headed to your house?"

Kenneth felt a wondering amazement come over him. "I have no idea," he answered. His throat felt dry all of a sudden, and the dizziness returned. "What else was on the scanner?"

"I don't know, I just caught the end of it when I was walking by. Kenneth...are you in trouble? Did you call the police?"

"No, I didn't...I don't know what's going on."

"Then *leave.*" Matthew's voice had grown hushed and hurried. "Fuck everything else, just get out of there. Do you have a lawyer? Fuck it, do you have a car?"

"Yes, I –" But an alert from his phone suddenly buzzed in his ear. He pulled it back from his face; Jacqueline was calling. "Matthew, I'll call you back."

"Kenneth –"

He ended the call and swapped to her number. He was beginning to feel as though he were in a dream.

"Kenneth? Where are you?"

"I'm just over at my house," he said. "Did you get my note?"

"Yes, but that's not why I'm calling." She spoke in a rush. "I just got a call from Eric. He said he's over at *Caroline's.* He says he's been there since last night."

"*What?*"

"He said she didn't want to talk to him, so he had to follow her back home to convince her to speak to him, because he was worried the demons might go back to her place. I guess she let him stay, and he stayed the night in case they came back, but he says they didn't. They must still be in the woods...he said he's there now, and –"

"Did Eric call them demons?"

"What?"

"Did Eric call them *demons?*" He repeated, slowly now, even as his heart began to beat much too fast. He tried to stand and only succeeded in sinking back down into the couch, his legs giving out.

"Yes...yes, he did." She sounded uneasy. "And he told me he's talked to Caroline, and he wants me to come over right now and tell her everything, convince her to run. I told him I would wait for you to come with me, but he said there's no time..."

He said nothing. The colors were spinning. He held his head in his free hand, closing his eyes against the blur.

"....Kenneth?"

When he spoke, his mouth felt cottony, his mind still in a haze, but he understood. He didn't know *why* or *how,* but he knew, and the weight of it nearly crushed him.

"They got him, Jacqueline." He didn't even know quite what he meant by that, but he knew it was the truth. "The demons. They got to him. Don't....don't go over there."

"What do you mean?"

"Eric told me he'd meet me at my house. I just got a call from Matthew over at the *Times;* he said he heard that police are heading my way. I think it must have been Eric. I wonder what he told them..." He remembered Matthew warning him about how odd coincidences could look on paper, how crimes that were left unsolved for too long begged for easy solutions...

"Then they're there," she whispered.

"Who?"

"The demons. They're at Caroline's...and they must have Eric. Kenneth, Eric has his faults, but he wouldn't betray us like this."

He let out a hollow laugh. Oh, he loved her – she really saw the best in people sometimes. She didn't see that Eric was luring her there, probably to save himself.

"Kenneth..." Her voice cracked. "I'm going. I'm going to save him."

He tried not to panic. "*Save* him? Jacqueline, *don't.* I'll come back to your house – we can talk about this together."

"How quickly can you get back?"

"If I leave now, I can be back within ten minutes, and we can talk about it then..."

"There's no time to talk. You get here, and we go."

"Jacqueline." He swallowed, trying to steady his voice. "We could run. The demons could kill Eric at any moment, if they're there with him. He might already be dead."

"I'm not running." Her voice was hard. "I'm *going.* And it's not just Eric, Kenneth. What about *her* – what about Caroline Lahey? If she's there, and *they're* there, something might have happened to her. I don't think she has any idea the kind of monsters they are. She can't possibly know, and if she does, they've probably threatened her, too. We have a responsibility to do something, to warn her...and we've got to save Eric. I want to leave *now* –"

"Jacqueline, *please* – can you just wait until I get there?"

The answering silence lasted only a few seconds, but it felt like an age. "...Okay."

"You promise?"

"Yes."

"Okay, I'll be right over..."

"Kenneth?" Another beat, frightened, and then, "I love you," she said, and hung up.

Kenneth looked down at the empty screen, his eyes unfocused. He had to get up, had to leave this place, get back to Jacqueline's, and then...

And then, they're going to kill you. The thought came upon him with enough force to knock the air from his lungs. He knew it like he knew the sun would rise again tomorrow; if he went to that farm, he was certain that he would die. He was up against a force he couldn't beat. They had played a gambit with the traps; they had failed. His body still ached with the torn flesh from demonic claws; his soul still hurt with the torture of the fox fire.

And when he failed again...what would they do to Jacqueline?

I can't...he thought. *But I have to...* Fear came creeping over him. He felt his eyes well up with the terror of it, and blinking, a drop fell into his lap.

Suddenly, the room seemed brighter. *Dawn,* he thought for a moment, but no; the light seemed to come from the very edges of the room, and with it, a gentle warmth. The warmth reached out and touched his back, caressing him; it felt so natural that

Kenneth closed his eyes and leaned back into it. With his eyes closed, he could almost feel it, this formless thing that reached over his shoulders now and felt like a pair of thin, small arms wrapping around him, hugging him. He reached up and could have sworn he could feel the weight of the flesh there, smooth, feel soft, feathery hair brushing against the side of his face...

But he knew that if he opened his eyes, it would be gone.

A voice spoke.

Kenneth, it said. *You have to save her. If you stay here, Jacqueline will leave without you, and she will die.*

"I know." His voice trembled. He didn't question what this thing was, this voice – everything in the world had narrowed down to terror and necessity. Everything had become too big, too unbelievable, and in the enormity of that realization, now everything was possible. In the back of his mind, he thought he was probably having a breakdown, which he figured had been a long time coming, anyways, but what the voice said made perfect sense: he didn't doubt for a moment that he needed to protect her, didn't need any convincing. Love was enough, would always be enough, to convince him, and even if it meant giving his life to save her, he meant to see this through. Even if it meant believing that some supernatural being, *an angel,* was speaking to him, right this very moment. "That's why I'm afraid."

You can't let Jaden kill her.

"I know," he repeated. Something inside of him felt like it was crumbling away. He was certain that Jacqueline was wrong; Eric *had* betrayed them. He knew it in the same way he believed his own life was worthless. He didn't even blame Eric, what with this warmth around him, encasing him in its protective embrace; he felt forgiveness already replacing the shock in his heart. Whatever had happened, whatever had moved Eric to do this, it was bigger than him, and it had probably destroyed some part of him in the process.

Who could fight back in the face of such things, and somehow win? *Him?* Here he was, coming apart at the seams. Kenneth drew a deep, jagged breath; he hoped Eric would be alright, in the end, whatever that end looked like for him. He hoped that maybe he could get to him in time, hoped that Jacqueline would change her mind, tell him they needed to forget Eric, forget Caroline, and just run, escape the demons –

His voice was strangled. "Why won't he leave her alone...?"

It sounded almost as though the creature sighed, or sobbed; a shudder passed through its incorporeal being. *We have people we belong to. People we are meant to love. And if we fall...if we let that go...we still find ourselves drawn to them. He wants to kill her. You cannot let that happen.*

He struggled to understand – it said 'we' as if it and the *kitsune* were the same. But Jacqueline had said an angel had told her that Jaden would never stop... "Are you...hers?"

She is not mine, the voice replied. *I am not hers.*

"Can you protect her?" This light, this warmth....it filled him with trust. Surely whatever this was, it could defeat a demon.

I'll do what I can for her, but I'm falling. I can't help much longer. I can't guarantee I'll be there when she needs me. I need you to save her from him. You cannot let him kill her.

He would do everything he could to stop it, but... "I'm too weak," he whispered. Eric, who he thought was made of stronger stuff, had somehow succumbed to those terrifying monsters of nightmare – what was *he* supposed to do now? Shoot a little straighter? "Tell me how to save her," he begged, "and I'll do whatever it takes."

The angel spoke. Kenneth listened, horrified at first, then so, so scared, and finally, shaking, clutching what he thought were the arms of this small, warm thing that had embraced his neck, its warm cheek pressed against his own, his eyes still squeezed shut, he nodded.

He would go through with it.

Are you frightened? It asked him.

"Yes," he whispered. He'd never been more scared in his entire life. Every part of him felt shocked into action by terror, but it didn't matter: he could picture Jacqueline in his mind now, telling him *there's no running from this.*

It might not have to happen, the angel told him. *It might not come to that. But if it does, that is the one thing, the single most powerful thing you can do. It might be enough to protect her, to grant me enough time to save her, because if it comes to that –*

Kenneth nodded, sick. Yes, if it came to *that,* it would take an angel, or something with equal power, to save her. There would be no escape at that point.

He didn't know if he would have the strength to stand up in a moment, let alone to go through with what the angel had told him. He hoped – desperately – it would not happen, for all their sakes. "I'll do it," he said. And then, his heart breaking, he whispered, "I wish...I wish I had been different. Or better." The angel made the sound again that resembled a sob, and it felt as though the arms tightened around him. "And I wish I could see you now."

Someday, you will.

That wasn't a comforting thought.

The angel, and its warmth, disappeared.

In the face of despair, Kenneth found the strength to stand, gathered his keys, and went out to his car. He could hear sirens in the distance.

FOURTEEN

Jaden sat up in bed, every sense tuned in for the sound of a car in the driveway.

He'd been feeding on Eric for nearly twelve hours, feasting on what tasted like spoiled meat now that the boy was haunted. At some point in the early morning when Eric had come in to check on his wounds, he had sunk his jaws in with vicious abandon, watching uninterestedly as Eric nearly fell unconscious from the pain of it.

The boy had fallen to his knees, white-faced and unable to breathe. When Jaden finally allowed him a reprieve, Eric stumbled to his feet, swayed, and then collapsed back down to the floor, ashen.

Jaden was troubled in the back of his mind by a niggling doubt; would he be able to eat Jacqueline's soul, to wrench it from her body? The haunted soul felt *looser,* somehow, yes, but it was still firmly in there – he could tear, shred, and maybe, he thought, considering, *maybe if I use fox fire and burn it away for a while...* but no, he didn't want to waste any of it. His fists clutched the sheets next to him.

He wanted it all.

He swallowed, tasting the desire of it; it was maddening.

Another thought, more troublesome: where had the angel gone? And: would it return? Would it try to stop him....?

He wanted the angel almost as badly: the angel could give him answers to everything he desperately wanted to know...but in the absence of its presence, he would be satisfied with just Jacqueline's soul.

Oh, *so satisfied.*

A sound alerted him; Caroline had gotten up, and he had heard Kuro leave earlier. Jaden's attention slid fell on Eric. The boy had sat up again, but his eyes were fogged.

"Get up," Jaden ordered him. He flicked his gaze toward the door, and with a silent, obedient nod, Eric stood, and left.

He could hear them talking, followed by the sound of her dog running around the house, barking. She must have let it out of the barn, he realized; what a pain...*the dog will be around.*

So he would kill it, a minor inconvenience. He knew Jacqueline would be there soon, summoned by Eric, and then...he would have her. Kenneth would be arrested, which would suit Jaden just fine: he made a promise not to kill him, and to break a promise of that magnitude, well...he wasn't sure what the consequences for himself would be, but instinct and the *holy dark* warned him that it would be commensurate with the gravity of the promise broken. It stood to reason, he thought, that killing Kenneth would most likely mean the death of *him.*

And what about Caroline?

He had a notion of how to be done with her. On one hand, Kuro wouldn't leave Caroline – he was smitten, and worse...*changed.* He shuddered to think of what had happened to him, but any change, he thought, could possibly be undone. Kuro was too simple-minded, too soft to see the easiest way... but Jaden was confident. He was of a curious, analytical nature, and the pattern of his mind followed a scientific process: a hypothesis, followed by a test, and lastly, an analysis of the data. The foundation of his theory was that at some point, Kuro had become a *myobu,* *her myobu* no less, which meant he was unnaturally bonded to that girl. It was important, if things were to go back to the way they were (and Jaden had every intention of returning things to the way they were), that the current state of affairs changed.

But the *how* of it would be a difficult knot to untangle.

There would be no persuading Kuro to kill Caroline; he knew that. But killing *Eric,* on the other hand...*yes,* Jaden, thought, that he could do; Kuro had been a *nogitsune;* he could become one again. He could persuade Kuro to kill *him,* and that would turn her away from him, might shift whatever invisible abacus moved the pieces of their unnatural bond.

And by then, he would have devoured Jacqueline. It would have been simpler to kill Jacqueline at her own home, but then he would have only been partially satisfied. No, he needed Kuro to return *here,* too late to save the girl; Jaden would promise Kuro that Eric had played a role in Jacqueline's death, which would be the truth...and Jaden felt certain that he could tip Kuro over the edge if he told him of Eric's other desires, convince him that he was a threat to his happiness, and inside the very walls of her home, Caroline would watch Kuro kill a man in cold blood. She would reject him, and surely that would cause her to release whatever strange hold she had over Kuro, so that he could once again feed from other humans.

And then nothing would hold them to this miserable pile of dirt, and they would move on.

He would have everything he wanted.

It was a gamble, of course; Kuro had grown unpredictable as of late, and obnoxiously *squeamish*...but his love for him would move him, or at the very least, his love for Caroline. He would see

Jaden's mangled leg, see the very real pain he was in, see the dead body of the girl in the dirt...and be reminded of how Eric knew and allowed it all to happen, would think of the greater threat Eric could become. Kuro would have his revenge, his *justice,* as Jaden would sell it to him, and they would resume their lives. *Together.*

The dog continued to bark.

He worked a muscle in his jaw; he hated that sound. The dog was running back and forth under the bedroom window, snarling.

There was another possibility, one that had occurred to him but that he did not want to entertain as a potential outcome: what if his plan worked, but Caroline did *not* reject Kuro? What if she overcame her horror and revulsion at the murderers who stood before her, looked past the dead bodies of Eric and Jacqueline, and *still* held onto his soul? Kuro would never be free...

Jaden looked down at his hand, considering.

Some knots were too hard to untangle. He thought of Alexander the Great then, drawing his sword, and slicing through his problem.

A door shut, and Caroline and Eric came back into the house. Jaden latched onto his soul and tore it a little more, just to try his strength; the *holy dark* was sustaining him, and for every ounce he used to numb the pain in his body, he replaced it with what the boy had to offer, contaminated as it was.

He could hear her telling Eric to sit down, that he didn't look so good. He tried to protest, mumbled something, and then Jaden heard her footsteps approaching.

There came a knock at the door.

She looked a little tired, but pretty in her rough, unpolished way. Her hair hung down loose over her back, and she was wearing a pair of overalls. *She intends to work outside today,* he thought. That was hardly surprising; a bright, clear day was coming through the window now, the rare sort of gem in the November autumn.

"How are you doing?"

He shrugged. "Better than I expected." He slid his foot down to the floor to test the weight, but she protested. He stopped and settled back onto the bed.

"Do you need anything? I'm going to make Eric some breakfast. Do you want some toast, or coffee...?"

"Eggs and coffee would be wonderful."

"Coming right up."

Jaden watched her leave; he rather liked being fussed over, though he had abhorred Eric's touch as he cleaned his wounds – deep down, in that part of him that he kept carefully concealed, he hated nearly all physical contact, but this was no matter: he often did things he did not enjoy, because they were the swiftest or most suitable means to an end, the surest way to manipulate and achieve the response he wanted in people. He had long ago mastered his own revulsion of physical intimacy in order to weaponize his body and capitalize on all it was capable of; his intellect had succeeded in strangling the part of his soul that recoiled against touch, and the result was a man bereft of any preference or desire other than the ability to conquer or dominate as needed.

But Eric especially disgusted him. He had told the boy what to do when Jacqueline arrived, told him what lies to say. He had given Eric two jobs: get Jacqueline out of her car, and *keep Caroline in the house.*

Jaden threw the sheet back and tested his leg on the ground; the pain was immediate and searing. He sucked in his breath and forced himself to stand, ignoring the agony that shot up the length of his body; behind him, an inhuman tail cracked out like a whip, and for a moment, he could see the ghosts of long claws instead of human hands. The *holy dark* settled him; he focused on it, letting it fill him, and felt the sense of his pain disappear until he could ignore it entirely; it felt like detaching himself from a part of his own mind, an act he was practiced and proficient at: it was the only way to cope with the constant roaring of wind in his head. He didn't understand why he suffered from it, what it *was*, because Kuro didn't experience it: if he did, he would have assumed it plagued all demons...but no.

It was the first of many questions he had hoped to ask the angel.

He froze when he heard the sound of a car pull up, its tires crunching over the gravel.

On cue, he heard Eric's chair scrape back as Caroline wondered out loud who it was, and Eric answered, "She's just a friend of mine. I called and asked her to bring me a change of clothes."

Caroline's answer was puzzled. "I could have given you some of Christopher's."

And Eric's response, too fast to sound natural, "That's alright. I'll go out and get them. Be right back."

And the front door opened, and closed. Jaden called for Caroline, and in a moment, she was there.

"You shouldn't be standing!"

"It's alright." He smiled and reached forward, taking her hands. She started and nearly pulled back from him, but his demeanor caught her off guard enough to allow him to turn her around, to push her gently down into a sitting position on the bed. He stood in front of her, smiling. His heart was nearly leaping with excitement, an unrestrained joy he had only felt once before. He was moments from it, he knew; he was *minutes* from it, from eating Jacqueline's soul, and he could reach out and *feel* it, just at the end of the driveway –

"Jaden, what's going on?"

His face had clouded, the smile frozen. There weren't just two human souls outside.

There were *three.*

For a moment, he had been unable to hide his expression; a snarl, a flash of anger came, and went. He snapped back to himself just in time to clamp down on his fury...but not enough, he saw, to prevent her from seeing. Caroline was worried; he felt the stirring of fear move in her soul.

Eric was supposed to come back inside at this point and, under some pretext, keep Caroline in the room, away from the kitchen, where the front window might give her a view she didn't need to see.

But Eric hadn't come back, and that third soul was familiar... Jaden ground his teeth; he hadn't imagined a version of these events where something went *wrong*. It was a simple plan: Kenneth was supposed to have been arrested by now, Jacqueline was supposed to be alone, and Eric was supposed to stall her, then come back inside. Jacqueline would be dead by the time Kuro returned and realized the part he had played.

But none of that was happening now.

A girl's voice – the only girl's voice he longed to hear, clear and bright – was beginning to shout, and she was saying –

"Caroline!"

"What?" Caroline jumped to her feet. Jaden reached out and shoved her down, just hard enough to startle her.

He locked eyes with her and spoke in his most commanding tone – the low, quiet one, smooth and dangerous.

"Do you love Kuro?"

"*What?*"

"I know you do," he said. She winced suddenly; he had raked across her soul and touched the embers of her love, as if to remind her of it. "Then listen to me. *Stay in this house.* Stay in this room. Do you understand me?"

"Why?"

His anger stirred; he wanted to strike her, or to pierce her soul in some painful spot, but he held himself in check, strangling his impulsivity with a single thought: *Kuro.*

"Because he loves you," he snapped, and turned to go.

"Jaden!"

"*Stay* in this room, Caroline."

Caroline was on her feet, already fast on his heels. He slammed the door and locked it from the outside, annoyed by her shouting. He had expected to over-awe her, to frighten her with his look, but it had been just the opposite; her soul had risen to the challenge and surged against him, ready to *fight.*

This would be tough to explain to her later on, he thought, but it wouldn't matter too much then; in fact, it would probably help to undo what she had done to Kuro. It was an evolving situation, he thought, his mouth quirking wryly. Not ideal, but workable.

He couldn't think of that now, though. His desire was all-consuming as he stalked to the front of the house; he imagined the moment the soul would let go of Jacqueline's body, imagined it coming into him, imagined some feeling, the gnawing emptiness being filled at last, being so totally sated and satisfied...and his mouth salivated.

Jaden stepped out into the sunlight, the screen swinging shut behind him.

"*Caroline! Caroline Lahey!*"

They had parked at the end of the driveway, back near the fence line. Jacqueline was standing outside the passenger door of Kenneth's pick-up truck, shouting as loud as her voice could carry. Jaden could practically already feel her skin under his hands, could picture the exquisite wonder of how it would be to wrap his fingers around that throat of hers, where the cords now stood out, and feel the delicate flow of her life under his fingertips...

And squeeze.

No angel, he thought, feeling the edges of her soul. *What a shame,* but also, *what a gift.*

He smiled.

"Caroline La –" The shout cut off in a gasp as their gazes collided.

Outside the driver side door, Kenneth McMahon stood, Eric beside him. Kenneth stared at Jaden near the house now, and a sad, knowing look came across his face.

"Oh, Eric," Jacqueline breathed. There was so much sorrow in her voice as she realized the betrayal. "How could you?"

Eric looked back at Jaden, his skin sickly, dark patches under his eyes, before turning back to Kenneth.

"You weren't supposed to be here," he said, his voice hoarse. "The police...you would have been safe..."

"Eric, stop talking." Kenneth's voice was oddly calm and devoid of judgement as he reached into his back pocket, and Jaden watched, ill-humored, as he drew out the gun and readied it with curiously steady hands. "You need to run."

"Kenneth –"

"Eric." Kenneth turned to him, and Jaden froze. Even from a distance, he could feel the change in the boy's soul: resolve so deep it sunk to its core. It was resigned, and with that resignation, there was certainty...and courage. *Warmth.*

The angel, Jaden thought suddenly, without understanding why...but no; it wasn't with him. He would have felt its presence.

Kenneth clipped the magazine into the gun. "You don't need to explain. Take Jacqueline, and get out of here."

Three things happened all at once: first, Jaden stepped forward, his human form melting away. He stretched his body out, tail and head erect, and ignited a wall of fox fire between Eric and the others. It blazed between them, and Eric fell backwards, scrambling on his hands and feet in the gravel.

At the same time, a gun shot rang out, exploding into the

front door, right where Jaden's head had been when he stood as a human, just as Feral came tearing around the corner of the house. For a moment, two thoughts went through Jaden's mind – first, how fortunate he was that the bandages seemed to have assimilated when he shifted, and how grateful he was that he had amassed so much power, to be able to stand on his injured leg; and secondly, that that miserable, wretched farm girl must have suspected something about him, deep in some hidden corner of her heart, and let the dog out *on purpose* in case he tried to leave the house today.

Feral charged him, leaping. Jaden pressed flat down and surged upward, slicing through skin, fat, and flesh with his front claws, and unseamed the animal from its inner groin to its throat. It fell down in a whimpering, steaming pile of offal, its intestines glittering wetly in the sun.

From the ground, Eric watched, horrified, his mouth moving in some sort of idiotic repetition of unspoken protest, a half-strangled scream that couldn't quite break free of his shock.

Jaden crouched and turned to Kenneth, a long, warning hiss escaping his jaws. A second gunshot nearly hit him in the flank.

"*Eric!*" Kenneth shouted. "*Get. UP! Get. JACQUELINE! RUN!*"

But Eric's eyes were locked on Jaden. "You lied...you lied..."

I lied, Jaden leered. He threw his head back and felt the *holy dark* rise, and from outside of him again, near each of his flanks, the blues flames of fox fire wheeled and suddenly ignited, surging toward them.

Kenneth flung himself forward and pushed Eric out of the way. The collision was enough to knock sense into him; Eric suddenly shot to his feet, leaving Kenneth struggling on the ground, and took off running toward his car.

"*Eric!*" Kenneth rolled over and struggled to stand, screaming for him. "*Take Jacqueline with you!*"

Jaden brought another wave of fox fire upon him, his snout pulling back in a snarl as he watched the boy collapse inside the blue flames.

But from within, *impossibly,* Kenneth still found the strength to aim.

Jaden dodged a third bullet and leapt, dashing around the back of the car now, the flames gone. He could see Jacqueline running around the front, heading for Kenneth.

"She's in the house!"

The *kitsune* drew up short, his ears flat. Eric was at his own car, the door wrenched open, but he had stopped, his eyes rolling back wildly, and the voice that came tearing out of him was desperate. *"Caroline is in the house!"*

Jacqueline had reached Kenneth and was helping him to stand. Jaden roared; if he had to summon an *inferno* to destroy them, he would do it, whatever the cost –

Eric looked into the demon's eyes, and in his terror, slammed the car door, the engine rumbling to life, and in another moment, a cloud of dust was racing after it as he hurtled down the driveway, abandoning the friends he had betrayed.

Cowards, all, Jaden grinned. *Just us now.* He slashed at the back tire of Kenneth's truck with his front paw, the sound of leaking air wheezing out. He came forward, slashed the front one, and lowered his head to the ground, ears flat back. *Let the girl go, boy. You don't have to die.*

Kenneth was on his feet now; he shoved Jacqueline behind him, and with all the strength in him, shouted, *"Caroline Lahey! If you can hear me, you need to run!"*

Jaden snarled and surged forward, heard the gun go off a fourth time, and felt a fiery pain trail along his back as the bullet grazed across his flank. He roared with the fury and pain of it, the *holy dark* crackling now as he fought the limitations of his own body.

The gun fired again, the bullet whizzing by the side of his chest; had he been in his human form, Kenneth would have had him through the heart. Behind them, Jacqueline screamed and fell backward as Jaden ducked low and leapt, slamming Kenneth to the ground, hissing as he batted the gun out of his hand, shredding the boy's forearm with his claws. The tip of one claw had touched the gun; for a moment, Jaden's leg had felt as though it were speared by fire, then went numb.

A spray of blood sent the gun skittering away in the dirt, and Jaden dug in his back claws, sending ribbons of lacerations down Kenneth's legs.

The boy reached up and gripped his forepaws with all his might, screaming wordlessly as he fought to hold him in place. Jacqueline ran for the gun and snatched it up from the dirt.

He wrenched away in time to avoid the bullet; it shattered the front kitchen window behind them. He crouched again, muscles tensing for the spring, and leapt for her, but he had been using too much of the *holy dark;* the pain in his back leg caught him unawares, and he screamed, stumbling.

Bleeding as he was, Kenneth was already on his feet and running back to where the girl stood.

Jaden roared and reached for her soul, gripping it. The girl gasped with the shock of it and stumbled. He approached, haunches low, a long snarl growing in his throat, as Kenneth struggled to pull her up, shouting at her.

"*He's –*" She was gasping, trying to get the words out, her eyes locked on him, and a hand flew toward her chest, where her heart was. The other hand gripped dirt and gravel, supporting herself up, but she was collapsing now, he was sure of it...

He was thirty paces away now, twenty-five; he dug in deeper, with everything he had, the *holy dark* rising up in him with the effort, the pain in his leg excruciating as he gripped her soul, wrenching, *heaving*, trying to grasp its haunted edges where despair had unmoored it and find some way to make it his, because *it IS mine,* he thought, just as he screamed *your soul belongs to me!*

"You can't have it!" Kenneth turned and raced straight at him, and before he could prepare himself, the human had collided with him, shoved him to the ground, and used the force of his elbow to try and crush his throat. Jaden let out of a yelp of surprise, his concentration broken, and in that moment, Jacqueline's soul escaped him, his grip lost.

"Run!" Kenneth twisted in the dirt, screaming. *"Run, Jacqueline!"*

She looked at him and saw the look in his eyes, so certain and reassuring, pleading, *begging* her to go, to *listen to him* and take this gift.

She gasped, turned, and fled for the trees.

Already Jacqueline's form was growing smaller, but that didn't matter to Jaden; he could catch her. He knew that forest very well now. He could track her to the edge of nothingness, if he had to.

He just had to get rid of *him.*

The boy had stopped him once; he wouldn't let it happen again.

An anger beyond rage broke through all of his tightly held control; the roaring in his head crescendoed, stripping his judgement away until all that was left was ungovernable, all-encompassing desire, and Jaden wrenched away from the boy's body, drew his front paw back, and slashed.

The first swipe cut down across his collarbone. Kenneth winced, insensible to the blood, and still screamed at her to "Run – *run!*"

He might have spared him if not for those words.

A flash of maroon struck out, and Kenneth screamed no more. Four streaks ripped open his throat. The boy had been moving too much; the wounds hadn't been deep enough to immediately sever those life-giving veins, but they had opened them up to the end. Jaden reared back and shredded the boy's core with one, two more swipes, the second deeper, and felt the tight slicing of organs bursting open beneath him, the rank stench of death and blood filling the air.

He bared his teeth for a killing bite, but he froze, some deep instinct moving in him, bringing him back from the edge of madness; the boy was dying, looking up at him from the ground with hurting, dark eyes, somehow not at all surprised, but pained.

His skin prickled as a promise almost broken began to crawl up his spine. *I've killed him,* he thought; the rage that had driven him from his mind receded, and he drew in a long, shaking breath. He backed away in horror, shuddering at the rage that had possessed him; Kenneth lay gasping on the ground, fallen near the rotting fence, dying.

He had ruined all of his own plans...

No, he told himself; *not yet – he's not dead yet. How long until the promise is broken?* He fought for control of himself, steading his breathing, and slowly drew the *holy dark* inward, numbing the pain in his leg and shoulder, his tail lowered. How long did he have?

He shifted to his human form and knelt by the boy, studying him with an almost tender expression. Kenneth was still gasping, his breath hitching as blood filled his throat. He wouldn't look away from him. Jaden reached out to touch his soul and burst into harsh, barking laughter.

It was desperately holding on to life.

"That's good," he whispered. It was so absurd that it would fight to cling to that frayed and beaten cage of flesh, but there it was – it was fighting to *live,* to *stay,* and it was nearly burning with the effort and determination to do so. Jaden knew it wouldn't succeed, but still: with that much spirit, who knew how long he would last?

Long enough for him to kill the girl.

He closed his eyes for a moment, sighing; he wanted so much more...but Jacqueline alone would have to be enough, now. Perhaps he would survive the broken promise; perhaps it wouldn't kill him...but even if it did, he would eat her soul first.

He pulled back from Kenneth's soul; any touch now might be too much for the fragile thing, and he didn't want to push it toward death and break the promise. He stood up and found himself chuckling again, amused at the ridiculousness of it all, his hands bloodied from where his claws had cut Kenneth down. "You keep fighting – you hold on as long as you can," he mocked. He studied the boy; the resolve was still there in those silent, dark eyes. "You know..." He leaned down, his voice quiet. "When I saw you today, I thought you looked different. I thought *the angel* was with you. I thought it would save you." He leaned in further, taunting; something had flickered in those fading eyes. "Do you think it'll save *her*?"

A sharp pain in his right eye suddenly made him wince. He blinked rapidly, annoyed. Unsurprised, he looked down at his palm, where the clear disc with the blue iris lay.

He took a step forward toward the trees, scanning. Time to go; he was working against the clock of Kenneth's impending death and the uncertain fate that awaited himself when it came. Perhaps the angel would return to Jacqueline, and if so, he would face it down, then...he would do as much as he could before the broken promise claimed his life.

He felt her just as he moved to step forward, the soul that had stepped out of the house. For a split second, he considered leaving. Jacqueline was out there; he could catch her now, easily. *Jacqueline*, he thought, longingly. But also...

Kuro.

Kuro, who was bound to the woman who now stood behind him.

Jaden sighed as he turned around.

Caroline had taken a dozen steps outside her kitchen door before she came to a halt. The shoulder of her shirt was torn, the skin scraped and bloody. She had fought against the door and finally freed herself by repeatedly slamming against it. He should have counted on that, he thought; hadn't he touched her soul in that moment, hadn't he known the spirit it contained? He must have realized, almost immediately, that she was not the kind of woman to stay quietly locked up in a room while screams and gunshots echoed outside.

Maybe he *had* realized it. Maybe he had wanted this.

Now there's a thought. He smiled.

She glanced down, saw the dismembered body of her dog, saw the boy dying in the grass, and looked back at him, silent. He didn't have to touch her soul to know that she had seen him strike the boy down, too. He could tell by the way she was looking at him...looking at his eye.

He reached up to cover it instinctually and stopped.

It didn't matter now.

Slowly, he let his arm fall away, openly looking back with one maroon iris that revealed everything in a single, silent stare.

For the first time, she really saw him. He expected horror, or even terror, but there was none; her response, so incomprehensible, angered him. Fear he could understand, fear he could *feed* off of...but she looked back at him with a great sadness, a near longing for something he didn't grasp.

"Caroline," he said, almost apologetic. He smiled again, a slow smile that resembled a sheepish apology, but even then she wouldn't look away. She only frowned. "I told you to stay inside."

As she looked at him, she thought for a moment that blood had suddenly begun to flow from an open wound at the top of his head, sliding down through his hair, but no; it was pure *color* that was flowing downward, and as it did, Jaden reached up, plucked the other contact lens away, and flung both into the grass. Without flinching, she watched as he walked toward her, his brown hair sliding into maroon, as he smiled warmly at her with the eyes of a devil.

She walked forward to meet him.

FIFTEEN

Kuro could smell blood before he could see it; his tail quivered at the thick scent of it. He ran forward, clearing the tree line, leapt the fence, and found himself skidding in the gravel, his mind racing in the effort to make sense of everything. There was the smell of gunpowder, acrid, stinging; and the kitchen window...glass was glittering on the ground, sparkling in the sun's rays. Blood, *human blood,* was drying, and blacker, thicker stuff, too...

Whose car is that? A truck sat at the end of the driveway, precariously lurched to one side, both right tires shredded. Another smell hit him – the smell of open, leaking wounds, of punctured organs, and he looked up and saw Feral in front of the house. He approached, his heart slowing; the sunlight was too harsh suddenly, blinding, and the sound of the flies that buzzed around the dog's carcass filled all the world with their roaring.

Caroline!

He reached out for her and felt her presence; it answered him from the garden. Kuro turned, his stomach lurching, and ran around the house.

At the entrance to the garden he slowed, his form shifting without his realizing. He stood on human legs, a human arm reaching out to steady himself against the fence. He tried to shout her name, but there was no air in his lungs.

She was standing in the middle of the garden, right where he had seen them the first time together, where they had picnicked so many times before, speaking with Jaden. He could see her lips moving, but he was too far away to make out the words, much too far away to hear. Jaden was listening intently, his arms folded across his chest. He seemed bemused; his brow was furrowed, a slightly smug, almost playful smirk on his face, like a parent indulging a child they weren't particularly fond of. Whatever she was telling him, she was saying it with adamant conviction; even from this distance, he could see it in her face, could feel it in her soul, that pure, shining strand of absolute faith.

But Jaden only smiled wider, kindly even, shaking his head: *no,* he seemed to be saying, his mind made up about something. Caroline was undeterred; she narrowed her eyes, insistent, her hands moving in the air in an effort to help make her point.

Jaden sighed, tilting his head, and only then did Kuro notice what should have struck him first: Jaden's hair and eyes were their true color.

He wasn't hiding any more.

Kuro managed one stumbling step forward, swallowing. "Caroline," he gasped. And then, stronger, *"Caroline!"*

They both stopped and turned to him; Jaden's expression was one of slight regret, and Caroline was momentarily surprised.

But she smiled at him suddenly, the worry lifting away. The sun caught in her eyes, and they sparkled as they crinkled around the edges, her soul flaring with its love for him. He tried to call her name again, found himself reaching forward, but she turned away, back to Jaden, her voice lower and the words coming more quickly now.

She reached out and took him by the hands, squeezing. Kuro had never seen Jaden so openly surprised, startled even, but he didn't pull away.

For a moment, Kuro had the impossible thought that Jaden would agree with whatever Caroline was imploring him to do, then would nod and turn to him, smiling and waving at him to join them. Kuro would walk over, and whatever bloody business had happened here, it would all be explained away, forgiven and forgotten. They would go inside; they would have breakfast. The rhythm of an uninteresting life would resume.

They would pretend there wasn't slaughter just outside her front door.

It was a comforting, fleeting fantasy, gone in an instant.

Kuro found his legs could still work; he took a stumbling step forward, then another, but it was like walking through quicksand.

And Jaden did nod at last. His face grew contemplative and serious, and Kuro watched as he gently pulled his hands away from her.

His throat was burning. He was telling himself to run, but his legs had stopped responding, frozen with a crust of terror that he couldn't break through. It felt as though his ribs were constricting his very lungs; he couldn't breathe, could barely bring himself to watch.

"Jaden," he managed, his voice breaking.

Jaden took a single, smooth step forward, slipping behind Caroline. Kuro could see her face; she was still smiling at him, but it was sad now; some weight had settled upon her, he could feel it, but her love, her assurance, was still intact, and it pushed through, reaching for him. *Holding* on to him.

Kuro watched as Jaden brought his left arm gently around Caroline's torso, his right arm moving around her shoulder, through her hair, the fingertips resting delicately on the left edge of her throat. He looked like a lover who had come up behind his intended, his body neatly molded to hers, arms wrapped fully around her in an intimate embrace, his lips on the edge of her ear. He said something; her smile didn't waver, but her lips – full and rich and soft – pressed together with the fleeting knowledge of regret and disappointment.

What had she tried to do? What had she said to him? Had she failed? She must not have thought so; this woman before him had never been meek. This was the woman who had raised a gun in the night and captured a demon, a woman who dared to touch him and came to know and love him. She would not lay herself down senselessly as a victim: this stillness in her now as she didn't move, as she let Jaden pull her back into the warmth of his body, was her way of fighting the demon she now understood and recognized for who he truly was.

She must have never considered that she could be wrong. Even now, on the very edge of death, with a murderer whispering in her ear, she believed she would succeed in whatever it was she had tried to accomplish.

She lifted her gaze to Kuro, and her eyes fixed him with more love than he thought he could ever deserve. He understood then that he had kept his promise: she understood everything now. She knew the truth, as inescapable as the arms around her...and still, she loved him.

"Please," he managed, begging, his voice a choked whisper now. "Please, no...don't..."

Kuro felt the stirring of the *holy dark* before he saw the ends of Jaden's hands fade away into claws. They sunk deep into her flesh and simultaneously ripped backward, opening her throat and abdomen in a single, fluid motion. The demon stepped back neatly as Caroline crumpled forward, then stared down at her body in the grass.

It had taken only a second.

Kuro screamed, but the sound seemed to come from a long

way off, as though it had traveled underwater to get to his own ears. At last his legs came unglued; he ran forward and fell to his knees, reaching for her. He tried to turn her over, his hands slipping in the hot liquid, her body convulsing. His hands flailed, pressing, grasping, trying first to stop the bleeding from her torso, to push the organs back inside, but her throat –

She was choking on her own blood, and it was bursting out of her in weakening but steady spurts. Both of his hands shook as he tried to stop the blood flow, his palms slipping across her skin in the slick horror of her receding life. Jaden had cut deep and true; the end would come quick.

Her right arm came up, reaching for his elbow. He was crying, he realized; he was speaking, pleading with her to live, saying her name over and over again. He could feel her soul now – it felt like it was melting, overflowing and spreading, like the thawing meadows in spring, rushing away from him.

Leaving.

She was trying to grip his elbow, trying to smile at him. The kindness and the warmth hadn't left her eyes even though their ability to focus was gone. He was sobbing, he knew, but all he could hear was the sound of her guttural, wet attempts for air. He held on to her soul with everything in him; if he could just hold on, he thought, she wouldn't die, *she can't die,* and she was looking back at him, a note of desperation and fear in her eyes now as she understood what was happening, holding on to him, too. No, he wouldn't let her go alone – he would *go with her,* through that place inside of every soul, that door where wind rushed through into a greater darkness than the one inside them – into the Dark itself, into whatever nightmare was beyond, he would follow her soul and stay with her –

You have to let go.

He gasped as a warmth stole over him. It came creeping like the sun over the mountains at dawn, first a gray lightening, a ray, and then the breaking of it inside of his heart. He felt it on his back, saw it in her eyes. *The angel,* he thought dimly, too numb to care. *I'm not going to let go, I'm going with her –*

A strange thing began to happen to him. He felt a sudden lightening in his body, as though the seams of himself were being gently undone. *I'll go with you,* he told her, silent, and somehow he was sure that she heard him; he had pulled her up into his arms, hugging her; something had slid out, wet and heavy, into the grass, and her arm fell away from his elbow.

They were both going to slip away. This was beyond his understanding, this feeling of dissolving...but he gave himself over to it, feeling her death pulling him with her toward the door in her soul, open now in the coming of death.

You have to let go of him.

Kuro looked up, wild and searching.

You have to let him go, the voice repeated more gently, insistent now.

Jaden stood apart from him, already distracted; he had not heard the voice. He was looking off into the trees, scanning for something. He was oblivious of the angel's presence *here,* right *here,* completely uninterested in Kuro at his feet. He couldn't hear the voice...

But Caroline could.

It's talking to her, he realized. The last of the light flickered in Caroline's eyes. They could both hear the angel; they felt it in their hearts. The warmth grew steadier, and with it, the voice came through again, clear and final, an insistent, commanding edge to it. *You can't take him with you. He needs to stay here.*

Her eyes had an unnatural glassiness, but then a single moment of understanding illuminated them, as though she had learned an answer to a question he hadn't heard her ask. Blood had collected at the edges of her mouth, but the corners turned up just slightly into a smile. Something solid reconnected inside of

Kuro, and the lightness, the feeling of floating, was gone. The door he had felt himself slipping through had slammed shut. His body was heavy again, the earth solid beneath him.

She was leaving him behind.

"Caroline, please," he gasped; he could feel her soul slowly disentangling itself, pulling away first at the edges, then the center, *lifting* away from him all at once – and the world opened again to everything in it, except for her.

"*No! Let me go with you!*"

But she was already gone.

He screamed until he felt blood in his throat, until his lungs burned for air. Her body slipped out of his arms into the dirt, her eyes open and empty.

Jaden turned toward him, glancing down at him in mild surprise.

His voice was maddeningly calm, intellectual in its callousness. "You won't believe me right now, but this wasn't my original intention. I told her to stay in the house."

Kuro looked up through his tears and stared at him in disbelief. Jaden reacted to whatever he saw in his eyes and bristled.

"You're understandably upset right now," he said dismissively. "But soon, it'll be better. She let go of you, didn't she?"

Kuro stared at him, unspeaking. He felt like a specimen that had been housed under the cloche of her soul; the glass had lifted away, and now in rushed too many sensations, too much of all the rest of the world. She had kept him just for herself, and it hadn't been a prison; her heart had been his home. He had been expelled from Eden now, thrust outside the gates, and the world was harsh, the sunlight too bright, the smell of the world the rot of decay and death.

He drew a ragged breath, looking down at his hands. He was covered in her blood, and the flies – already they were coming. The sound...

He turned and vomited.

Jaden looked away, disgusted. "I need you to pull yourself together," he said. "Jacqueline is in the woods...I can feel her out there. Caroline tried to stop me," he added, as if by way of explanation. He gestured toward her body. "I knew if I tried to go after Jacqueline, she would have just followed me. It would have led to this either way, Kuro. You knew her: she wouldn't have been persuaded to just...let it go." He turned his gaze back to the woods, his eyes narrowed, already forgetting about the dead woman behind him on the ground. "Jacqueline's still running. She'll be trying to get back up to the main road, up to her house. We can stop her –"

"I'm not going *anywhere* with *you*."

Jaden looked back at him, an eyebrow raised. "Yes, you are," he said. "We're going to kill that girl, and then get out of this place."

"*Go to hell.*"

Jaden knelt in front of him; he reached out and gripped Kuro's shoulder in an icy clamp. Kuro recoiled and tried to pull away, but Jaden held him, his hand pressing painfully into the flesh. Kuro could smell the blood on him now, both his and Caroline's and someone else's, and felt the *holy dark* suddenly surge and cut off the air to his lungs.

"*Kurobushko,*" Jaden growled, the *holy dark* crackling around them. Kuro shuddered and quivered inside himself, crushed by it. "You can take a few moments to collect yourself, and then you *will* come with me into that forest. You *will* help me kill that girl." The grip tightened further yet, and the flicker of a whipping tail appeared, and claws pierced through him in sharp knives of pain. "Do you understand me?"

The *holy dark* suffocated him; he tried to reach out instinctively for Caroline's soul, but there was nothing there. It felt like falling over the edge of a cliff, and the only thing that kept him from crashing was the leash of Jaden's power over him, using the full extent of the *holy dark* to compel him with his name. He tried to resist: a brief war raged in him with the silent need to scream, but unseen, cold fire raked down his spine with the fury of Jaden's power as he repeated, "*Kurobushko:* do as I say."

He could only nod, sick with the compulsion to obey.

Jaden let him go; Kuro fell backwards, gasping as the other demon stepped over him, walking toward the forest.

He paused only to say, "Come," and then shifted forms, already running.

Kuro struggled up in the dirt, turning over. He wanted to run in the opposite direction, but he could feel the chains of the *holy dark* circling him, tightening around his throat. He found himself taking one stumbling step forward toward the woods, fighting against himself.

I don't want to kill that girl, he thought, and a wordless cry tore out of him, pained and desperate. He hadn't been strong enough to resist the power of his name before; he had no chance now. He remembered the way she had struggled against him, screaming...

No. He would kill himself first: he would rip open his own chest, his throat if need be, and die before he helped that monster to torture and kill again.

One last time, he reached again for Caroline, feeling for her soul to ground him, give him an anchor, let him fight against Jaden's command –

Something reached back for him; he grabbed it, searching; he hadn't felt another soul besides her in months, and the feeling had become frightening, foreign to him now.

It was a human. There was someone else here...

He held on to it in desperation, pulling himself back from the current of the *holy dark* that was carrying him toward the woods. The first steps away from that direct command were almost impossible, a shuffling on legs that felt like lead, his body unwilling to go anywhere other than the direction he had been compelled toward, and *Caroline was behind him, laying there*...he closed his eyes, trying to shut out the image of her lifeless eyes, staring.

But the human soul that reached for him now was insistent, determined in its grip of him. Each step away was a little easier as the feeling of the soul grew stronger. He had never touched this soul before and didn't recognize the hues, but as he came around the corner of the house, he could begin to make out the patterns of its emotions: it was *fighting*, kicking against its own fate, fierce and insistent, holding on to something...

Life. He drew up short, searching. *Where are you?*

It answered him with the blended feeling of wild hope and crushing sorrow, like a prisoner mounting the steps of the guillotine, knowing the release from torture that would come... and the cost of that freedom.

Kuro shifted his form and followed it, following the scent of blood...and then he saw him.

Kenneth was lying in the grass by the rotted fence post, near the front of the barn, right where Kuro himself had once been shot. He shifted forms and knelt beside the boy, shaking.

Kenneth stared back at him, his eyes wide. Kuro reached down and gently pushed back the hair from his eyes; it was plastered to his face with cold sweat. He had rolled onto his side, his hands gripping his torso, his shirt soaked with blood. He had been wounded, slashed by familiar claws, the death blow across his throat certain but not immediate like Caroline's deep and rending wound: he had been discarded, left to die a slow, lingering death. His legs, his back, his life bled out of him...but still he stared, holding on, his mouth twitching in an effort to speak.

Kuro's voice caught in his throat. "Don't," he mumbled. He knew the boy was going to die, and soon. "Don't try to speak." He took a deep breath; he could feel Kenneth's soul; it was so frightened, terrified of him and some other nameless horror. "I'm sorry," he told it, his whisper strained. "I'm sorry about everything."

Jaden's order pulled at him, clawing its way into his resolve; he refused its call with all the strength he had, even as it tore into his mind. He wouldn't let this boy die alone.

Kenneth's mouth twitched again. A weak sound choked out, but Kuro shook his head.

"It's okay," he tried. His mouth was dry, his voice a rasp of pain. He felt too numb for tears anymore, but a horrible, cutting sadness had sunk into his bones. "I'm not going to hurt you," he whispered. "I'll stay with you..." *until the end,* he thought.

Something was shifting in the boy's soul; a flare of indignation, of frustration...the boy let go of himself and reached forward suddenly, gripping Kuro's shirt, hauling him closer with the absolute last of his strength. Kenneth's mouth was working furiously now, desperate.

He was trying to speak, but no words could come out. Blood speckled onto Kuro's shirt as Kenneth's breath gasped out, failing.

"I don't know what you want," Kuro protested. He sounded scared and desperate now. The boy clutched him tighter, insistent.

"M-my..." Kenneth managed, gasping; a wet, wrenching sound came from his throat. The boy collapsed downward, choking on his blood. His hand slipped from Kuro's shirt but remained outstretched, reaching for him, as though offering him something.

"I don't know what you want!" Kuro screamed. "Do you want me to kill you?! Do you want me to end this!?"

Kenneth's movements were growing sluggish. His legs kicked out ineffectually, his face contorting in pain as he worked to speak. His eyes bulged suddenly with a wave of agony, teeth clamping shut, then forced themselves open, his voice thick and pained.

"*T-take it,*" he panted. He coughed, blood flecking his lips. "*My soul.*"

Kuro stared at him, shocked. Kenneth sank back down again, fighting his death with everything left in him. Kuro began to shake his head, slow at first, then faster, horrified.

"I'm not going to do that," he whispered. The thought of that, of feeling a human soul *inside* him... "I'm not going to do that," he repeated more loudly, terrified. He had the sudden urge to give himself back to the *holy dark* and obey Jaden and run, run far away from this dying boy.

A familiar warmth settled on his shoulders.

Kenneth's eyes lit up. Kuro knew he could sense it, too. He wanted to tear that being from his body, drag it out of whatever hidden world it occupied, out into this world of death, and rip it open, dig out its fire, and see if it could bleed.

Kuro, the angel spoke, pleading. *Take this boy's gift.*

"I won't." He was trembling now. "I *can't.*"

You can. He's giving it to you.

"Jaden can't even do that!" He shouted at it. "How do you expect *me* to?"

A soul's power cannot be taken, it answered. *It can only be given.*

Kuro's eyes widened. He shook his head again in mute protest.

Take it.

"No."

If you do, you will be stronger than him, the angel promised. *He will have no power over you...and you will be able to help me save Jacqueline.*

"*Her?*" He rounded on it, fresh tears and fury in his eyes, but there was nothing there. "I don't care about *her!* Why didn't you do something to save *Caroline? What are you?!*" He shouted, the blood ringing in his ears. "WHERE are you?! *Why couldn't you do something?!*" His voice broke on a fresh sob. "Why...why did you tell her to let me go..."

Kuro, the voice spoke again, patient. The warmth came around him once more; he tried to fight against it, but it was insistent. *I won't compel you, but you have a choice... You could take this soul. You can take this boy's gift. He has waited here, fighting against death, for this very moment. For you. He knew it might come to this, and still he fights. If you take his gift, you can still stop Jaden. You can at least save* her.

He wanted to scream at it *save her yourself* or demand to know why it had done nothing to save Caroline, why it had told her to let him go...but he was exhausted almost beyond speech now. He took a deep, shuddering breath and looked back down at Kenneth. He could feel the soul there, reaching for him; it was decided, but frightened. Pleading.

"What happens if I do?"

You'll be alright.

"I don't care about me," he snapped, fury rising. He was still looking down into that boy's eyes; it was like staring into a mirror. The angel had ignored his questions earlier, had let Caroline die... and now was sacrificing this boy, too. Whatever this creature was, it was as cruel as Jaden. This was no mercy; this was calculation, and he knew he was being used without understanding why or even to what end. "What happens to *him*?"

He is so close to death already...the shock of it will kill him.

"You want me to be a murderer, too?" He laughed, bitter. "*No.*"

Slowly, the warmth withdrew, and Kuro understood; it was leaving him to make the choice on his own, without his influence. In that moment, he hated the angel more than he hated Jaden. It had power, he thought; surely, there must have been *something* it could have done – in all this bloodshed, there must have been a moment where it could have stepped in, could have prevented all of this...

If it could have, don't you think it would have done so? It was every bit as limited and useless as he was. He closed his eyes and tried to slow his breathing; he had to believe that was the case, because the alternative truth – that the angel could watch on, an observer, and let these people die for reasons known just to it, reasons it would not share, and only work to spare that girl *Jacqueline* for reasons it would not say – was too terrible to think about.

He opened his eyes and looked down.

Kenneth was waiting.

Kuro sighed, his decision made, already crushed by this new sorrow.

"I don't know how to do this," he said. His face burned; his own heart beat with almost paralyzing horror at what he was about to do. He leaned down and took the boy's hand in his, squeezing. "And...I'm sorry."

Kenneth managed a final smile. Kuro closed his eyes again and reached out for his soul; it felt much like Caroline's had at the moment of her slipping away, a spreading, expanding warmth... but then it began to contract, coalesce. He closed his eyes tighter in concentration, and in some unseen, dark place, he could almost *see* the soul in his mind, could picture himself reaching out for it – it was glowing, *shining*, a moving ball of light and being. Kuro reached out and pictured himself in his mind holding it.

It fit neatly in the palm of his hand, this glowing orb...this person.

Feelings flooded him at once, feelings that didn't belong to him; he felt the terror of being attacked in his own home by a pair of strange creatures, felt the cut of the betrayal of a friend, the heavy, shuddering despair of a winding melancholy, and *love* –

He pulled away from it, scared. *I don't want that in me,* he thought. *I don't want to feel those things again...*

But the soul was insistent. Kuro reached for it against his will, his hands trembling as he cradled it. He brought it close to him, lifting it away; a final instinct urged it to fight back, frightened, and for a moment, it tried to hold on to itself, reaching backwards to the life it was abandoning.

It's okay, Kuro told it. *You can let go. I'll keep you safe.*

It shimmered, and with a feeling of release, the soul spread within his heart, and became part of him.

Kuro opened his eyes to a quiet world. His hand was still gripping Kenneth's, but the body had gone lifeless, the eyes the same empty glassiness of Caroline's. Kuro reached down and touched the edge of his face; *I did that,* he thought, and then, ...*I did all of this. I killed him.*

He stood up, his legs shaking, and promptly fell back down, his head spinning. He could *feel* Kenneth's soul inside of him, even reach inside *himself* and touch it...but he recoiled from doing so.

It lacked the dynamic pulse of its living body; no ripples touched its still waters. It would never grow, never change; it was a dead thing, static now, yet somehow a living part of him. He didn't understand this, yet he could already feel it changing him.

He fought the urge to throw up again and found himself suddenly scrambling at his chest with the sense of the invasion; *get it out of me,* he thought wildly, his heart racing – *get it out!*

No, there was no time for this, this terror; he fought against his panic, hauling himself to his feet.

Something had changed. That feeling of being commanded beyond what he could resist, of being pushed and controlled by the *holy dark* had lifted away entirely. Even the command of his name had cooled. He felt inexplicably *free.*

Kuro took a step forward, shifting forms, but his balance was off.

Where one tail had been, *three* now stretched, black as the night sky at new moon. The *holy dark* moved in him, heavier and more powerful, with the rolling, gathering strength of the deep ocean tides.

He had done what Jaden had tried so hard to achieve...*because he didn't know,* he thought. *He didn't know he could never take a soul without its consent. He'll try until it drives him mad.*

But understanding dawned with the next thought. *It already has.*

A feeling stirred in him, foreign and yet recognizable. Love and longing suddenly gripped every part of him, the final throes of Kenneth's soul before Kuro pushed it down into a dark, hidden place.

Are you with me, angel? He snarled, his tails thrashing. He wasn't afraid of it anymore; whatever it really was, it was a pathetic, useless thing, a hateful, weak creature that let humans die, alone.

The light shifted, and he knew it was there. He mocked it, his fangs flashing. *Are you going to let her die, too?*

Never, it answered. *I'll be with you, for as long as I can, until I break entirely. But you have to hurry. You have to run.*

Kuro ran.

Sixteen

He found Jaden deep in the forest, moving with the patience of a practiced hunter. At the sound of his approach, the demon came to a stop, shifted to a human, and turned to face him.

Kuro stood there on human legs, staring after him. The ghost of a smile lighted on Jaden's face before drawing down into a frown.

"Kuro?"

Kuro walked forward, his fists clenched, and stopped twenty paces away. Jaden studied him, puzzled. He spoke quietly, searching his face.

"For a moment, I had the strangest sensation...that there was a human in the woods. I thought I felt its soul...But it was just you."

"You were the one who killed Kenneth, didn't you?"

"Oh. You found him." His face grew animated suddenly. "Was he dead, then? That's fortunate." He looked down at his hands. "He was fighting to hold on, and I thought that he must still be alive; I thought if I broke the promise not to kill him, the consequences would be..." His laughter fell away into a somber grimace. "Severe. But nothing has happened to me yet. Is he still alive?"

Kuro glared at him; he had never wanted to hurt someone so badly. Even in the moments when he thought he had hated Kenneth, it was nothing compared to this. Jaden saw the animosity in his face, and his expression clouded again, amazed at his hatred. When Kuro spoke, his words were bitter. "No. I delivered the death blow."

"So *you* killed him?" Jaden's eyes lit up. "Then you have my thanks." His smile returned. "You kept me from breaking a promise. How appropriate; we kept each other's promises today. Caroline found out 'the truth' in the end. I think it would have been worse to break the one I made, though," he mused. "I think you probably saved my life."

"That's unfortunate."

"Kuro." Jaden's voice grew stern. He took a few steps forward and watched as Kuro's face clouded over into a deeper anger. That look struck him, hit him hard; he stopped, stunned. "You may think that I don't care about what you're feeling, or that I can't understand it..."

"You fucking bastard," Kuro hissed. "*You killed her!*"

Jaden spoke patiently, but his eyes flashed with new danger. "I did it for *you*. A life as a *myobu* is no life, Kuro – look what she had already done to you. Even then, I told you the truth – I hadn't meant for this to happen. I told her to *stay in the goddamn house.*"

"What happened? *Why* did you do it?"

Jaden waved his hand in exasperation. "It doesn't *matter!* It won't change anything."

Kuro advanced a single step. Jaden froze; he could feel the *holy dark* moving, but something was *different,* heavier and more potent in its dark fury...

"You told Eric he could have Caroline." The words escaped Kuro's mouth in a hiss. "I *heard* it."

"It was a lie to get him to bring me Jacqueline – that's all. It worked, but Kenneth...he wasn't supposed to be there. If you want someone to blame, blame *him*. Caroline would be alive if not for him."

"And then what?"

"What?"

"*And then what!?*" Kuro beat his fist against a tree, the energy around him building now.

"And then I would have found a way to get her soul to *release* you," he said. "I had a plan, and it didn't involve her death. She would have let you go."

"I didn't *want* her to let me go. Did you ever think, even for a single moment, about what *I* wanted? Did that *ever* matter to you?" Jaden stared back at him, silent. Kuro drew a deep, shuddering breath, and continued. "What did she say to you? In the garden...at the end. She was smiling." His voice broke. "She took your hands. She was saying something. *What did she say?*"

Jaden's face became carefully blank. He remained perfectly frozen, studying Kuro. Jaden could feel him moving farther and farther away from him somehow; he thought the anger in those eyes was a temporary, passing thing, but it was so much deeper... and growing wider by the moment...

For the first time, Kuro saw a flash of fear in his face: the fear of abandonment.

"Kuro." Jaden stepped forward and held his hand out. There was a slight breeze in the air, and between them, leaves the color of burnt umber were drifting down in the lazy delight of a slow, cool morning. He caught one in his palm. "Kuro, *listen to me.* We live for *a thousand years.* Every human we've ever met will be *long* dead by the time we're a quarter of the way through our lifespan. Can you imagine *two hundred and fifty years* from now? This world – these people – everything changes, *rapidly*. Their lives are so brief. I know this one...Caroline," he said, forcing himself to use her name, "was first, and hurts very deeply right now. But people are like leaves, Kuro; we're going to see them fade and fall, and it will come with the rapidity and repetition of the seasons. We're going to meet many people in our lives, and before we know it, they'll fade. And they'll die. And it'll all repeat, over and over again, in a cycle...while we live on." He crushed the leaf in his hand and let it fall to the forest floor. "You and I will remain. We're destined to outlast all their lives. *We have one another.*"

"You used that exact same reasoning to tell me I could spend her life with her...because her whole life would have only been a moment for us. I didn't *need* your permission," Kuro snarled. "I only needed *hers.* But *you...*" He took another step forward, and the *holy dark* intensified – but something else, too; something *warm.* "You pride yourself on being so *intelligent.* You lie to humans; you've lied to *me*...and you're lying to yourself. It wasn't about what was best for me. Everything you've done has been purely about what's best for *you.* What is it you want from me, Jaden? Some sort of pet to keep around?"

Jaden licked his lips; the air was growing drier, and it wasn't his imagination – the dust in the air seemed to be lifting *up* from the ground with the growing force of some unseen current.

"You're not a pet," he answered. He stood a little more firmly, his eyes sweeping the trees for the hidden being he could now sense. "I did what I thought was best, Kuro. Caroline saw me – *really* saw me. Things would have been...difficult. I did what I thought I had to because *you are my friend*, and *I will not abandon you.*"

"You are *nothing* to me." Kuro slashed at the air, the *holy dark* crackling around him. He was having trouble keeping himself form-bound, and where human hands would have been, angry, sharp claws, dark with the dried blood of two human deaths, his and hers, had formed. Kuro was crouching, getting ready to spring, and behind him, three tails were steadying him.

Jaden's eyes widened at the sight. "Kurobushko...what have you *done?*"

This time, the use of his name felt only like a lash, not a collar; he felt *insulted,* not compelled, recoiling as though he had been touched without his consent. "I did what you always wanted to do." Kuro advanced forward so fast, Jaden wasn't prepared for it. He grabbed him by the front of his shirt and slammed him against the nearest tree. A shower of leaves began to fall upon them. "I *ate* that boy's soul. It was the last thing I did before I came out here to *kill you,* you *fucking bastard!*"

Jaden's eyes widened in disbelief.

Kuro slammed him back against the trunk a second time. "And you're never going to touch that girl," he snarled. "You're not going to get your hands on her today, tomorrow, or the next day." Inside of him, Kenneth's soul stirred, and a name came up from the depths of his soul, his heart pouring forth now. "You will *never* have Jacqueline."

Jaden's voice was menacingly low. "Is that so?"

"*I promise.*"

Something snapped in him; Jaden shifted and sprung forward first, roaring. Kuro met him and dug his claws deep into his shoulders, fighting him into the ground, his back legs sliding in the leaves. Both their jaws opened, fangs aiming for each other's throats; Kuro succeeded in biting him deep in the fleshy side of his throat as Jaden writhed away, snarling. There was a strange, blurry movement, but Kuro's eyes followed, seeing: *two* maroon tails stretched, quivering in rage.

He wasn't the only one who had changed this morning.

He had just enough time to think *how? And when?* before the *nogitsune* lunged for him again.

He fought away from him, slashing at his eyes. Kuro fell back, hissing, then stretched himself upward, the *holy dark* surging.

In the bright morning, the forest was awash in shadow, long

strips of darkness in the form of tree trunks. The shadows retracted swiftly, faster than he'd ever been able to move them before. Jaden retreated a step, his back arching for whatever was coming. Kuro understood now what *power* was; they had known in some instinctual, indefinite way, just as he had always known Jaden was more powerful than him...until *this*.

The shadows shot forward like whips, lashing themselves to Jaden's legs. Once, they had raced up Jacqueline's body, an insubstantial illusion, the mere warping of light. He had changed now: the *holy dark* within him had grown, and a new form of his power was unleashed. The shadows clung and held on, strengthened by the new force inside him into forms both corporeal and deadly. Jaden tried to rear up and leap, but the darkness clutched him, dragging him down.

Kuro leapt forward, his claws ready just as Jaden summoned the fox fire. An inferno leapt up between them, massive and blazing.

Even in death, Kenneth's human soul inside him was still susceptible to the fire; no longer was he impervious to the blue flame. Kuro snarled, steeling himself to run through the flames anyway and ignore the pain, but his legs remained rooted to the ground. He shivered suddenly; he felt a foreign need to protect the thing inside him. No life would replenish anything burned away; once gone, it would never reflower, and the pain – he had felt it for just a moment at the edge of those flames – would be *his*.

Jaden could burn the soul right out of him.

Kuro ran the length of the fire, searching for its end. It began to diminish, the blue flames lifting away harmlessly into the trees, and there, a glimpse of maroon –

He leapt at the demon and collided, claws and teeth slashing at each other like knives, their screams filling the forest.

Jaden reared back on his feet and struck him hard across the chest. The rosary he had forgotten he was still wearing flew out as he fell backwards. He felt warm blood begin to pour down the front of him, coating the onyx beads.

Get out of my way, Kurobushko! Jaden roared.

You can stop using my name, Jaden. His jowls drew up into a mocking, bloodied smile over his fangs. *You're outclassed.*

Another scream tore from Jaden's throat. He leapt again, and this time, his aim was good; each paw sunk deep into Kuro's shoulders, knocking the wind out of him. Kuro fell down and moved away just in time as the *kitsune* swiped at his face. He twisted and slashed in turn. Jaden moved back a second too late; the blow caught him across the right shoulder. His eyes were blazing, infuriated.

I've only ever been your friend, Kuro, he tried, backing up, ears flat. There was no retreat in that pose, Kuro knew; he was merely readying himself, his tail high and stiff as he prepared to leap.

Kuro barked at him, enraged. *You will NEVER be ANYTHING to me ever again!*

The fox fire came lunging for him. Kuro crouched, unable to avoid it, and braced himself for the agony to come.

It never reached him.

Real fire, hot and golden red, spread out between them, the force of it extinguishing the fox fire where the two collided. Kuro backed up, frightened; it was just like yesterday, an age ago, in the woods with the humans, only this time, the fire did not disappear. There was something bright in the center of it, something small with wings outstretched, *burning*, and the fire grew higher, an impenetrable wall between them.

The overwhelming, unfurling power of the angel pressed him to the ground.

Kuro, it spoke. His tails curled beneath him. It sounded so *substantial*, powerful, as though it had rallied every ounce of power that it possessed for this single moment. *Ready yourself.*

He tensed his body to spring. The flames disappeared in an

instant, but around him, the bare trees had ignited from the angel's fire.

Kuro leapt before Jaden could recover, pinning him to the ground. The moment he was upon him, he shifted forms. Human hands turned into fists, punching down at the *kitsune's* head below him. Jaden shifted forms in an effort to avoid the blow, but Kuro merely redoubled his efforts, two humans now grappling in a world steadily igniting around them. He hit him in the side of the throat; Jaden gasped, and then a second blow connected with his temple, and the demon lay still.

Kuro pulled his hand back, stretching himself between forms purposefully just as Jaden had done when he killed Caroline. He felt his claws at the end of his fingers, his tails at the base of his human spine, and aimed for the throat –

And froze, his body nearly paralyzed with the force of the angel holding him back. The light had appeared and *touched him,* grabbing his hand. Kuro wrenched from it; the skin around his wrist was burned, blistering from the touch.

It was too bright to stare directly at, but it was there, tangible. Around him, the forest was ablaze; black, heavy smoke was billowing into the sky. The fire was climbing fast, and what began as mere crackling was escalating into a hungry roar, the hiss of wet leaves and sodden limbs cutting through the air like a knife.

You mustn't kill him, the angel was saying. *You've done enough. She'll get away. I'm going to take her somewhere –*

"I don't care about her!" He shouted. "I want him *dead!*"

You mustn't kill him.

He screamed with the utter frustration of his despair and anger. "You wouldn't save Caroline...you didn't even save the boy...but *him?* You'll spare *HIM?*"

All I have done, I have done to pull them apart, and keep them from one another. I tried to keep her from approaching him. I warned her. I've tried, and I've failed.

"Then let me kill him," he pleaded. "He'll wake up and come after her again. You think he'll *stop?*"

He will never stop.

"Then I'll finish it, here and now."

No. I will take her far away. I will hide her. Kurobushko...I do not want him to die.

Kuro laughed. He stood alone in hell and felt its burning heat, felt the smoke choke his throat and dull his senses, and laughed at the senselessness of it. To hear an angel speak his true name...it was like the crash of a cymbal in his mind. There was no disobeying that power. Understanding hit him suddenly, tears coming to his eyes now. Perhaps he wasn't laughing at all; maybe he was sobbing again.

It was growing difficult to hear his own voice over the sound of the flames. "He would have been her *myobu,*" he said. "That's why...that's why he wanted her, isn't it?" The pull he felt toward Caroline, that feeling of *rightness*...had somehow gone wrong for Jaden, had had some uncanny, opposite effect...a reversal; a perversion. The *nogitsune* at his feet was still, unconscious to this revelation, but maybe, somewhere in some dark, unacknowledged place in his heart, Jaden might have known, or at least suspected.

It is an unforgivable thing to kill your intended, the angel answered, its voice heavy with sorrow.

Kuro let out another bark of bitter laughter. "Why would you care if he kills her?" The angel hadn't cared if he killed anyone else; how many bodies were piled at Jaden's feet, but *that* single one, that girl, was to be spared...?

Someday, you'll know. Someday, you will know the answer to every question you have asked me.

"No," he said. "I hope, as long as I live, I never hear your voice again. I hope Jacqueline lives every day knowing you let them die for *her.* You're *pathetic!*" He screamed.

Kuro turned to go and felt another burning sensation on his wrist. He yanked it away, yelping. The light drew back.

Take him, the angel pleaded. *If I touch him, I'll burn him...and I'm fading. I must get to Jacqueline. This place will be engulfed soon. Take him somewhere safe, out of the way of the flames...and then run, Kurobushko.* The voice hardened, the power coalescing, and once again he felt the bit and reins of power slip over him. It enraged him, but he was helpless before the command of the angel, restraining himself from cowering before the light. It was growing, expanding now, and the heat was rising. *Do this last thing I command of you, and someday, I promise, you will understand why you were forced to do it.*

Kuro felt a jolt in his heart; his voice hitched when he spoke, and a strange feeling stirred inside him, a feeling that wasn't his but kept him rooted to the spot. Kenneth's soul was reaching through him, desperate. "What about Jacqueline? You're going to...to take her somewhere? She'll be safe?"

The angel spoke, and Kuro heard fresh sorrow in its voice. *I will do all I can to keep her safe from him. You have given me the time to do so.*

There was a lump in his throat; he tried to swallow and found he couldn't. His eyes were stinging again; tears were pouring down. *The smoke,* he thought, but no; the last active stirring of Kenneth was there, and his love hurt so badly...

"Do you promise?"

It isn't the same for me as it is for you, the angel answered. *But yes. I promise.*

"Why?" He had to try, just one more time. "Why do you want me to spare him? Why did you tell her to let me go?"

There was no final answer, just a feeling: a warm secret, slipping away, and Kuro thought again of that final glimpse of understanding he had seen in Caroline's eyes...

And just like her, the angel was now gone.

Kuro turned and yanked Jaden upward by one arm, hoisting his body over his shoulders. Yesterday he had carried him out of the forest, desperate to save his life; today, every step revolted him, but as powerful as he had become, the angel was stronger yet, and it had issued a command.

He headed in the opposite direction of Caroline's house, emerging at last near the road, the roar of the fire behind his back. He dumped Jaden down near the edge of the asphalt. In the distance, he could hear sirens already wailing. The sunlight, choked by the smoke from the forest fire, had turned a sickly yellow, and ash had begun to drift down.

Kuro turned and watched as a flake landed on Jaden's face. He wanted to pull his leg back and kick that throat, crush it beneath him...he reached up and gripped the rosary, knuckles white with the force of it. It was wet with his own blood.

He felt Caroline's presence on it, strengthening him.

It didn't matter what the angel promised. *Jaden will go after her...and not just her,* he thought. Jaden would seek *him* out, too, perhaps even find him someday...and what then? The angel had told Caroline that he was needed here – why? For the next moment when Jaden would find him again? To fight, over and over, until one of them killed the other? Better to kill him now... He didn't feel the angel's presence. He drew his hand back, readying his claws. Perhaps, if he was quick –

Shaking, he lowered his hand to his side, and turned away.

He stared at the road, seeking something – an answer, a path. Back to the mountains, maybe...but no. A heavy feeling was settling in his chest, a grief that pulled him down, crushed his breath, and it demanded he go somewhere new, somewhere far away from here, somewhere where *nothing* could remind him of her...

He touched the rosary again and felt the loss of everything;

*Caroline...*his eyes rolled down to where Jaden lay, blood drying on his temple now.

...and Jaden.

A single, wailing cry came from the deepest part of his own soul. He clamped his teeth down on it, trying to swallow his sorrow, and found that grief was a monster of many heads, all eating with its many mouths from inside him. He took a shaking step into the road, and then another. Behind him lay the fire and the blood, the loss and the unknowing – *why?* He kept asking himself. *What had she said to him?* Perhaps someday Jaden would stand before him again, and he would reveal her final words then.

Where was it taking Jacqueline?

Why wouldn't it let me just kill him here?

Why couldn't I go with Caroline?

And where had she gone? Kenneth's soul was safe inside of his heart now; Caroline's had slipped away – to where? What became of them, after death? And could he follow her there, *find* her...and be with her again?

The answers were on the other side of a closed, locked door, and behind that door lay the Dark.

And he could not yet go inside, or follow her.

It didn't matter that the angel had promised him answers; for now, there was only grief.

Kuro cried out again and shifted. A silver fox, black spare the white tip on its tail, stood next to the road. When Jaden awoke, he would seek Kuro, no doubt, but there would be no trace, nothing for him to follow, no presence to sense for... and if the angel had succeeded, then Jacqueline, too, would be lost to him. Jaden would be alive and utterly alone, and what he would do then... Kuro didn't know, or care.

The inferno grew louder.

The fox turned from it and ran.

That afternoon, a firefighter stumbled back from the ashes of the burned forest, winded. The ground had been damp enough, but the days had been dry lately, and the bare trees had gone up quick. He'd been startled earlier when a gorgeous, 10-point buck had thundered out of the scorched trees, its eyes rolling back in terror. It wasn't uncommon to see wildlife come streaming out of a forest once their world went up in flames, but it had surprised him nonetheless.

But as the truck barreled down the road, he'd seen something strange about a quarter mile off from the edge of the fire: a black fox running. It had stood out to him at first because of the color. He knew they were called 'silver foxes,' though he'd never seen one in person before.

It had been running in the opposite direction of everything else: south.

It was racing towards the sea.

KEEP READING

FOR AN EXCERPT FROM THE THIRD BOOK IN
THE COLOR BY NUMBERS SERIES BY
DANIELLE THOMPSON: CARIBBEAN BLUE

In the city of St. Augustine, a demon had come to mourn.

Tucked in a small, cobbled courtyard with a fountain, partially shaded, he sat drinking hot chocolate under a perfect noonday sky.

'Perfect' was a relative term; it was perfect for Florida in the sense that it was hot, oppressively so, and cloudless, which meant that the sun ruled with maximum brutality in August. To breathe was to gulp water, to exhale was to sweat; the air here was characterized by a persistent, clinging dampness and heat, driving even the tourists indoors, which meant that the demon was able to sit in relative solitude and sip his drink, a fixture in this courtyard. He wore a pair of dark pants, which alone might have been enough to ignite the suspicion of the locals, but it was his eyes that arrested attention: they were so dark, so black, that at first glance one had to squint to discern where the pupil began and the iris ended.

Or rather, one would have had to squint, if anyone could hold his gaze long enough. His eyes were often narrowed, scowling, his mouth turned down in a snarl of displeasure so etched that it become a permanent aspect of his expression. It was the sort of look that drove away polite smiles and shy glances, as if bitterness was a disease that was catching. He was the sort of man who looked as though he would break before he would ever smile.

But his money was good, and he paid promptly, and so every morning, for almost a year, he had been served hot chocolate at a little table set out beneath a palm tree in a quiet courtyard of a section of the city otherwise relegated to the tourists. The young woman who worked at the coffee shop was startled the first time he appeared: he was *tall*, broad-shouldered and well-toned, muscular in a carved way that spoke of brutal strength and power.

At first, she had tried to learn his name with a smile and the usual chatter. She had persisted in these efforts for the first few weeks when he became a regular, but like all good waitstaff who instinctually understand the ebbs and needs of people, she lapsed into silence and no longer tried to get him to enter a conversation; she never even learned his name. In return for her gift of silence, she no longer received pointed glares or grunts; one morning when he came in bleary-eyed and tired, he even managed a stiff nod when she put a shot of espresso into his drink – or rather, *half* a shot.

And even that was almost too bitter for him. She saw the way his nose scrunched up, blanching at first sip.

For Kuro, those were the sort of mornings that followed long nights prowling the city.

St. Augustine was a city of ghosts; its cobbled streets still pulsed with the presence of time passed, and a few locals were even believers in the unseen. Strange lights, they said, glowed in the swamps; eerie things could be spotted out at sea from the fort. That a rare black fox had been spotted walking swiftly along the coquina walls at night, hopping lithely up into the low-hanging limb of an oak tree, all but its white-tipped tail lost among the Spanish moss, was not an unusual thing, though it was a thing to be remarked upon. After all, St. Augustine was also a city of much drinking, and many visions could be chalked up to the blurred hallucination brought upon by too much merriment combined with too much sun beating down upon heat-baked minds.

But too many people had seen the fox slipping away into the shadows to discount its existence, and even one guide who conducted one of the city's many ghost tours had mentioned it two weeks ago, pointing at a small, gated cemetery it had been known to haunt.

It was the feeling of the city that kept Kuro restless at night; he had come to this place to be lost and stay lost – to himself, and to the world. A feeling inside of him had driven him three years ago, running and grief-stricken, to the coast. He had never seen or felt the ocean, let alone imagined the salt breeze. The first time he came to the beach, dawn had been breaking. The sound of the surf had been thunderous in his ears; his legs had ached to lift themselves up from the sand, to push himself forward. His feet had sunk into the border where the ocean swelled and touched the beach, the cold water rushing over him. Here was the very edge of life and death. Salt stung his eyes, and the reek of decay from low tide had choked his nose. He stared out at the horizon, feeling his heart tighten, searching inwardly...and found nothing.

He stood there for an hour, and as he stood, the waves began to pound higher, cresting with more violence, his paws sinking into the sand as froth swirled around him, churning. Shells with jagged edges lashed out and cut him. He realized that if he remained much longer, the current would drag him out, and he would surely die.

It had been tempting to give himself over to death, but he had pulled his legs out of that wet sand, licked the foam off his chest, and turned back to the shore.

And Kuro had run south.

There were many places that called to him along the way, but the compulsion to keep running had kept him from staying anywhere too long. Sheer exhaustion had collapsed him in the old city by the sea; one evening, in the shadow of the Spanish fort, he had fallen asleep, and waking, found himself in a place of so much *energy* that he felt himself breathe with the striking relief of it. The *holy dark* was everywhere, and there was so much to sense, so much happening in the hidden currents of the world, that a *kitsune* who didn't dare to take its demon form could stay lost and hidden here for a long, long time...and might never be found.

He had shifted then, shedding his humanity, and assumed his *myobu* form. For the first two years, he lived life undetectable as a common fox. It wasn't until the third that he began to stretch human legs again, to crave a cup of hot chocolate once more.

In all that time, Caroline's rosary had never assimilated. Whatever form he chose, it always hung around his neck.

Kuro now stood and left his cup on the table, stretching. August was a pregnant, heavy month; people confined themselves to the shadows on days like this to lay supine and bloated, and for a moment, he considered doing the same. It would be nice to find a quiet corner, perhaps against the cool stone of a crumbled grave, and curl up, his nose pressed into his tail, and sleep through the heat. He passed a store front, where the temperature – 102 degrees, and expected to climb – blinked from a red, neon sign. A line of sweating humans had gathered at the ice cream store for a sweet breakfast, two umbrellas open in a desperate bid to shield them from the early heat of the day.

He felt the ache of the distant surf in his bones. It happened every now and then, ever since that first time he'd touched the ocean three years ago, and on days like that, it was best to answer, rather than fight, the feeling. The heat was a gift; there would be a few humans at the beach, but not as many: the sand grew so hot that it burned painfully underfoot, and people kept away. He set his feet moving without haste; he walked with his hands shoved into his pockets, brooding.

He walked often and everywhere, with no care for human sensibilities or danger. A cloud of fearlessness and anger had settled on his shoulders, a near palpable warning to others that told them to stay away.

He drifted across the bridge, the sound of traffic roaring in his ears, lost to his own thoughts, always the same. He didn't *think* so much as he *felt*, or remembered, and the images and emotions had become well-played and well-worn in his mind.

He passed a cyclist and reached out for his soul, feeling the buzz of the young man's frustration. His front tire had blown, and he pushed the bicycle past Kuro, cursing.

Within the hour he came to the park he liked best; its high

sand dunes sprouted tufts of sea grass that whispered strange secrets to the wind. He came out here often at night to listen and decipher their sayings, but so far, no meaning had come to him. Further inland stood the oaks with their wise beards of Spanish moss; they, too, danced strange dances in the night, their black forms twisting under the moon, but their silence was equally maddening, their knowledge unknowable...but still he came, seeking, and still he left, empty.

He kicked his shoes off and let his bare feet sink into the sand, ignoring the burning pain. A few towels and umbrellas spotted the beach, but it was as he suspected – mostly empty.

He could be alone.

He jogged down to the surf and kicked at it as he went, splashing the waves and mud up, hunched and scowling like a schoolboy dismissed with homework. There had been times when he had run out into the ocean in a mad frenzy, a black fox fighting against the surf, but always, he had come back to the beach, dripping and gasping, too much of a coward to just drown himself, and angrier for it with each failed attempt.

He'd walked on for almost thirty minutes now; there was no sign of any humans. Alone, Kuro paused, staring down at a crab at his feet. It had died and been partially eaten by whatever scavenger had found its remains. The outer shell had been cracked open, lost somewhere to the ocean, and its innards had been gnawed away, one of its prized claws ripped from its body. He leaned down and sniffed; it reeked of sun-rot and salt, brine, and the distinct fishiness that comes from dead ocean life.

He straightened, then kicked it. It flopped over, and loosened from the sand, the ocean swelled and pulled it back into itself, and then it was gone.

Everything is death, he thought. He watched the place where the crab had been, then gazed out at the waters. *Everything leaves.*

He thought of taking a step into the ocean and having another go at suicide, just to see if today was the day he could finally manage it, when a sound floated to him on the wind.

It was a cough.

He turned back to the beach, searching...but he could see nothing. It had come from ahead, that was certain, because the wind was blowing his dark bangs away from his face. A person, then, over that dune just up ahead. Not a good place to die, he thought.

He turned to head back the way he had come, but the cough came again; it was a raw, rasping sound that spoke of struggle and pain.

Kuro hesitated, searching the beach for someone else...but there was no one. Tentatively, he reached out with the *holy* dark; if the person was in trouble and needed help, he'd know instantly... and if not, well, he could go.

He could go anyways, of course, he told himself, but that sound...

His face screwed up, confused. He reached out again to the farthest edges that he could...and there was nothing, no soul to be touched.

A third cough, accompanied by a desperate gasping.

Before he knew what he was doing, his legs were pumping hard in the sand. Whoever was up ahead couldn't be more than fifty, maybe seventy feet, just over the crest of that little dune, but he had felt *nothing*.

It's a ghost, he thought. What else could produce a human *sound*, but had no human *soul*?

Is a ghost a human soul? Came his next thought; if that were so, wouldn't he have felt the ghost...?

There's no such things as ghosts, he cursed at himself, and of that, he had to be certain, because otherwise, wouldn't she –

He clamped down on the thought with a violence that surprised himself, cresting the dune. Kuro staggered to a halt.

A human lay on the sand, naked.

He was a young boy of indeterminate age, perhaps seventeen, perhaps nineteen, with flaxen hair that rippled like ripe wheat under the Florida sun, the ocean breeze stirring the damp ends against his forehead. His eyes were open, staring at Kuro. They were a blue he couldn't recognize or place, yet familiar in a distant way; crystalline, almost, brighter than these green waters here...and they were staring at him.

The boy coughed again, rasping, and began to move, struggling to sit up.

Two competing forces stirred inside of Kuro; the first told him to turn and run from this eerie, dead thing, because despite its movements, he could feel no soul, which meant a corpse lay in the sand before him. The second was more rational, and it told him that this moving, breathing human was clearly no corpse, and that he needed help, and it reminded him, very gently, that there was a time when he had been unable to feel any other souls besides a single, certain one, but that didn't mean that all the rest of the world had died.

It had only felt like it had.

Kuro slid down the sand and took two halting steps forward. Every step increased his anxiety, and instinct was moving in him with a rapid current, prickling him to caution. The hair along his forearms had shivered even in the heat, standing on edge. Inside of him, the *holy dark* wreathed with unease, warning him to turn away.

"Are you okay?"

His own voice surprised himself, rusted from disuse. He spoke to no one and, when he must, very little.

The boy was doubled over in the sand now, wracked with coughing, and Kuro watched as he suddenly spewed saltwater out of his lungs. With a pained, wrenching gasp, he fell backwards onto the sand, his arms wide and open, his face beaming.

"I can breathe." He smiled, the sunlight sparkling in his eyes. His face held the joy of a bridegroom on the dawn of his wedding day, and the boy burst into delighted laughter. Kuro felt a bit of jealousy stir in him to see such happiness in another, and with it, a hot spike of hatred. He turned to go.

"Wait! You can't leave!"

Kuro walked faster.

"Kuro, *please*! You *must* wait!"

He froze, his nerves ringing now with cutting fear. He turned slowly, fists clenched, and took three halting steps back to the boy. When he spoke, his voice came out in a low growl.

"How do you know my name?"

The boy sat up again, this time with more strength, and coughed once more, clearing his throat. Kuro saw now that the sand clung to the back of his legs and arms, but his hair was drying, lifting in the salt breeze; he must have been washed up by the ocean, like that crab...

And why was he *naked*?

He tried to feel for the soul again, but it was like touching air. Nothing responded to him. The boy searched his face and seemed to know what he was doing, because he said, "oh no, don't bother with that – that won't work, Kuro."

Realization hit him too late. "*Demon*," he hissed. He took a step back involuntarily, preparing for a fight. Behind him, three tails cracked across the air, a shimmered illusion, and then were gone. The *holy dark* moved, summoned within him, ready to kill.

The boy burst into laughter that bubbled up like champagne. "No, no, please, don't be afraid," he said. He tried to stand up and then promptly fell down again, his legs buckling beneath him. He caught himself with his arms and laughed with the surprised wonderment of a child. "Oh, my," he managed. "I...I am quite winded." He sat backwards again, panting; some of his earlier joy had dissipated, replaced by a brief flash of worry, a momentary furrowing of his brow. "I don't believe I have the strength to stand quite yet, and this sand is *quite* hot. Would you help?"

"*No.*"

He had no intention of touching this strange creature in front of him. In three years, Kuro had learned many things, most of the lessons hard won; one of the lessons he had accepted was how *little* he knew of the world – or rather, *his* world. *Kitsune* were not the only demons out there; the world lurked with monsters in all manners and shapes, and this creature here, though no fox, was something new, and new things were threats.

"I am sorry to hear that," the boy said. He brought a hand to his chest and gulped air again, his breaths shallow and rapid. "But nevertheless, I am *so* glad you're here. I *knew* you would be, but it's...foggy now," he said. He passed a hand in front of his eyes, and Kuro watched as the boy's emotions flickered with open transparency: worry now gave way to genuine misgiving...and a touch of fear. "I seem to have.... lost something...or, quite a bit...? Wait now, please don't go!"

Kuro had begun inching backwards again. He froze, nervous now that those blue eyes were on him. He was preparing to bolt.

"My name is Iwalani," he said. He held up a hand to Kuro in a gesture of goodwill. When Kuro didn't move to shake it, he let it fall away. "Kuro, I came here to get you. We have so much to do, and it all begins tonight."

He felt his stomach turn over. "What begins?"

"Our journey. My task. But it's the strangest thing..." The boy shivered despite the intense heat, and Kuro watched as his earlier happiness evaporated. The creature was disturbed and unsettled. "Everything was so clear only a minute ago...or at least, I think it was a minute ago...? But now...I can't remember most of it... Perhaps this is still so new, this body...perhaps I need a moment to think, and then it might come back to me..." But he trailed off, lost in his own thoughts, his expression darkening. He looked down thoughtfully at his hand, opening and closing it, eyes narrowed. "Why can't I remember...? I remember I came here for *you*, but..."

Kuro had heard quite enough. He shifted forms and bolted with the swiftness of a scared, small thing, fleeing toward the safety of the oaks and the city.

There was a stifling, humid dampness to Florida that Kuro liked. He didn't mind his own sweat, or the slickness of his skin; he didn't mind the glare of the sun off of the stones, either, or even the mosquitos. The world was a warm blanket he could close his eyes and suffocate in, engulfed and cradled by the heat of the hot day.

He did so now, stretching backwards in his chair outside the café. The noon shadows were pooled neatly below him, and the buzz of the city had settled into the soft murmur of fatigued tourists and sensible locals who had disappeared now that the heat had climbed to 110.

Something inside of him was rattled, shaken; he could admit it. That creature – that *thing* – on the beach had looked at him hours ago, had spoken to him...*and he knew my name,* he thought, shuddering. In all the world, there was only one other person who knew he even existed...

Not person, Kuro, his mind reminded him. *One demon...and two other people.*

He didn't want the demon to ever find him again, didn't want to even think of his name. And the people? The *humans?* What did *they* matter?

Maybe Eric doesn't matter, but he knows about you, his mind warned. *And he died to save Jacqueline...she matters.*

He felt the sudden urge to be sick. There were things he didn't think about, places he didn't go in his memory. He didn't dare dwell on the soul inside of him, the dead thing he had consumed, the girl gone missing...He felt Kenneth's soul stir at the presence of Jacqueline's name in his thoughts and shoved it roughly away, frightened of that feeling of the dead somehow living in his heart.

It's been a strange day, he told himself, willing his mind to find some other, safer route to explore. *Forget it.*

In three years, he had never yet succeeded in forgetting.

He knew he never would.

In the semi-darkness behind his drooped eyelids, the bright orange of the sun baked through, blinding him, and the quiet gurgling of the fountain behind him lulled him into a half doze.

"Oh thank goodness – *there* you are!"

His eyes flew open.

A fair-haired boy sunk into the seat across from him, exhausted, his hair limp and plastered to his face with sweat, nevertheless beaming with breakaway delight.

Kuro's chair toppled backwards as he sprung up, heart racing.

"Oh no, please, do sit down!" The boy gestured quickly to the chair. Nearby, the café barista had appeared in the doorway at the sound of the clatter, and she put her head out now, squinting.

Kuro steadied his shaking hands and put the chair back in place, waving her away.

"Please, have a seat," the boy said again, but Kuro shook his head adamantly, his body nearly pulsing with energy and the bolting need to flee. He gripped the back of the iron chair to steady himself, gritting his teeth.

"How did you find me?"

"Well, it wasn't easy," the boy said. He seemed genuinely pleased that Kuro was interested, and he sat up a little straighter, like a child presenting an excellent report card. He was clothed now, thank goodness, but the fit was all wrong. "You've done such a wonderful job of hiding yourself – I commend you, truly. Your efforts have been extraordinary, and I have to say, you picked a perfect city to tuck yourself away in. But please – *do* have a seat, Kuro," he repeated, and a little line of worry appeared above his eyebrows. He gestured again to the chair. "You'll summon that poor woman out here again by this continued behavior of yours, and we both know how abhorrently hot it is."

Kuro's limbs jerked him forward. Stiffly, he sat down, pressing himself as far back into the metal as possible. His palms sweat and itched, but his feet wouldn't budge, even as he began to shout *run! RUN!* in his mind.

"There, now," the boy beamed. "Isn't that much better? But, listen, I am so sorry – could I trouble you to get me a water? I'm *extremely* thirsty. I actually think I might be critically dehydrated." He laughed as though there were no funnier joke in the world, but the flush in his cheeks and neck, Kuro noticed now, had not abated. "You see, I have no money. Not that it would matter if I did. And I am *quite* dizzy."

Kuro swallowed, his mind spinning. "...If you have no money, how did you get those clothes?"

"Oh, these?" He was wearing a white collared shirt and a pair of khaki shorts, both slightly too large for him. "I met the *nicest* police officer as I was walking along the beach, and he explained that I should not be naked in public. I agreed and explained that I didn't know why I was naked to begin with. He then escorted me to the station in his patrol car, which was extremely convenient, as I don't think I would have had the energy to even get back to the city, let alone here!"

Kuro's skin was prickling all over with fear; earlier, on the beach, he had felt nothing...an unsettling *absence* of being, but now... The boy was giving off a *tremendous* energy, and it was crushing the *kitsune*, sucking the air from his lungs. His voice was strangled. "And he let you *go*?"

"Well, I have to admit – and I'm sorry to say this," he said, and his eyes cast themselves downward with real shame, "I just walked out, after I put on the clothes. I thought I would have to devise an elaborate escape plan, but in the end, no one was paying me much attention, and it was simple to slip away before they booked me. It was perhaps not the kindest way to return his generosity, but you see, I had to come find you. But I – well, I really am sorry, but I *desperately* need water. Would you – please?"

Kuro stood up again and moved like a broken wooden solider, shuffling forward into the café. He considered, briefly and insanely, the possibility of running again, but even his instinct had recognized the futility of it: he knew now not to try, because this boy – this *creature,* this horrific demon – had found him once.

He would do it again.

And if *he* had found him...might not someone else be able to?

"You okay?" The barista measured his expression as she rang him up. "You look like you've seen a ghost. Everything all right out there?"

It was the most she'd ever said to him in nearly a year. He managed a weak nod, swallowed, and then uttered an unconvincing, "yea."

The boy was still breathing irregularly when Kuro put a large bottle of water in front of him. He sat back down and watched as the boy unscrewed the cap and drank deeply, pausing only to gasp for air, before returning back to the water.

When he was done, he settled back, his chest rising more slowly.

"Thank you so much, Kuro," he said.

"How do you know my name? Who – *what* are you?" Without realizing it, Kuro had slipped his fingers through the iron of the chairs, gripping the bars, his elbows locked. He forced himself to relax a fraction, trying to affect a mask of calm.

"My name is Iwalani," he repeated. He took a deep breath and spoke as though he had rehearsed these lines for some time – or, at least, the last few hours. "And I know you because I have come to ask for your help in a most important task of some complexity."

Jesus Christ, Kuro thought. He could barely follow what this creature was saying. He waited for him to go on, but the boy's face, confident before, fell into a pained half-smile of embarrassment.

"And, well, I am prepared for your frustration as I tell you this, but the fact of the matter is that...I have quite forgotten what it is *exactly* that I am here to do. The task, that is," he added, a sheepish smile stealing across his face.

"*What?*"

"You see, when I took this form," he said, and Kuro caught himself retreating back into the chair again as one would withdraw from a particularly poisonous snake, "it required a great deal of... transformation. When you change your forms, it's *meta*physical. For me, it is quite a – a violent, physical affair." He was troubled now; Kuro noticed how swift and genuine his emotions came and shifted, with no pretense at concealment. "And with that transformation, it seems that I lost quite a bit of my memory... although, 'lost' is not the most accurate term." He chewed on his bottom lip, puzzled. "You see, there's no reason why I should have lost *anything*. It's possible that I lost my memories *accidentally*, or at the very least, *unintentionally*, but that seems unlikely to me... though possible. But if that's the case, something went very, *very* wrong, and I don't remember *how* or *why*." He perked up for a moment before continuing. "The alternative explanation is that I intentionally sealed a great deal of my memory away from myself, and naturally, if that were the case, it seems that I also intentionally sealed away the *why*, as even knowing the *why* would have perhaps led me to remember *what* it is I felt I must not know while in this form. Either way, regardless of *how* or *why* I've lost my memory, I can assure you, this is *incredibly* unpleasant for me."

Kuro gawked. All he had gleaned from the demon's ramblings

was that it had lost most of its memory. When he found the strength to speak again, his voice was full of dread; a second little detail had just gotten through to him. "And just – what – is your...form?"

But the boy snapped back into a cheery smile and waved the question away, as though Kuro had asked him when tea would be served. "Oh, you needn't concern yourself with that – it would be absolutely terrible if you were to ever see it – really, *dreadful!* We would be in dire circumstances if such a thing came to be!" He laughed again, chipper; he reminded Kuro of a little bird, innocent and fluttering with delight in the sun, like an oriole sunbathing. There was nothing sinister about him, no ossature of threat hidden as the foundation of his words, and yet Kuro's skin crawled with the ancient recognition of a being that was far, far more powerful than him. Being in his presence felt like being a grasshopper held in a human palm; at any moment, the fingers could close...and crush him.

But Iwalani, if that was truly his name, was smiling with the bright sincerity of a toddler. He was a bizarre creature of feeling and whim, and Kuro's head swam with the effort to keep up with the conversation.

The creature was mainly talking to himself, anyways.

"When I try to remember, it's like seeing...well, not quite a puzzle with missing pieces, because at least then I know the shape of the thing – or I have some idea of what is missing. With a puzzle, you *know* what to look for...and that troubles me," he continued, musing. "I *want* to know what it is I've forgotten, even though I recognize that if indeed I *chose* to forget it, I must have surmised that forgetting it was for my own good – for the very success of my purpose, that is. Alternatively, if I've lost nearly all my memories on accident...well, that would be *quite* terrible. Regardless, I can't help but search for them within my mind, and when I do, I see instead of a puzzle a shifting watercolor, the colors spreading, touching. I can't quite make out the shape...just a few hints, a few clues...and you, of course."

He fell silent, considering, then launched on. "But I am choosing to believe *this has happened on purpose.* The alternative is...too terrible to consider...but oh, I hope I'm not boring you," he said, blushing with embarrassment. "I hope you're not finding this uninteresting. You see, let me come back to what we were talking about. I *do* have a specific purpose for you, as I do at least recall the absolute *essentials,* the *beginning,* if you please, and *you* are at the very heart of that. And it all starts here and now – in fact, what time is it?"

Kuro fought off the urge to throw up as he answered, "It's... nearly 12:30."

"Yes, excellent, it's almost time!" He exclaimed.

"What do you mean? Can you...see the future?"

"I think there was a moment when I somewhat *could,*" he confessed, cocking his head. "Though it wasn't....certain, or *solid.* At any rate, you *must* listen to me."

He sat up straight and suddenly reached forward, grabbing Kuro's hands and squeezing them, his eyes wide in sincerity. Kuro would have wrenched away if terror hadn't utterly paralyzed him to the spot. "Kuro, you *must* help me."

"W-what?"

"There is a girl." He spoke rapidly, confidentially. "She is going to appear here any minute. I need you to protect her."

Kuro ripped his hands away, startling the boy. He felt as though a bolt of lightning had gone through him, striking right at his heart.

There had been a girl once – a beautiful, tall girl – whom he could not protect. And there had been *another* girl, a slip of a thing, whom he had saved, and never seen again, and something inside of him, something he avoided thinking about, ached at the very thought of her, wherever she was.

He would not be drawn into human affairs ever, ever again.

When he spoke, his voice was hoarse. "Get away from me."

Iwalani's eyes widened, pained. "Kuro, I'm so very sorry – I'm not sure what I said..."

"Find someone else," he hissed. "Find some other demon to do your bidding."

But the boy shook his head, his eyes the brightest blue Kuro had ever seen. "I'm sorry, I can't – it has to be you. You're the one that I remember – *you're* the one I needed to find."

"*No.*"

"Kuro, please, I –" But he stopped mid-sentence and looked past him, his eyes huge, and then he dropped his voice to the lowest whisper he could manage. "She's here."

Kuro grew supernaturally still, staring down determinedly at the table. Iwalani, too, seemed unobtrusively small, his head bent over the water bottle, each of them appearing very interested in anything other than the sound of the steps that drew closer to them.

Kuro heard her footfalls on the stone before he saw her, and as she passed, her shadow touching his, he risked looking up.

She was lanky, like a colt not yet out of adolescence, which she wasn't; perhaps just past eighteen, her legs and arms were too long, her stride the unnatural, unbalanced sway of a young girl who hadn't learned to accommodate the fluid movements of a woman's body, and aware of the change, had over-compensated by trying to control it. As a result, she walked like an awkward stork, too conscious of herself. Her skin was the deep, even tone of a Pacific islander, the coppery warmth of terra-cotta. Dark hair fell to the small of her back in loose, natural waves. Once more, that place inside him, the tender spot he tried not to touch, flared with fresh pain; he knew the feeling of hair almost like that, in a different place, in a different time.

She was wearing a simple sundress, flip flops, sunglasses

pushed on top of her head, and he watched as she turned to the cashier and purchased a bottle of water. Her eyes were almost too large for her face, wide and naïve, he thought. She wore silly bracelets that jangled backwards when she lifted her wallet.

He carefully reached out to touch the edge of her soul, but before he could, Iwalani had kicked him under the table and shook his head swiftly in a silent, admonishing *no!*

Kuro retracted, glancing back at her. She was chatting with the cashier pleasantly...but there was nothing special about her. She was awkward in the way that every young girl coming into her own is awkward, with no grace yet, though the promise was there. She possessed little distinguishing factors other than uncommonly pretty hair, which he knew only stood out to him because – because –

He jerked his head away with an angry hiss and stared pointedly at the fountain until Iwalani let out a breath of air, his eyes following the girl as she walked on.

"She's gone."

"So what?" He snapped. Demon or no, he was just about done with this maddening creature. If they were to come to a fight, *fine.* Let it be so. He turned to snarl at the boy, but Iwalani's expression took him off guard.

He was looking at him with deep pity, and on his lips, a sad smile lingered.

"I see your love, Kuro," he whispered. "I am so sorry to see how it has led you to such anger."

"Just what the fuck do you want?" He demanded. He pushed his chair back, but Iwalani gestured for him to stay.

"I told you – I need you to protect that girl."

"From what?"

"A demon," he said. "A *kitsune.*"

The skin on Kuro's neck prickled again, and the *holy dark* began to move through him, heightened to danger.

"...Is it him?"

Kuro couldn't bring himself to say his name.

Iwalani shook his head, and then horror dawned upon Kuro. *He knows who I'm talking about.*

He knows about Jaden.

Kuro didn't even like to *think* his name; he wouldn't admit it to himself, but he feared that thinking it – let alone *speaking* it – might somehow summon him out of the darkness and into his life once again.

"How do you know who I am? How do you know...about *him?*"

"One thing at a time, Kuro. You asked who it was we needed to protect her from. No, it's not *him,*" he said. And then, pointing again over Kuro's shoulders, he lowered his voice. "It's *him.*"

Kuro waited a second time for footsteps to pass him, but this time, the footfalls stopped back by the fountain. Kuro could feel the presence of the demon, the *kitsune,* behind him, reluctant to go on; no doubt the *kitsune* could sense the tremendous power Iwalani was giving off, even if he didn't know who or what it was coming from, and he wasn't stupid enough to just walk into the quagmire of it...

And yet, one, then two, and then a succession of trepid steps drew nearer, the cautious creeping of hunted prey, and Kuro glanced up, watching as a young man made his way through the courtyard, passing them, clearly nervous and trying to hide it.

He looked to be about the girl's age – no, just a bit older – and he walked with the frightened slinking of a beaten animal, shoulders hunched, eyes darting about the courtyard. For a moment, he met Kuro's gaze, and with a start, he looked away much too quickly.

But not quick enough. Kuro had seen that his eyes matched the exact shade of his hair: the cheerful orange of a California poppy, an autumn color made bright with gold. It was an unusual enough hue to be memorable but still pass within the realm of human possibility. No doubt his eyes drew a few looks, but Kuro could imagine that in the right light, they might pass for an odd variant of amber that would be mistaken for light brown, perhaps. He was far shorter than Kuro and not built for battle: he looked utterly unremarkable.

Kuro watched as the demon nervously pushed long bangs out his face.

His hands were shaking.

The *kitsune* glanced into the café, saw no one inside, and continued out of the courtyard, following the path that the girl had gone, nearly tripping over himself in his haste to get away from the unseen thing giving off the sickening waves of dangerous power behind him.

When he was gone, Kuro snorted. "*That* is what you want me to protect that girl from? That *whelp?*"

"Kuro, I am really quite surprised at you." Iwalani folded his arms over his chest. "That's a *demon* you're talking about."

"A second-rate demon. He's not strong – he was scared to even step into the courtyard." Kuro didn't need to admit that he himself was almost too scared to *leave* it.

"Don't underestimate him. He's here because –" but Iwalani stopped suddenly, two pink spots appearing in his cheeks. "Well, it's not important right now."

"It's not important, ever." Kuro finally gathered the courage needed to stand up, startling the boy. "I'm not going to help you."

"Kuro, I –"

"And I never want to see you *again,*" he growled. All around him, he gathered the *holy dark,* letting it surge and build in a warning, pushing back against the creature's power with his own. "I don't want to know how you know my name, how you know about *him,* or anything else about you. I want you to *leave me alone.*"

But the boy was unperturbed. "You're going to just let that girl fall victim to that *kitsune*?"

"I don't give a shit about her! I don't fucking know her!" He shouted. He didn't care if his words carried and drew attention from any passerby or not. "And I don't give a shit about that demon, either! She's not my responsibility!"

A dark cloud passed over Iwalani's face, and his voice grew stern. "One's responsibility is independent of one's *interest,* Kuro. Jacqueline was your *responsibility,* at the end, even though you didn't care about *her* – and even though you still don't, you *still* have a responsibility to her, and what I am asking you to do *fulfills* that responsibility to her."

He felt as though the boy had struck him, but the demon had moved only his eyes. They were glaring into him now with a ferociousness that left him utterly incapacitated, and all his boyishness was gone, replaced by the weighty gaze of judgement.

"How," he managed. "*How –*"

"You saved her." His voice was cold. "You fought a demon just long enough to give her time to run. You have the chance now to save someone else, someone who needs you just as badly, and these events are not unconnected."

But that wasn't important to him. A desperate feeling leapt up inside him, fighting to get out; all of Kenneth was burning within him, moving. The soul's struggle was nearly overwhelming. When he spoke, his words came out in a rushed whisper. "Do you know where she's at? Jacqueline – is she safe? Where is she?"

"You don't need to know that right now, Kuro."

Not a yes or a no, he thought. He could feel the blood rushing in his head as Kenneth's soul urged him to ask again –

No. He fought it down, his gorge rising. *No,* he was done with all of this: he had run once, down here to the south, and again this morning. He would run again. Whatever responsibility he had toward Jacqueline was *done.* He snapped angrily in his own mind, snarling at the soul within him and felt it melt away. A temporary feeling of guilt troubled him; had he hurt Kenneth just now?

Kenneth's dead, he told himself. *He doesn't feel anything.*

And yet, Kuro did...all of the time.

"*Demon.*" He forced the word through clenched teeth, his hands balling tightly into fists. "I've done enough for people I don't care about in this world. Fight your own battles."

He turned to go and made it one step before the boy's voice, cold as the edge of a knife pressing under the chin, stopped him.

"*Kurobushko.*"

The name fell upon him like a clap of thunder. Kuro sucked in his breath, freezing. All around him, the air grew with the energy of some unknown, furious thing, and it grabbed him now, choking him. "I had hoped to do this the pleasant way, with you listening to me, and trusting me. I see now that is not to be. *Turn and face me.*"

He did so without wanting to, but there was no disobeying that command, that voice that spoke his true name, winding it around him like a leash. Once, Jaden had enough power to compel him through his name, and the touch of Kenneth's soul had been enough to set him free.

There was no escaping this.

Iwalani's steely gaze met his, displeased.

"Kurobushko, I am no demon." Iwalani stood up, and even though his head barely came to Kuro's mid-chest, Kuro shrank back from this terrible creature that wore the form of a harmless, slight young man. All his earlier pleasantness was gone.

"I am an *angel*," he corrected, "and I compel you now: *protect that girl.*"

About the Author

Danielle Thompson likes a strong cup of coffee in the morning and a stronger cup of tea in the afternoon. Born and educated in the United States, Danielle spends most of her time trying to find her cat, a Somali named Moxie, who is inevitably never where she should be.

A Splash of Burgundy is her second published novel, and the second in the *Color by Numbers* series.

For more information, follow her on Instagram at @author.danielle.thompson or visit her Web site at www.writer-daniellethompson.com.